TORNADO PINBALL

STORM SEEKERS 2

BY

CHRIS KRIDLER

Published by Sky Diary Productions, Rockledge, Florida

Learn more about the author and storm chasing at ChrisKridler.com

Cover design and photo illustrations by Sky Diary Productions

Paperback ISBN: 978-0-9849139-5-4

First edition

THE TWISTER TRACKER

The tornado siren filled Jack's ears when he wasn't listening. It crept into moments of silence when his mind wandered off into that dark place without permission. He heard it the way the storm's victims hadn't, a vibration more than a sound, a ghost glimpsed out of the corner of his eye. Then a word or a noise or the wind on his face would bring him back, and for an instant, all he heard was the void.

"Jack, it's full."

He looked up, back in the present, to see Michiko eyeing him with her usual wry expression. She stood under the service station overhang, headphones around her neck, trying to keep her boom mike and field mixer dry. He realized he was still squeezing the gas nozzle's trigger. It had shut off, and so had his brain.

"Where were you?" she asked.

He wasn't going to mention the siren. "Just wondering why I decided to use my PhD to consult for a television show."

"I thought it was for the money." She glanced over at the

gas station's store, ready to jump when their star came out of the bathroom. Her dark, spiky hair — not unlike Jack's, he mused, but more shaggy — glistened with tiny drops as the fine rain blew sideways into their faces. "You're pretty bitter considering we've only been doing this for three days," she said. "We might be doing this for three more weeks."

"Bitter? More like resigned to my fate," Jack said, squeezing a few more drops of fuel into Van One. "And I'm not doing it for the money. He's doing it for the money, and for the fame. I'm doing it because I'm getting paid to chase tornadoes." And there were no desirable forecasting jobs available, he noted to himself.

"What's the difference?"

"I still have my self-respect. He's still an ass."

The ass, or as he now billed himself, Brad "The Twister Tracker" Treat, came out of the gas station's shop clutching an energy drink and a bag of corn chips. Instantly, two high-definition cameras were in his face, ready to catch any whiffle in his expression or any ruffle of his carefully gelled, short brown hair.

"Thanks for not following me into the stall this time," Brad said to the cameramen. His dark eyebrows scrunched together, perpetually broadcasting his concern over what might happen next.

"I gotta go," Michiko said, pulling on her headphones and rushing over to stick her boom mike above Brad's head. The fuzzy microphone dangled like an orbiting rat.

Gas nozzle stowed, Jack leaned against the white van, lit a cigarette against the advice of all signage and watched with amusement as a petite figure in a bright blue rain jacket hopped out of a sport-utility vehicle and got into the fray.

Wynda, their rosy-cheeked producer, spit out staccato orders in a persuasive English accent.

"Brad," said Wynda, whose red hair kept escaping from her hood in the wind, "we need you to talk with Saffire and Devlin on camera about getting the Bubble into the storm. You know, talk about your strategy and your forecast and what you plan to do."

This was Jack's favorite part, watching Brad perform, knowing how little Brad knew. How Brad had to be rescued, despite the myth he'd created about himself online and in interviews. How Brad let his tour van be sucked up by the Prairie Rock tornado, even though he claimed the dash-cam footage he later retrieved was completely intentional. How Brad agreed to become a human tornado probe for this documentary miniseries despite his almost beautiful ignorance of what he'd let himself in for.

"Where's my team?" Brad shouted. He was getting pretty good at playing the demanding leader.

Devlin, an engineer with a minor in meteorology, and Saffire, known more formally to her fans as Saffire Soulliere, were sharing a bag of popcorn inside Van One. Upon hearing the call, Devlin was the first to emerge. The staff geek sported a thin shock of light-brown hair, black-framed glasses and a small build that hid an enormous brain.

Saffire was next. She ran a hand through her loose, honey-blond curls as she brushed past Jack, offering him a modest smile. He got a whiff of her scent, a touch of lavender, fresh and subtle, as she parted his cloud of smoke. An entertainment-show host until recently, she was, Jack presumed, their series' requisite eye candy. He had to hand it to her. She was a pro, and she was immediately "on."

"So, Brad, where are we headed? This rain doesn't look good, and it's bad for Devlin's hair," she joked with a twinkle.

"This storm has petered out, so we've got to choose our next target," Brad said, a little too loudly for the sensitive mikes. "We have to look at radar and figure out where to go. Devlin, what's the latest?"

As the conversation continued for the cameras, Jack's smartphone buzzed. He pulled it out, noted the alert and flipped to a radar image, trying to quell his desire to jump in the van and leave these posers behind. These posers were paying his tab, he reminded himself. As much as he longed to be alone with his supercells, instead of alone in his thoughts, he was woefully short on gas money.

"We don't want to deploy the Bubble in these gusts without a reason," Devlin was saying. "You'd probably just get seasick. We've got to find a tornado."

"I love it," producer Wynda cut in. "Just dumbed-down enough for the audience. You're getting better at that, Devlin."

Devlin scowled. "Gee, thanks."

"Jack Andreas!" Wynda shouted.

Jack walked over to the group, noting the lenses were aimed nowhere near him. Usually, he manned the computer in the back of the van and was almost never on camera. Yet he was the consultant, the only guy who knew how to chase tornadoes.

"I suggest we go here," he said, showing them the image on his cell phone.

He'd zoomed in so they could see the first words of the bulletin superimposed on the radar: "TORNADO WARNING."

"Really? Let's go!" Wynda shouted, then stopped herself.

"Wait! No, you guys film Brad getting in the van. Actually, you film Brad telling everyone to get in the van. Brad, say something, you know, really boffo action stuff about how you've just heard there's a tornado, then run to the van."

Brad looked pale. "Fuck," he said.

VAN ONE WAS STARTING to smell like Doritos. It was inevitable, even after a couple of days, as the storm-chasing crew found itself grabbing meals wherever it could on the road, most often at truck stops and convenience stores.

Now, with the weather radio periodically screeching and the regular radio turned off — it was so tough to clear TV rights later for all those pop songs — official hero Brad drove. Riding shotgun was the photogenic Saffire, whose cleavage, as captured in the wide-angle cameras mounted above the windshield, looked as if Julie Andrews should be running atop it, singing emphatically that the hills were alive.

Destination: the possibly even more hilly jungles of northeast Oklahoma, one of Jack's least favorite areas to track tornadoes. Still, chasing a tornadic storm was better than those five days of shooting B-roll in March, when he'd led Wynda and the cameramen around the prairie. They'd shot fields and barns and clouds that would never in a million years produce a raindrop, let alone a storm. This was the most interesting weather they'd had since their May shoot began.

Seated in the third seat of the large minivan behind a laptop mount, Jack used an Internet connection that wavered between a cellular signal, when he could get it, and a much more costly satellite link. When he wasn't forecasting, he kept an eye on the radar and their position on the map. It was a lot like the university research he used to do, only less satisfying. They were forever interrupting the chase so they could get a drive-by shot of the vehicles or a thoughtful sequence with Brad standing along a country byway, looking concerned.

Next to engineer Devlin in the middle seat was shooter Andre, ebony-skinned and handsome, trying to catch with his camera any rare pearl Brad might drop. Andre twisted back and forth to film conversations as if he were covering a tennis match.

"Brad?" called Devlin.

"Yes, boy genius," Brad answered.

"This landscape doesn't lend itself to safe recovery of the Bubble," Devlin said, "but if we find a good spot, we should probably try to deploy it and see how long it takes to get you inside and strapped in."

And then we leave him there, Jack thought, and chase some storms. He picked up his CB, one of two in the van, and spoke so the crew in the other two vehicles could hear. "It looks like this cell has a mean core. Let's get east of Bartlesville and then get north, and by all means, let's avoid the Interstate."

"I like the Interstate," Brad said.

"It's great if you want to get shredded by a tornado or hail with no exits at your disposal," Jack replied. A little tic in the back of his brain brought up fleeting images of car wrecks and terrible losses and things he'd rather not remember before he pushed himself back into the red and green of the radar, figuring out their next move.

The convoy zigzagged through the south side of Bartlesville, whose meager skyline claimed a little class from Frank Lloyd Wright's only skyscraper. "It was finished in 1956, just three years before he died," Saffire noted, playing tour guide. "But if you really want some history, you'll have to visit the oil well."

"We're going to see plenty of them if we ever get back to Texas," said Brad, a note of homesickness in his voice.

"I'm talking about the Nellie Johnstone, Oklahoma's first commercial oil well," Saffire said, adding choice facts for the camera. She'd made it her mission to study up on the attractions, an effort Wynda encouraged so they would have something to fill the show if they didn't catch enough tornadoes. Jack could already foresee a return trip so they could shoot the rickety old well structure from every angle in order to get five seconds of video to lay over Saffire's chatter. As much as he despised the filler, he had to confess he could listen to her talk for hours, and more and more, she surprised him with flashes of wit that belied her Hollywood rep. His studied disdain eroded each time she uttered one of her melodic monologues. In her voice was the place where bourbon met vanilla ice cream.

While he could get almost enough bourbon, he could never slake his thirst for women. They were usually easier to chase than tornadoes, given his good looks and sinewy figure, but he had other things to do right now. *Focus on the storm, Jack. That's why you're here.* And it was starting to get interesting, even if it was losing its tornado signature. A hint of a second rain core had appeared on radar, and he wondered if the storm might be splitting. A splitting storm could complicate their approach. Jack smiled.

They were out of town now and into the country. The hills and trees threatened any chance they had of seeing anything, and with so few arteries to carry residents from place to place, the road was surprisingly busy. Oklahoma rush hour. Jack noted a few chaser cars on the road, too, easily spotted with their antennas and spinning anemometers.

It had been several minutes since there'd been word from Wynda. As a rule, she didn't like to talk over whatever cinematic action might be happening in Van One. She rode in the support SUV with sound gal and frequent driver Michiko, along with unkempt cameraman Razor, whose abundant tattoos had started to creep onto his bearded face in the form of an uncoiling snake.

Bringing up the rear was their prize: the Bubble, secured in a modest cargo truck Wynda insisted on calling the Bubblevan, driven by meteorology dropout Paul Pole. He had a hint of a receding hairline and the sunglasses of a 1970s TV cop. Like Van One, Pole's truck was wired with cameras, and all his activities would be captured on film, from his skittish reststop dashes to his meticulous nail-biting.

Their target storm was finally in view, but it was splitting in two, its updrafts conjoined twins that were ripping themselves apart. The edge of a ragged anvil blew off the top of the clouds, forming a feathery disc in the late-afternoon sky. The radar-indicated tornado warning hadn't verified, as far as they knew, and Jack doubted there was a tornado in there now. Still, they potentially faced two severe storms, with hours of daylight left for the chase.

"All right, team," Brad said. "We paid our quarter. It's time to play."

It was a punchy line. If only Brad had thought of it himself. Jack had spotted it on the loose script provided by Palatable Productions.

Van One, Wynda's crew car and Pole's Bubblevan approached the splitting cells like a squadron of ants about to tackle a pair of layer cakes. Jack could see lightning in the clouds, especially in the burgeoning southern storm. A look at the quickly changing radar made it clear that north wasn't the way to go.

"Change of plan," he said over the CB. "We're going to turn south, before Nowata if possible. This storm is splitting, and the right split should be our boy."

Their turn would be precariously close to the substantial hail core. They were already getting rain. They had to edge south and get east of this beast before it ate them alive. Jack liked his adrenaline rush as much as the next guy, but putting their convoy through a hail grinder was not his idea of a wise move. Besides, they had to stay intact if they wanted to catch a tornado. If they actually succeeded and launched Brad in the Bubble, Jack would get a sizable contractual bonus. It should be enough to buy him some chase time on his own, and that was all he wanted.

Just before they made the turn, a stray, icy baseball slammed into the windshield.

"Awesome!" Devlin exclaimed as the spider crack made its initial march across the glass.

"A palpable hit," Saffire said.

Pole radioed: "Did I just see a projectile cross your path?"

Brad grabbed his CB mike. "Hail! Wynda, should we turn around? Should we turn around?"

"No," Jack said to the group, keying his own mike so everyone would hear. "We keep going. We should be able to get around this and get east. Otherwise, no tornado. No happy stormy fun time."

"And no shot," Wynda's voice came back. She still had the mike keyed as she said, "Michiko, drive faster." Through the back window, Jack could see the support vehicle right on their ass, with Michiko driving, Razor shooting in the passenger seat, and Wynda peering from the back. So they *were* still alive. We'll see how long we can keep that up, Jack thought.

The caravan turned to get on the main route heading south and soon crept up behind a two-vehicle convoy whose lead van, a silver one, was plastered with logos for Zane Films.

"What's that?" Brad asked into the radio as they got closer. The extended-cab pickup truck that rode behind the Zane van had a machine mounted in the bed.

"Yes, what is that?" Wynda asked. "What does Zane have now?"

"Wouldn't you like to know?" came a deep voice over the radio, someone not of their crew, as smaller hailstones pinged off the vehicles.

"Aurelius!" Wynda said.

"Aurelius?" Jack muttered. Then, missing his ham radio, he added over the CB: "Looks like a UAV to me."

"A what?" Brad asked.

"Unmanned aerial vehicle," Jack said to the others in the van. "A fancy drone. A remotely flown plane. A *very* fun toy for storm chasing."

Wynda's voice was irate as she spoke into the mike. "Zane, don't bother. Go back to your documentaries about monkeys."

"Oh, Wynda," came the deep voice again. "I did enjoy our time in the jungle."

The silence that followed gave Jack an excuse to see Wynda in a new light, and perhaps in a cheetah-print bikini. But the storm demanded his attention. He looked ahead and saw their east turn. "Forget about it," he said into the radio. "Take the left. We have to get ahead of this thing."

Their storm was developing rapidly, while the left split had become the incredible shrinking updraft — a pretty little corkscrewing thing, rotating anti-cyclonically, a smaller mirror of the storm to the south. The right split they were chasing was developing a series of towers, back-building. Jack hoped it didn't split again. It was meaty and starting to spit out spears of lightning.

One brilliant stroke was followed by an almost instantaneous crash of thunder, and a transformer on the telephone pole Van One was passing erupted with a bang and a flash of green light. The van trembled in the concussive rumble. "Harness that, and you could power your house for a month!" Saffire said.

Devlin nodded in approval. "There's a good way to fry your UAV."

Brad looked pained. "Does the Bubble have lightning protection?"

Funny, Jack thought, that Brad was just asking this now.

"It's built around a lightweight metal frame," Devlin said. "It should shed lightning, a little like an airplane."

Brad still looked worried. "Um, you tested it?"

"Yeah, we got great footage of it in the artificial lightning lab. It'll be like a flying Faraday cage. Well, not quite, since you won't be fully enclosed in metal, but it works thanks to a few tricks. Mesh where you can't see it. Shielded electronics. And wait till you see it bounce. Did you know one of the Mars rovers bounced thirty-one times when it landed? How cool is that?"

Cool or crazy, Jack mused. If the thing ever did get off the ground, which seemed unlikely, lightning would be the least of Brad's worries.

There was a certain arrogance in all this tornado probe stuff. Every time he saw a new armor-clad chase vehicle, he recalled the loaded hundred-ton train cars he saw tossed by the Pancake tornado. As close as Jack liked to get, he knew a camera wasn't a magic shield against a twister's power.

Just beyond where Jack's crew planned to turn, the truck carrying the drone pulled over, letting the Zane van get far ahead and park. A film crew jumped out of the silver van as a couple of guys emerged from the UAV truck and tinkered with the machine in the back. In a few moments, the tiny plane shot off a rail mounted in the bed and soared in a graceful arc that would bring it toward the top of the storm.

"Christ," Wynda said over the radio, seeing the prospects for being the most extreme tornado show of next season's sweeps in serious jeopardy.

Even Jack was impressed. And Devlin was practically drooling.

"I want that," he whispered.

AURELIUS ZANE CHOSE his team carefully. First, he needed professionals to back him up on the camera work, especially since all the popular shows these days were personality-driven, and he was the personality. He needed to be in front of the camera, to drive the audience to that place where they would feel electrified and seduced and hungry for more. So he hired two freelance shooters who between them could handle the cameras and the sound and his very insistent direction as they rode in the van. They were a gaunt and listless married couple who eerily, strongly resembled each other. He called them Thing One and Thing Two, to simplify Things.

Next, he needed gophers and sycophants. Enter Ernie, meteorology grad student and chief forecaster, who did indeed understand the importance of being earnest, and Evie, an intern who wanted to document their trip for her college newspaper. She was here for credit, so she had to be paid very little to look gorgeous, her chocolate tresses flying, as she took photos of absolutely everything and wrestled with their gear.

Gear was a big part of Aurelius's adventuring, and it was expensive. He'd realized as a boy that he didn't have to act out his quests via video games and science-fiction conventions; he could make them real, as long as he had the right toys. So since he started adventuring, leaving his puzzled parents' rural grocery store in western Pennsylvania, he'd been borrowing. He'd made almost enough money now to break even, but it always took a bigger loan or better begging to make his latest enterprise happen. For this venture, he'd hired a startup to provide the flying drone and its twin, now stored in a garage in Wichita. The miniature planes were owned by two young techies who seemed unworried by knotty FAA rules. To afford the gizmos, he'd had to turn to a Hollywood producer he knew, Rodney Mezner, who lent him the money at an exorbitant interest rate while taking a financial interest in the show Zane Films was shooting for the Excursions Network. Aurelius had to get six episodes in the can in a month of shooting and, according to his contract, he had to get a tornado. Quality footage. Two minutes, at least. Otherwise, no payday, and he would face a new assault of debt collectors when he got back to his one-bedroom apartment in Pasadena.

Unlike Brad Treat, he was unclouded by doubts. At thirty-five, he had always survived and flourished, and looked good doing it, with his dirty-blond hair falling over his forehead in smooth, perfectly cut bangs. For this adventure, he'd spent some of Rodney's money on a tailor-made, double-breasted, knee-length black rain jacket that, especially when falling open in the breeze, made him look especially dashing. Success, he'd learned, took looks, guts and a reckless disregard for physics, whether he was flying a helicopter into the crater of an erupting volcano or tying himself to a cement post in Guam in the middle of a Category 5 typhoon. The footage just kept getting better, and when it came to television, there was always an appetite for destruction. More than that, there was an appetite for anything at all, as long as it was shot in high definition, given that the number of TV channels seeking original content grew almost daily.

Chasing tornadoes was a piece of cake after what he'd been through.

"The surface flow is weak," Ernie said from the back seat as they rolled south to a less serpentine east road than the one Wynda's crew had taken. "I don't know if this one is going to do it."

"See what you can do about that," Aurelius said from the driver's seat, and for a moment, gullible Ernie had a scared-rabbit look only enhanced by his wide blue eyes and dark buzz cut. Aurelius laughed and picked up the ham radio they were using for car-to-car communication. He had a CB and a scanner for backup and monitoring, but he liked the idea that fewer people might be listening to amateur radio. "Keep it flying for another twenty minutes, and then get it to the field," he said. They'd lined up a series of out-of-the-way spots, far from official scrutiny, to set up nets to catch their drone. If they had time, they set up a net on the truck. In a pinch, the drone could skid to a stop.

"All set," said Duncan, one of the techies, over the speaker. "Our feed looks fantastic."

"When it gets a tornado, then it will be fantastic," Aurelius corrected them.

"You're fantastic," Evie said cheerfully from the passenger seat, where Thing One and Thing Two and the on-board cameras could get loving shots of her profile as she took photos of Aurelius.

He smiled his best camera smile. "I'm just doing my job," he intoned deeply, "bringing the most extreme phenomena of nature to the world's living rooms." He thought for a moment. That sounded a little too PR-speak. "Try this instead, guys," he said to Things One and Two. He rolled down his window and stuck his head and left arm out, pointing to the top of the supercell as lightning flashed. "This thing could put down a tornado any minute!" he shouted with authority. There. That could be repeated in any number of commercials. He needed to remember to scream when the time came. They ate that shit up.

WYNDA WAS BACK on the CB. "Ignore it," she said in her clipped British tones. "Ignore it. So he has a bloody toy plane. We have the Bubble. Jack, find us a spot to deploy."

The three-vehicle caravan headed east, now ahead of the supercell. Jack eyed the radar on the laptop. The reborn storm looked powerful but not very well organized. He took a moment and broke away from the computer, craning his neck to look out of the back of the van, where the towering, knuckled cumulonimbus loomed large and dark against the declining sun. It was pretty, and its shape was suggestive of weak rotation, but he didn't have that tornado tingle. They might as well strap Brad in the Bubble and give it a test run. At least their meal ticket would live to see another day.

"We need a clearing at least," Jack said. The tree-lined

secondary road they were on resembled an undulating snake more than a highway. "That might be a challenge here. Let's get a couple of miles ahead of it."

"Find a level spot, a field, a parking lot, anything like that," suggested Devlin.

Jack, envisioning their very round piece of gear, couldn't help responding with sarcasm. "But a hill would be so much fun."

Andre put down his camera for a minute. "Now, I'm no director," he said, "but you have to remember, you're on. This deployment sequence could be important to the show. You've got to keep focused and energetic here, because you think you're going to see a tornado."

"Actually, I don't," Jack said, going back to the radar.

Andre sighed and returned to shooting Brad, who cleared his throat, working himself up to hero mode. "Devlin, this storm could tornado any second," Brad said. "Let's find a good place to deploy."

Saffire flashed a smile at the camera staring at her from the upper right corner of the windshield. "This is *so* exciting. This is when science is at its most fun — when it confronts the violence of nature." A shiver seemed to run through her amber locks and breasts in the same moment. Jack had a feeling the camera guys would be fighting over that footage later.

"Here we go," Devlin said from the second seat. "Here we go. This might work." They were crossing a long, low valley.

"I suggest getting a little higher on the hill so we can see it coming," Jack said. He didn't like the idea of the entire crew hiding obliviously behind a knoll if this storm really did put down a twister. That could be a bad, bad day.

"Pole!" Brad called into the radio. "Pull off up here into the parking lot."

Parking lot was an exaggeration. It was a wide dirt and gravel clearing off the right side of the road next to what apparently used to be an ice-cream stand. Although it was nearly level, it was, indeed, at the top of the hill. A weathered, broken neon ice cream cone supported by a large, rusted metal hand protruded from the boarded-up yellow brick building. The only letters left on the sign spelled out "I ... REAM."

"Ouch," Jack noted to himself as their Van One, Pole's Bubblevan and the crew SUV pulled up, side by side. As Jack slid his door open, he could feel the warm air, carried by decent southeast winds that could still give the storm the fuel and spin it needed.

"Let's deploy!" Devlin said as they piled out, all cameras and colorful rain jackets and hair blowing in the wind. Wearing a headset wired to the radio at his waist, the engineer pulled open the Bubblevan's double doors. Devlin and Pole slid out a ramp and jumped inside to disengage the Bubble. Lightning hit nearby with a quick report of thunder, prompting Saffire to emit a little whoop. It was kind of cute, Jack had to admit.

A few minutes later, after fighting with a sticky clamp, the guys rolled the Bubble slowly out of the van. They brought it to a halt on the gravel, where it rested and rocked slightly. A clear globe about six feet wide, framed by gleaming metal struts, it was a hamster ball for storm geeks. Inside, a contoured chair hung in the middle of three gyroscope-controlled rings.

The inner walls were crisscrossed with conduits and boxes for wires and electronics. The outer wall was mostly smooth but studded with instrument and camera housings attached to the shiny metal supports that encircled it. Wide airbag boxes were attached to the struts, too. While a car's airbags were internal, the Bubble's were on the outside. They would help the probe bounce if a tornado picked it up.

Brad was starting to look uncomfortable. "Does that thing have a kickstand?" he asked.

"Come on, boys!" Wynda shouted. "Action time. Get him in! Brad, look enthusiastic, for Christ's sake!"

Pole and Devlin unlatched the door of the sphere and pulled it open. A nearby flash of lightning shot a blue gleam off the curved surface.

Brad hesitated, then looked at Jack. "Well?"

Jack turned to the storm. It was getting closer and now had a wall cloud, a possible precursor to a tornado. But it still didn't have that *thing*, that magic. Not yet. His reply was low, pitched so not everyone could hear. "I don't think it's going to do it."

Jack saw relief cross Brad's face as the fearful, er, fearless leader shifted into movie-star mode. "All right, team, this thing could put down a twister any minute. Strap me in and get to safety! I don't want any of you hurt!"

The words gave an urgency, however fake, to Devlin and Pole. With swift movements, they got Brad's tall frame folded into the chair suspended inside the Bubble's rings and proceeded to lock in the web of safety harnesses that were meant to keep their star from becoming a human maraca. Brad stuck a key into the manual override control for the external airbags and unlocked it so, in an emergency, he could open the clear plastic box that protected the button. The guys popped a helmet over his head, and Brad did a sound check with Michiko and Devlin. They all should be able to hear Brad through the long-range radio monitors installed in each vehicle.

"All right, Brad," Devlin said. "The internal and external cameras are running now. All you need is a tornado to pick you up. We seriously don't think the Bubble will be lifted higher than tens of meters, and probably a lot less. If by some freak happenstance it goes so high you have to deploy the 'chutes, an alarm will sound. But the external airbags will deploy automatically when the Bubble senses a predetermined altitude increase and then a sharp descent. You can also deploy them manually at any time. I can't see a reason you'll need the manual override, but with the key in the control, you just have to flip open the cover and press the button, if it comes to that. Once the air bladders inflate, you won't have much of a view, other than whatever the cameras show on the monitor. And then you'll bounce to safety. Piece of cake." Devlin waved at the primary outside camera, and his face showed up on a small color screen mounted above and in front of Brad. "Good luck!"

"With a team like you behind me, I know I'm already lucky," said Brad, getting into his brave role.

"All right, time to hit the road and get this on camera!" Saffire said.

Jack hung back for a moment as the others rushed to the vehicles. The storm was probably going to miss them. But there was a distinct change in the wind where they were. It was stronger, warmer. The storm was breathing, sucking in the moist, hot air that had traveled all this way from the Gulf of Mexico. Inflow. It was getting stronger. He took a last look at the Bubble, met Brad's confused eyes with his own and shrugged, not without pity. Then he joined the others in the van, and the caravan spun out of the I ... REAM parking lot, hauling east toward a vantage point on the next hill as thunder crashed around them.

THIS WAS the spring of Brad's discontent. He was on the skids with his fiancée, Willa, whom he still called his fiancée because she was hanging on to the pawn-shop cubic zirconia he'd purchased for her as an engagement ring. At twenty-five, with a degree in business but not the will, he was pretty much unqualified to do anything except for what he'd fallen into. And that was storm chasing and the occasional part-time job.

This was better than running Thor's Tours, though, and having to face the disappointment when tourists paying a few thousand bucks saw little more than broken windshields and dust devils after Brad led them around in circles, usually nowhere near the tornado. All that changed outside Prairie Rock, where Jack and his research buddies saved Brad and the tourists when their tour van got stuck in the path of a monster twister. That's not how it all came out in the media, however. Brad emerged a hero as his van became a flying tornado probe and his camera caught incredible footage inside the monster. The bits about the terror and the rescue and Jack's selfless act later that day never did find legs when the story was retold, but Brad got a job offer out of it, as the star of this new reality show. Sure, there was competition on TV, lots of it, but he was getting paid quite a bit without having to get a real job. And they had the Bubble, which made his show unique.

All that said, it wasn't comforting to be in it as the brooding supercell, tinged with black and mint-green, bore down upon him. Through the clear walls, between the

Bubble's struts, the storm looked a lot more real than the drawings on the white boards in the production company's modest L.A. offices. He could see a milky wall of rain to his northwest and a blocky lowering under the storm's base. The anvil spread above his head. Lightning hit in bursts around him. The Bubble's straps cut into his shoulders, and he had to pee.

His one comfort was that it looked like the worst might miss him, but he noticed the grass bending toward the storm, worshiping its might. Or, as Jack might have pointed out, the southeast inflow was picking up. The storm was sucking in fuel, and the wind made the Bubble rock slightly and then, slowly, turn half a revolution toward the supercell. Brad bobbled in his chair and harness, getting a brief look at the ground as the computerized, gyroscope-controlled servos slowly righted him.

"We have movement," Brad said nervously.

"Copy, Brad," he heard Devlin say. "How far have you moved?"

"Just far enough so that I was looking at the ground for a second. I'm upright again."

"Are you steady on top of the hill?" Devlin asked. "Are the cameras working?"

That's when it really sunk in for Brad that he was on top of a hill. A pretty big hill, with tussocks and pits and … was that an armadillo running past him, away from the storm?

"Uh, yes, still on top of the hill," Brad said. But not steady, he thought to himself. He pressed a button on his armrest that made the monitor above his head flip through multiple camera views. "It's getting good shots, I think." The Bubble trembled for a moment. The wind shifted a little as the storm got closer. Then the probe rolled west again, a whole revolution this time. It was almost to the edge of the parking lot and the slope.

"We saw that roll," Devlin said over the radio. "That looks cool."

"Yeah, uh, real cool."

That's when the storm inhaled.

The southeast winds picked up abruptly. The Bubble rolled another revolution and a half, this time coming to a stop against a rock. It took a few seconds for the gyroscope to catch up. Brad felt nauseous.

"I hope all these electronics can handle vomit," he heard himself saying.

"Now, Brad," Wynda said, "keep it positive. This is for posterity."

"I thought it was just a test," he said, his voice pitching higher.

The Bubble bumped against the rock, and then again. And then harder, like an obsessive rocking chair, as a few fat raindrops spattered the clear enclosure. As the wind whistled around the pitching orb, Brad let out a slow and strangely harmonic whine.

ON THE NEXT HILL, where the vehicles had parked by a derelict windmill, Jack stood outside and looked at the Bubble through a pair of binoculars. Perhaps foolishly, he was the only one who braved the lightning. He always needed to get the flavor of a storm. As the rotation and inflow picked up, this one had started to get a stacked-plate look. But Jack could see that the rotation wasn't Brad's problem right now. The inflow was rocking the Bubble against some kind of blockage, a rock or something, in the increasing wind. Jack was having trouble standing steady against the gusts, and he estimated they had topped fifty miles per hour as the storm greedily sucked up the warm, moist air. It was just a matter of time before the Bubble was set free, and then they'd see what earthbound deployment was all about.

It turned out, it was a matter of about ninety seconds. Jack felt the gust first, as he was east of Brad's location. The Bubble felt it second.

Like a wave wearing down a wall in a hurricane, it took that one good push to send it over. Then the Bubble was off and running — or, to be more accurate, rolling and occasionally bouncing down the hill, without the help of airbags. Jack could hear Brad's shrieks over the radio even from outside the van, and he jumped in the side door.

"We'd better go get him," he said to Devlin, who was behind the wheel.

"This is awesome," said Devlin. "A great test run!"

"Or roll." Jack couldn't help but be amused as he thought of Brad spinning inside the Bubble, but he knew he needed it to work, and needed Brad to get through it, if he was going to get his bonus — if not this time, then next.

Jack picked up the radio as the van accelerated. "Come on, everybody," he said. "Let's play catch."

The Bubble had vanished from sight after several yards, with the hill blocking their view. They drove down, then up, and were halfway down the "I … REAM" hill before they spotted it, sitting still in a trickling brook, which parted to spill around its curved bottom. Whatever the bottom was at that moment.

"Brad?" Devlin called over the radio. "Brad, are you all right?"

All they heard was a guttural sound as they parked on the shoulder. The storm was bypassing them, though they were still in brisk wind and light rain, and a plume of dust advanced in their direction. Not a tornado. "RFD," Jack said as they jumped out and ran toward the Bubble. It was about twenty-five yards from the road and looked intact. It could have been worse.

Michiko caught up with him, microphone boom in hand, running beside him. "I heard you say something back there," she said. "RFD?"

"Rear-flank downdraft. That wall of dust. We need to get him out of here. We should be OK, but this will be a lot more pleasant if we hurry."

Andre and Razor, cameras in hand, and the others got to the Bubble about the same time. The surface was muddy and scratched in some places. It had been clearing trail, too — weeds were jammed into every seam and gizmo that dared to stick out a few millimeters. Brad was OK. They could tell by the way he was screaming.

"GET ME THE FUCK OUT OF HERE!" They could hear it through the curved walls and the shielded air vents. Devlin and Pole looked for the door and found it, halfway in the water — the reason Brad couldn't open the door himself — and started to roll the ball. "DON'T YOU FUCKING ROLL ME!" Brad screamed again, but they had to do something, so roll him they did, onto drier ground. The lagging gyro slowly flipped him upright as they got the door open. Devlin and Pole painstakingly unstrapped Brad, and as they pulled him out, he leaned forward a little and threw up.

"Language, Brad, language," Wynda scolded, handing him a small towel she pulled from her jacket pocket. "Get your brave face on and tell the cameras what you went through."

"Hurry up," Jack said, as the first bits of dust and rock started to sting their skin. The dust plume was overtaking them, and the winds were increasing.

Shaky and pale, the Twister Tracker visibly tried to pull himself together. "What do I say?"

Wynda looked thoughtful. "How about, 'I can't wait to launch this into a real tornado!' "

Brad looked at her incredulously, then pointed west and screamed, "TORNADO!"

It was indeed a column of rotating dirt, but it wasn't the tornado they were looking for. The weak gustnado spun through their group, carrying dust and grass in a cyclonic swirl, scattering them and sending them to the ground as they tried to cover up their mouths and eyes — except for the camera guys, of course, who dropped to their knees and risked exposing their gear to get footage of the chaos. At the least, it made for good video and a lot of dust in their teeth. Wynda looked rumpled but ecstatic as it passed. Jack laughed for the brief thrill of it. The spin-up weakened and dissipated as it climbed the shallow slope. They caught their breath and dusted themselves off.

"Oh, look," said Saffire from a spot near a pile of rocks where she and Michiko had taken shelter. "A tarantula!"

"Yuck," said Michiko, who edged away from her and sat on another rock, picking debris out of her fuzzy mike.

"It's an Oklahoma brown," the actress said, reaching down and, to Jack's astonishment, gently picking it up and laying it on the sleeve of her jacket. "No worse the wear. Just have to make sure I don't get its nasty little hairs in my skin. Right, boy?" She held the fuzzy creature up to her face and looked lovingly into its eight eyes.

"How can you tell it's a boy?" Michiko asked.

"I'm not a hundred percent sure, but the boys are smaller."

"Adorable," Wynda said dryly. "OK, now's your chance to say something heroic, Brad. Oh, wait a minute." She was looking down at Brad's jeans, where a wet spot darkened the crotch. "Pole, go back to the car and fetch another pair of Brad's trousers."

THE TEAM WAS EXHAUSTED, and no one except Jack wanted to continue the chase. Brad, especially, sulked in the passenger seat of Van One as Devlin drove back west, blasting a country station, about the only frequency he could tune in. Even Jack recognized that, one, their storm had entered horribly hilly chase territory in Missouri; and two, the Bubble was going to need a thorough going-over before they could think of launching it again. They headed toward their temporary headquarters near Oklahoma City to see what they could do.

Jack flipped through radar images anyway as they rolled, armchair-chasing, considering what it would be like if the Bubble really worked. To be able to see a tornado from the inside — or even to flip around one once or twice, to be lifted by the updraft and actually feel which way the winds around the funnel were blowing — would be an incredible experience. At the same time, he knew the risks were huge. The airbags would help the Bubble bounce or float, but they had been tested on sharp rocks, not, say, church steeples. And the chances of the Bubble getting good elevation or a panoramic view were small. The large airbag boxes, camera housings and other gear attached to the struts already limited the view. Once the airbags inflated and surrounded the Bubble, Brad would be stuck watching the fun on a little monitor. Who'd want to risk his life to fly into a tornado just to watch it on TV? Apparently someone who wanted to be on TV, and that was Brad.

The only one among them who seemed born to be on TV was Saffire, whose yellow jacket now partially hid her tempting décolletage. She sat next to Jack in the back as they took a break from filming. In the middle seat, Andre dozed, a tiny drop of spittle clinging to the corner of his mouth and threatening to drop onto the camera he still clutched tightly, unconsciously, under his arm.

"It was a great day, wasn't it?" Saffire made it a statement more than a question. "How is that storm doing?"

Jack wasn't sure if she was really interested, but he was always ready to talk about the weather. "It started to fall apart, but since it crossed the border, it's showing new signs of life. I wouldn't be surprised if it produced after dark."

"A tornado, you mean?"

"Yes, a tornado. The low-level jet is kicking in." He sounded grumpier than he felt. At least he was chasing and not stuck in some office somewhere, though that could be next if this job didn't pan out.

"Cool. I haven't seen one yet."

"We'll do something about that."

"How can you be sure?"

"I've never gone a year without seeing one, at least since I've been chasing," he said. "I'll get us to a tornado. Whether we'll get Mr. Twister in it, that's another question."

They heard a growl from the front seat, where Brad had stirred from his funk long enough to snarl at them. "Mr. *Tracker* to you."

"I can't wait to see him fly," Saffire said, nodding toward

Brad. "You heard about that tornado he filmed in Kansas, didn't you?"

Jack gave her a half smile. "He was almost a tornado probe in that one, too."

"I know! It was amazing footage. I got to see it when they cast me in this show. How did you hear about it?"

"Besides the TV shows that have told and retold the *story*?" he said, making it clear he meant something different by "story." "I have good sources." He flashed back to that day, to the van full of Brad's tourists stuck in the mud, to the massive tornado and the Chinese fire drill with the research vehicles that saved Brad's ass and sent Jack off to sound the alarm in Prairie Rock. It was dreamlike now, everything happened so rapidly. He was glad he had his own video to go back to. The only other things he'd taken away from the last few moments in the town were his memories, a laptop full of data, and his life. And the siren.

"So you know more than you're saying?" Saffire asked.

"Always," Jack teased.

"You don't have to tell me everything." She winked one of those big golden-brown eyes at him. "I always find out anyway."

"That's what makes you such a good reporter." He couldn't keep the derision out of his voice.

"I know, *Star Beat* is not *60 Minutes,* but we had a much better wardrobe. Anyway, this is a lot more fun. I can see this leading to a regular gig on a TV show. A science show, I hope. Those geek shows are always looking for a techno-babe to fill out the cast."

"That's how you see yourself? A techno-babe?"

"I'm whatever they want me to be, baby," she said. "But I do have an inner geek that's dying to get out."

Jack liked the lilt in her voice, the way she said "baby." It was cute. That was the second time he'd noticed her propensity for cuteness, which he usually found cloying in anything but women, and sometimes even then. Still, since the events of the past year, he'd noticed in himself a subtle, disturbing softening of his attitude, manifested in involuntary reactions to such stimuli as sentimental commercials and puppy calendars. So what? Saffire was no puppy. She was persuasive when she spoke and magnetic when she moved. And she was a lot more than cute when she folded her body into a car seat or unfolded it to stand outside in front of a camera, showing off all the right angles.

"How'd you know about the tarantula?" he asked her.

"Studied entomology in college before I started getting cast in a bunch of things," she said. "Had to pick up the last few credits while I was filming *Star Beat*."

"You studied bugs?"

"What did you think I studied, hairspray?"

"I don't know. TV, maybe?"

Saffire showed her dimples. "Majored in bugs. Minored in film." She leaned closer, and he caught another whiff of lavender. "Hey, are those eyes real?"

"I could be a cyborg," Jack said.

"My co-host used to wear these weird violet contacts. I called him Elizabeth Taylor."

"I don't wear contacts. They're green and they're real. I know. I'm a freak." But he said it as if he were saying, *I'm irresistible.* Experience had taught him the allure of his green eyes.

"I like them," she confirmed, offering a coy smile.

"So, is that name real?"

"Reality is relative."

"True. Kind of like this show." He wondered how much of

her was real. All of the important parts, at least, he thought. "You want to get a drink later?" He said it without thinking. He couldn't help it. There was something about her, more than she let on. And what else did he have to chase on this trip, besides storms? Michiko looked like she might be fun to hang with, but she was apparently involved with some hipster guitar player from her home in Phoenix and quite possibly immune to his charms. Wynda was too damn manic. Besides, you don't fuck with the boss, figuratively or literally, and she was his paycheck.

Saffire, though — women had gotten him into trouble before on chases. And except for a tragic moment or two, he'd enjoyed it.

"Sure," she accepted his invitation, her smile broadening. "What else is there to do?"

Oh, he could think of a few things.

IT WAS dark in the gravel lot of the low-rent business park, where rows of numbered metal buildings concealed mysterious enterprises only sporadically labeled by signs. Jack could hear the whine of a power saw in a unit half a building away and saw a couple of pickup trucks parked in the light that spilled out of its garage door. A few tractor-trailers had parking lights on nearby, but they were quiet. There was no other activity, except for here, at the unit rented by Palatable Productions, where Van One was parked next to Pole's Bubble transport.

Jack spotted the light shining from around the door of the garage and frowned. He'd been hoping for a little privacy, because right behind him, dancing out of the darkness, was

Saffire. A pure optimist, she seemed to have a gift for enjoying wherever she landed, even if it was one of the ugliest spots in Oklahoma City. She executed a graceful turn in her black jeans and olive-green peasant blouse and skipped up to him.

"We need some bubbly before we see the Bubble," she whispered in his ear.

"We've already had our share of Manhattans," he said, and he was feeling them. Unfortunately, the bar where they'd spent the last couple of hours — a short walk away — hadn't been as intoxicating as the drinks. The neon-lit faux-cowboy joint was decorated chiefly with animal heads, including a creepy jackalope. The stuffed rabbit had watched them slowly get drunk, its tacked-on antlers looking as askew as Jack now felt.

"I need bubbly, or I'm going to have to repossess my evening," Saffire said, swaying a little.

"There's no place to get bubbly around here."

"We don't need a liquor store. Do you have the key to the van?"

Jack dug into his pocket.

"I have a key. What will that get me?"

"Bubbly!" Saffire said, reaching into the same pocket as his hand and giving him more of a thrill than he'd expected as she grabbed the keys.

She hopped over to the back of the vehicle, opened it and dug beneath some bags. There hid a small cooler, the type that plugged into the accessory outlet. She opened it and pulled out a bottle of inexpensive California champagne, or whatever they called it when it came from California.

"Clever," he said as she shut the van door. "Does Wynda know about that?"

"I told her I had to have a cooler to store my fruit juices. A couple of them fit in there, too, but I find champagne is more crucial to my health." She gave him a sly look, caressing the bottle's neck seductively.

"Works for me," he said, feeling his blood rise. "But if you don't want her to know about it, you might want to hide it now, because I think she's in there."

They both listened, and Jack heard it again — the clipped, irate tones of Wynda seeping through the closed doors. He couldn't tell exactly what she was saying, but they were about to find out.

"I'll stow it in this handy champagne storage area," Saffire said, tucking the bottle behind a trash can between the garage and the people door. Jack pushed the latter open and held it for her, lightly touching her shoulder as he entered the work space after her.

The overhead lights were on, and the Bubble shone brightly under the added glare of work lights that showed off all its recent scratches. It was stabilized on a rack Wynda's crew had set up for the purpose. Devlin was polishing it, and so was Brad, probably because Razor was filming him do so with a tripod-mounted camera. Pole sat in front of a computer at a table full of cables and test equipment, playing digital solitaire.

"I can't believe this is going to take you another bloody day to fix," Wynda was saying to Devlin.

"It will take about ten minutes to fix, but the parts won't be in until tomorrow afternoon," he said.

"What's wrong with it?" asked Jack, feeling a little of his buzz wear off as curiosity took over.

"I ran some tests," Devlin said, "and the mechanism to automatically inflate the airbags is indicating failure in about one of ten simulations. I want to replace both the sensors so we're absolutely sure it will work."

"I could always push the button," Brad said as he stepped back, admiring his distorted reflection in the surface of the Bubble, where the clear walls gleamed between the struts.

"The auto mechanism is there in case you get knocked unconscious or something," Devlin said matter-of-factly. "You don't want to get four or five stories above the ground and fall with no airbags."

"Oh." Brad blanched. It was clear he hadn't thought of that possibility.

Wynda looked frustrated, but she caved. "That would be an unfortunate ending to our program," she said. "So I suppose we'll wait until you get it fixed. Jack, where have you been?"

He stood warily under her scrutiny as she took in his expression and the glowing Saffire. "Dinner, of course," he said.

"Fine." Wynda relaxed, a wee smile playing around her mouth. "We should all get some rest, then, and do laundry, since it looks as if we're going to have another day off. Except Devlin, of course," she added, the annoyance creeping back in. "Jack, why don't you use the computer here and work on a forecast? I'll give you a call in a little while to get the gen. Pole, take Van One into the shop and get the windscreen replaced in the morning. Razor, a word?"

Razor left his camera and walked over to Wynda. Devlin and Brad approached Jack and Saffire. "Want to go get a beer?" Devlin asked. "I told Michiko we'd pick her and Andre up at the hotel."

"I think we're good," Saffire said.

"Rain check?" added Jack.

Devlin looked at both of them and got it. "Tornado check," he grinned.

Pole gave up on his game and wandered over to the Bubble to turn off the work lights. Razor and Wynda broke apart, and Razor made one more tweak on his camera. The three of them headed for the door. "Last person out, lock up," Wynda said to no one in particular as she left.

Devlin shrugged as he followed the rest in a cloud of tension. "This could be a long spring," he murmured.

Jack and Saffire walked outside behind them, and once they were sure the others were gone, Saffire grabbed the bottle she'd hidden and pushed Jack back inside.

He found the light switches and flipped off all but one of the overheads, the one over the Bubble. It cast an eerie, greenish glow on the clear sphere, and he could feel them both drawn to it. It was magnetic, alien, like something out of a movie.

"Didn't Glinda the Good Witch ride in something like that?" Saffire mused.

"Only she didn't need airbags," Jack said.

"Just an enormously puffy pink dress."

"Let's take a closer look," he replied, walking toward the Bubble. He ran his hands over the smooth surface between the struts and found the latches. He pulled the door open and climbed inside the tall chair, which was padded and contoured for maximum survivability. Even if the sphere was six feet wide, it felt as if he barely fit, with the gear and walls circling tightly around him. Still, he pointed at Saffire, crooked a finger and gave her a "get over here" gesture.

She chuckled, placed the sweating champagne bottle on the concrete floor and somehow climbed in. It was immediately clear that this was not going to work for Jack's unscientific purposes, but she sat in his lap anyway, putting her arms around his neck. They looked at each other for a few seconds, and Jack recognized in her the thing that so often propelled him forward without thinking, a lust for the moment. That, and more than a touch of drunkenness. He leaned in, and their lips met and melded. He slipped his tongue into play, tasting hers, lightly at first, then probing, until their hands were wandering and Jack was wishing they'd stayed back at the hotel. The Bubble creaked, and they paused, breathing heavily.

"Not built for two," Jack joked.

"Can you imagine — not just, you know — but flying in this thing?" Saffire's eyes were bright. "Seeing something — surviving something — no one has ever seen before?"

Jack held her lightly, distracted by the idea as he looked at the gadgetry surrounding them. "I wouldn't mind seeing a tornado from cloud level," he said, "but scientifically speaking, I'd rather fuck in zero gravity." He caught her eye again, realizing what he'd said in his sozzled state and wondering if he'd gone too far.

Saffire raised her eyebrows but granted him a mischievous smile. "Got a rocket in your pocket, baby?"

Just then, the thing in his pocket buzzed. The smartphone. He extracted it with difficulty, answered and recognized the voice immediately.

"Jack, do you have that forecast for me?"

Wynda, Jack mouthed to Saffire.

"It's been *ten minutes*." Jack let himself sound as irritated as he felt. Smiling with anticipation at Saffire, he quickly finished his conversation with Wynda. "Give me at least twenty."

THIS WAS THE NEW REALITY, thought Aurelius Zane as his silver van and the UAV truck made their way west on I-40. Every storm was subject to a fucking storm-chaser traffic jam, and even though his crew didn't expect to chase until tomorrow, he counted dozens of antenna-topped, ad-clad chase cars passing them as they headed through Oklahoma toward the Texas Panhandle. He didn't mind the ones who played nice, but making it seem as if, on camera, he was a rare adventurer in the wilderness was getting harder and harder. At least they wouldn't be chasing in Oklahoma, where tornadoes were a live TV spectator sport filmed from helicopters, and the clueless curious couldn't help jumping in the family van to check out the tornado at the intersection of Road X and Highway Y, exactly where their favorite meteorologist told them it would be. Aurelius marveled at the ability of people to believe in TV shows about ghosts and Bigfoot while refusing to give credibility to the warnings the storm-chasing shows posted to cover their legal asses. While most locals seemed storm-aware, there were always some who thought they were immune. One would think they'd learn from the damage they had seen personally, given that they lived in Tornado Alley.

Though Aurelius was aghast at people's capacity for self-deception, he knew it was possible he also exploited it. He excelled at becoming what they wanted him to be. To promote his bestselling book, "Life Is an Adventure," which was part memoir and part self-help, he gave motivational speeches. He talked about following dreams, climbing that volcano, surfing that big wave, and so on and so forth. Audiences were enraptured by his PowerPoint presentations, and they left thinking they could do anything, at least until the baby spit up on their clothes or the car broke down on the way to their job at the discount store, if they had a job or a car at all. Handsome and fearless, he was in the business of hope and excitement and flash. Escapism at its finest, the illusion of purpose. And despite being endlessly dogged by creditors threatening to shatter his illusion, he was good at it.

"Open your mouth! Cootchie-cootchie-coo! Here comes the little airplane!" he heard a staccato voice say over the CB. British. Female. The scrumptious and infuriating Wynda. As Zane drove, he looked in the side mirror and saw the Palatable Productions caravan creeping up in the other lane behind his silver van and the truck that shouldered the miniature aircraft.

He couldn't resist picking up the radio: "I'm sorry, whose mouth is open in this scenario?"

Thing One and Thing Two, sensing action, pulled out their cameras and started filming him and the vehicles, while Ernie and Evie tittered.

"A real storm chaser would fly *himself* into the tornado," came a voice he didn't recognize.

"Very good, Brad," said Wynda. "Andre, I hope you got that."

"We're doing this for science," Aurelius lied.

"And we're doing this for the sunburned polar bears in the Arctic, you bloody ball bag," Wynda retorted.

"You would have to bring up my balls," Aurelius countered, "given how impressive they are."

Evie looked at him, confused. "What is she talking about?"

"It's British, my dear," he said. "It doesn't matter what they say, as long as it sounds good."

Ernie looked interested. "It *does* sound good."

Aurelius shot him a look. "She's mine. Or was," he added, glancing at Evie, not wanting to diminish her distant admiration of him.

As if on cue, Wynda's voice came back on the radio. "What

are the chances of me running into you in the middle of America? I'm reminded of the twenty-four hours of belching that followed our visit to the Pickle and Jodhpur. You just keep coming back."

"I'm at least as persistent as that shepherd's pie. Those were some chewy shepherds." He remembered with fondness their evening at the London pub, and with horror the extreme indigestion that followed. Why was everything he did extreme?

"I am torn between asking where you're going to stay, if only for the sake of avoiding you," Wynda said, "or telling you to go to hell."

"Why don't we talk about it tonight over a seventy-two-ounce steak, and you can tell me to go to hell in the morning?" Aurelius replied.

"You're *not!*" Wynda said over the radio.

"The Big Texan makes fabulous television. Everybody knows that. We gonna see you there?"

"Not if I see you first," Wynda replied. Aurelius suppressed a laugh as he heard her keep talking, forgetting to release her microphone. "Brad, remember, no snacking. I want to film you eating that dinner, and I don't want you sparking out until you've eaten at least two pounds of meat. Oh, damn," he heard her mutter as she realized the mike was still on, and gentle static resumed.

"I'm sorry, who's eating meat?" Aurelius asked suggestively.

"Brad is," came her reply, and Zane heard multiple voices laughing on the other end of the radio before she unkeyed the mike again.

He'd heard rumors about her show, her device and her crew. Brad, he was pretty sure, was that Twister Tracker guy who'd been all over TV after the Prairie Rock tornado. As for the Bubble, which he'd heard them mention on the radio — he could only guess. If it was some sort of probe and had to be inserted or launched into a tornado, that meant it involved danger. Ergo, it should involve him. And there was no contractual reason he shouldn't be on *two* television shows next season.

It was definitely time to reacquaint himself with the lovely, carnivorous Wynda.

JACK LIKED A GOOD STEAK, but he was superstitious, and he didn't feel it was right to eat one on a storm chase without seeing a tornado first. Still, Wynda was hell-bent on going to The Big Texan, seeing as how its steak challenge and wandering singers and attractive young cowpoke servers would make decent TV to fill in around what, so far, were pretty uneventful chases. Brad would try to consume the massive slab of meat, plus all the sides and fixin's, in one hour under the glare of HD television. This might be the one thing Brad actually could do, Jack thought.

That morning, after a day of laundry and sleeping off hangovers, the team had stowed the repaired Bubble in the Bubblevan and grabbed a big, greasy-spoon breakfast. As they'd loaded up the vehicles with their bags and gear, Jack had snuck up behind Saffire and run a hand through her smooth curls, while giving Razor a dirty look as the tattooed one pointed his camera their way.

"Not the hair," she'd said, her voice a sexy, gentle slap as she pulled away. Now in cool professional mode, she seemed a little unsettled around him since their drunken encounter two nights before. They hadn't succeeded in consummating their cocktail-fueled date. The Bubble was simply too awkward, and when they'd staggered back to the hotel, he had escorted the increasingly drowsy Saffire to her room only to see her pass out, her green and black outfit clashing with the maroon and teal Southwest motif on the bedspread. He'd taken off her shoes, covered her with the blanket and left her to sleep, placing the unopened champagne bottle by the television. Instead of breaking what had been an unusual dry spell for him, he got to return to his uncomfortable room, light up a cigarette, unwrap a flimsy plastic hotel cup and have another drink from the bottle of sipping bourbon he carried in his bag. Soon he was seated at the faux-wood laminate desk and doing a forecast on his laptop, a task he found actually became more intuitive when he had a couple of drinks in him. Somehow his brain connected all the pieces more quickly: the upper air, the surface winds, the highs, the lows, the moisture and temperature and geography, the boundaries that might trigger storms, and the subtle mesoscale features that revealed themselves in elegant water vapor loops. Though he hated waking up with a computer keyboard imprinted on his face.

Tomorrow did look promising: a classic dryline setup with a nice cold front moving in. And he loved chasing in the Panhandle, with its marvelous, dusty flatness. Usually only a thread of barbed wire stood between him and his view of the sky, unless, of course, they ended up driving up and down the craggy slopes of the Caprock.

As Devlin drove the van west and into Texas and past the colossal cross in Groom, which always made Jack imagine a giant Jesus rampaging among tiny tourists, Jack settled into watching for dust devils. Winds were light today, and it was warm. Soon, he saw what he was after, rising from a recently

plowed field. It started small, barely a swirl of almost invisible
dust, then grew into a respectable column of reddish brown, a
spinning dancer entranced by itself. Its steps were so light and
rapid that its feet were a blur, and its arms whirled and feath-
ered through the air with delicate randomness, nature's chore-
ography. It was so caught up in its own forward motion that it
failed to notice the green field looming in its path, a recently
watered patch of earth where it died and was buried in an
instant. It was no tornado, but if Jack closed his eyes and used
his imagination, he might be able to justify that slab of meat
tonight.

Amarillo was familiar, a strip of a city along I-40 that mate-
rialized out of nowhere and beckoned travelers with the
promise of a multitude of hotel rooms, the American Quarter
Horse Hall of Fame and the Big Texan. The billboards had
been haunting them for miles: *FREE 72-oz. STEAK* followed by
an asterisk and the minuscule footnote, barely readable while
whizzing by at seventy miles per hour: *dinner if eaten in one
hour.*

Jack was relieved they weren't staying at the Texan. While
he secretly loved the rooms, with the kitschy swinging saloon
doors that led to the bathrooms and the Texas flag shower
curtains and the cow print blankets, he would need triple-
crown-fast Internet in the morning. And he knew from experience that web-surfing at the Big Texan was more like riding a
mule.

They checked in at their generic, mid-priced hotel, which
had the exact same patterned bedspread in the room as the
one back in Oklahoma. Saffire was on a different floor, he
noted, but there might be an opportunity later to warm her up
again. There was a pool, and they had social time ahead at the
Big Texan. He took a quick shower, left his chin stocked with

manly stubble and pulled on a black T-shirt. As The Weather Channel's Jim Cantore had proved repeatedly during hurricane chases, you could never really go wrong with a black T-shirt.

A few minutes after Jack met the rest of the crew in the lobby, the Big Texan's limo showed up. "No," Wynda said as they all moved forward. "Just Brad, Saffire, Devlin and the two shooters. I want only our stars on camera. Even if you *are* looking well in that T-shirt." She patted Jack's rough cheek, gave him a bright smile and led the rejects — Jack, Michiko and Pole — to Van One.

Pole drove. "I don't drink," he said in his typical flat, nasal tone. "However, I may be soporific by the time we're done, depending on my beef intake. You'll have to check my breath for excess meat molecules."

Jack laughed, surprised to hear Pole talk, let alone say anything interesting. A corner of Pole's mouth lifted when he realized his one utterance of the day had been acknowledged.

After navigating Amarillo's elevated highways and loopy U-turn exits, they pulled up and parked in time to see the limo unloading. The setting sun had cast the sky in peachy orange and blue, streaked with clouds of red, backlighting the enormous fake cow that stood sentry outside the restaurant's long, creaky, wooden porch. For a moment, Brad looked like somebody important, surrounded as he was by an entourage and two intense-looking camera guys as he climbed out of the shiny car in his sunglasses. Mitigating his gravitas somewhat was the fact that the white limo had cow horns on the front and a taxi-style Big Texan sign on the top.

Michiko helped Razor and Andre shoot Brad walking into the restaurant four times, from every possible angle, before Wynda allowed them all to enter. A blast of country music and the tinkle of arcade machines greeted them inside. Light spilled into the lobby from the gift shop, which carried the latest in hot sauce, horse figurines, John Deere lamps, cow-poop "art," Western paraphernalia and stuffed rattlesnakes, eerily frozen in coiled strike position.

Within a few minutes of their approaching the vast dining room, a friendly cowboy showed them to seats at one of the many long tables surrounding the stage. On the dais, in front of the grill, a table for six with a cowhide tablecloth was set up in the shadow of six large digital clocks mounted on the wall above.

"This will be perfect," said Wynda. "Andre, Razor, get ready. Brad, tell the server you want to do the thing."

Brad had been starving himself all day, to the point where he confessed to feeling queasy. "Couldn't I just get a little bread first?" he asked.

"Nonsense," Wynda replied. "You have to save room! Look, here comes Gene Autry now."

A brief look crossed the waiter's face that told Jack he'd heard Wynda's remark, but he was smooth, twangy and relentlessly friendly as he asked if he could take their drink orders.

"I'd like to try the seventy-two-ounce steak," Brad said, a note of defeat already in his voice.

"Well, we can fix you right up," the waiter said in that Texas style peculiar to cowboys and airline pilots. "I'll put in the order, and when I bring back the drinks, we'll set you up. If you want to call folks at home and have 'em watch you, we've got you on the web cams right there." He pointed up and to the back of the room.

Razor and Andre were still filming. "I think I'm covered," Brad said. Michiko, quietly efficient as always, made sure his wireless mike was working before she ordered a flight of the restaurant's microbrew beers and a steak that would make Paul Bunyan quiver. Jack had begun to realize that the slight young woman got up before all of them on most mornings and ran, whether they were in the city or surrounded by fields. He'd bumped into her yesterday when he was walking back from the corner store, a newly purchased cigarette in his hand, and was greeted only with a slow shake of the head as she ran by.

All of them ordered steaks except Saffire, who went for the catfish platter. "I'm a fishatarian," she said to no one in particular. Devlin almost had her talked into the Mountain Oysters, but Pole's snickers prompted her to look them up on her handheld. Bull testicles, which is what they were, didn't seem so tempting.

Jack was fortunate to have a lean figure that seemed unaffected by several weeks of road food each spring, but he didn't go whole cow. Instead, he went for the classics: an eight-ounce center-cut sirloin with mushrooms, the salad with blue cheese, a baked potato, and an extra side of fried okra, one of the few good things he remembered about growing up in Virginia. He added a top-shelf margarita. It was a tourist drink, but this was a tourist place.

By the time the food arrived, Brad was already ensconced in the pig-out chair. Two others joined him on the platform, ready to take the challenge. One was a slight, weather-beaten fiftysomething woman dressed in a "Mother Trucker" T-shirt who looked as if she could use a seventy-two-ounce steak. The other was a guy in a large, freshly purchased cowboy hat, maybe a couple of years younger than Brad — British, judging by his chatter with members of the camera-wielding storm-tour group who gathered around him. Jack had noted on more than one occasion that the Brits couldn't get enough of Yank beef, especially after the whole mad cow nightmare.

Out came the platters, and the truth of "seventy-two-ounce steak-asterisk-*dinner* if eaten in one hour" finally came home. The slab of meat was almost impossibly huge and, given its size and texture, which so vividly declared it a piece of dead animal, somewhat grotesque. The sides were respectable — baked potato, salad, roll and shrimp cocktail — and they were usually a challenger's downfall. Jack could barely imagine the revulsion generated by a starchy baked potato after eating four-plus pounds of meat.

The cameramen had managed to gobble just a couple of mouthfuls of their dinners before they were forced to film Brad's epic attempt. He had an hour, but anyone who watched food television knew that the first twenty minutes were crucial, and he didn't look so good. He ate the roll first, shooting Wynda a defiant glance as he did so, and then dug into the steak.

Wynda was transfixed by this grand television event, at least until Aurelius Zane and his team walked in. They were seated across the room but close enough to where, Jack noticed, she couldn't help glancing over at him. He wasn't sure if her expression meant hostility or love. He confused the two when it came to figuring out women, and the closer he got to see which it was, he found women often defaulted to love.

Watching the gavotte between Wynda and Zane was almost as entertaining as watching Brad shovel in the beef. The Twister Tracker's eyebrows came together in his customary manifestation of anxiety as he saw the British boy and the Mother Trucker advancing on him, finishing off their sides well before they were halfway through their steak. "I'm racing the clock, not them," he told the cameras between mouthfuls, affecting confidence. He began eating faster, then with an impressive rhythm, slurping water, taking a bite of potato or shrimp, stuffing an enormous hunk of fibrous meat into his mouth, chewing a few times and swallowing with effort before going through each step again. With seventeen minutes to go, he had about a pound of meat left. It was then that he made a sound that a nervous walrus might have attempted in his first singing audition for a Broadway production of *The Walrus King,* a kind of snuffly warble. And he began to turn blue.

THERE WAS an essential moment when all noise in the large room dimmed, like the flickering of a light bulb. Servers halted in mid-step and looked toward the stage. The trio of cowboy musicians who'd been making the rounds trailed off in the middle of "Yellow Rose of Texas." Wynda made a slight squeaking sound.

It was one of the servers who made a move first, flopping down her tray on the nearest table and clambering onto the stage. But as she tried to get her arms around Brad to give him the Heimlich, he stood and staggered and struggled and waved her off, choking all the while. The girl knew what she was doing, despite the impression given by her fringed outfit, but without a cooperative subject, she was lost. The other contestants looked alarmed but continued to eat, unstoppable as the clock ticked down in slow motion. Jack and the rest of the team stood up as the microseconds ticked by, subconsciously waiting for someone better trained to do something. "He should be passing out about now," Devlin whispered, looking terrified behind his glasses. Then Aurelius Zane snapped into action.

The barrel-chested adventurer made it in two strides, bounding from across the room, and leapt upon the stage like a gazelle. He dashed behind the table, pushed the server aside and grasped Brad so forcefully that Brad's brown eyes grew three times larger in an instant. With one mighty Zane squeeze, the Twister Tracker exhaled a grisly projectile of half-chewed steak and potato. It landed in the lap of 43-year-old Maude Erringsforth of Dallas, who had worn a dress that was far too nice for The Big Texan in order to please her businessman husband and who, especially after this incident, really didn't want to be here anyway.

Brad sucked in a wad of oxygen and blew it out in a big *booof!* The room erupted in applause. Zane patted Brad on the back absentmindedly while grinning and nodding at the crowd, enjoying the adulation. Jack heard Wynda sigh and immediately sensed a subtle change in the temperature of the room as Zane caught her eye. What could go wrong? Jack thought. The host of a rival TV show just saved our host from death by steak, and our producer has the hots for him.

Wynda gathered herself quickly and addressed Brad. "Would you like to give it another go?" she asked. "You still have fourteen minutes."

Brad looked at her incredulously. "I ... I ..." he sputtered. "I'm full."

Wynda appeared only mildly annoyed this time, perhaps softened by his brush with fate. If he were going to die, apparently she'd much rather it be in the Bubble and on a lot more than two cameras. "All right," she relented. "But it's going to make it a challenging day in the editing room."

Devlin and Pole patted Brad on the back as he stepped off

the stage and returned to their long table. The cameramen looked doubly relieved, as now they were able to sit down and finish their meals. The steaks were a little cold, but hey, they were steaks.

Zane sat with them, too, next to Wynda, forcing an irritated Pole to find another seat.

"It's been far too long," he said smoothly.

"Since getting drunk in London or you abandoning me at that boat ramp in South America?"

"I explained that." He looked sheepish as his perfect dark-blond bangs fell in a line just above his gray eyes. "I had to pay a debt."

"They have wire transfers, you know."

"Those aren't always — effective."

"Still a scarper, eh?"

"I'm more or less caught up, as long as I get some sweet tornado footage, which is pretty much inevitable given my team and my gear."

Saffire interjected. "Nothing is inevitable. Where would be the fun in that?"

"That's why storm chasing attracts gamblers," Jack said. "Don't count your tornadoes before they're hatched."

"Lovely to meet you in person, Ms. Soulliere," Zane said to Saffire with a slight bow before reaching a hand out to Jack. "And you are?"

"Jack Andreas. And you are?" Jack replied as he shook the proffered hand, even though he knew very well who Zane was.

"Aurelius Zane. Perhaps you have heard of me."

"I'll have to Google you," Jack said innocently, taking a sip of his drink. "And have you officially met the man you saved tonight?"

"Brad Treat," their hero said, looking embarrassed as he tentatively sipped a glass of water. "Thanks."

"My pleasure," Zane said. "I know your name. Prairie Rock, correct? I could not deprive the world of a fellow adventurer. What would people's boring little lives be without us?"

"Perhaps free of meaningless television shows?" Jack offered.

"Which are paying your bills," Michiko quietly noted, popping the last bite of her massive steak into her mouth.

"Which are paying all of our bills," Wynda said. "But we do it for the love of it, don't we?"

Jack smiled. "It depends what you mean by *it*." He was not quite sure what he meant, but he knew *it* wasn't television, not for him. It was tornadoes, or that intangible thing he found in the delicate contour of Saffire's neck, matched only by the curve of her breasts, which were barely shielded by a thin, white cotton blouse. Yes, that was *it*, too.

"I am an adventurer by nature." Zane looked into Wynda's eyes. "But I am also here for the company."

"No matter how accidental?" she asked. "Regardless, we're quite happy to have you tonight. Our star lives another day, and tomorrow, I have no doubt that our flying machine will trump yours when we see our first tornado."

"Oh, it flies, does it?" Zane stated lightly. He took her hand and pressed upon it a leisurely kiss. The buzzer sounded. The Mother Trucker arose from her seat on the steak-eating stage, raising her fork and knife in victory, and Aurelius released Wynda and strode across the room to his crew.

"Damn him," Wynda snarled with reluctant affection, pushing a lock of red hair behind her ear as she watched Aurelius Zane settle into the center of his universe, laughing, while his crew orbited around him in admiration. "Beautiful bastard."

🔻

JACK WAS near the end of his third margarita when his mind began to blend the colors and textures around him into a pleasant kaleidoscope. There was Zane, popping up to sing "Your Cheatin' Heart" with the wandering musicians, garnering Wynda's rapt attention. There were Michiko and Pole, playing a hangman game with their phones amid all the racket, laughing quietly as they chatted about their favorite sci-fi shows. There was Brad, regurgitating the Storm Prediction Center's discussion for tomorrow with helpful insertions from Devlin, as Razor and Andre affixed them with their glass-lens gaze.

"It's getting to you, isn't it?" Saffire asked him. She was next to him, leaning in slightly so their arms touched, and probably only half as drunk as he was.

"The trip or that braying?" Jack murmured, nodding toward the singers as he took another sip. This was when he was usually at his most relaxed, after a few decent drinks, or right after a tornado. About now, he should have the feeling that nothing could touch him. Unless she wanted to. That's what was missing.

He felt the compulsion welling up in him, a need for a woman to burn away his doubts, a supernova to reboot his corner of the universe. Saffire, in particular, exuded a force that enticed him, something more than her looks. It was the flame of life that burned so brightly in her. He sensed no hesitation about her, no insecurities. He wanted her, not just to feel her body next to him, but to feel what she felt. He offered her a roguish smile.

"You're dangerous to be around," Saffire said, "because you don't give a damn, and not giving a damn is contagious."

"I have a few damns left to give. Just wait until we get on a good storm tomorrow. You'll see me giving several damns."

"Don't give them all away." She smiled, sipping her drink, a martini-style concoction in a godawful blue color. It was making her tongue blue. He wanted to taste it. He leaned slightly toward her before reining himself in. This wasn't the place. He saw Wynda give him a look he couldn't read before she turned toward Brad and offered him prompts, getting him to outline his team's brilliant strategy for the cameras.

"We should go to the gift shop," Jack said suddenly.

"Why?" Saffire asked. "Do you need to buy a souvenir for someone?"

"Yes, I do. Someone very important."

"A girlfriend?"

He gulped the last of his drink. "Noooo," he said slowly, his tone a question.

"Who, then?"

"You'll see. Come on."

"The check," Saffire said. "Wait a minute."

"I'm getting this one," Wynda declared. "I think tonight definitely qualifies as work."

"Thanks!" Saffire said, perkier than cowboy coffee. Jack stood up unsteadily, then took her arm and weaved with her among the long tables toward the dining room exit.

WYNDA NUDGED RAZOR, who turned his camera away from Brad and trained it on the departing Jack and Saffire.

She let him get the shot until they escaped the glow of the wagon-wheel chandeliers, then turned to him, speaking low so the others couldn't hear. "I see you are taking our little conversation to heart."

"'The story is more than the storm,'" Razor quoted her back to herself, his gravelly baritone nothing like her mezzo-soprano. The cameraman's baseball cap was on backward, his brown hair was tied in a ponytail, and his shaggy beard made him look as if he'd rather be riding his motorcycle.

"That's right. If we don't get what we need out of the Bubble and Brad, we still have plenty of drama to work with. *Intimate* details are important to a really good show."

"I think I get you," he said, scratching the head of the snake tattoo that curled up onto his cheek.

"Within reason, of course, and according to the high standards of basic cable."

Razor, who had shot video for any number of dating shows that involved hot tubs, smiled knowingly.

"This is reality," Wynda continued, "and reality does not fit neatly into the chase vehicles."

"Of course not," Razor said. Brad, loosened up by several beers, got up to sing with Zane and the pickers. Andre leaned into Wynda's conversation.

"They aren't going to like it," he said simply, his dark, chiseled face serious.

"They're getting paid, aren't they? We all are," Wynda said. "Don't worry. This is just a backup plan, and everyone will look good, I'm sure. They'll look good, or it'll be a good story."

Andre's brow furrowed for just a moment. "I have to hit the head," he said abruptly and left the table.

"Pay him no never-mind," Wynda said to Razor. "Thanks to your enterprise the other evening in the garage, you've already got enough to make this show very interesting, and we haven't even had a decent storm yet. And I'll pay you more than a steak if you get me what I want."

"I'm on it, boss," Razor said with a grin, then got up with his camera and eased his bulky form across the room toward the lobby, looking for the story outside the storm.

Wynda signed the receipt, paying the tab with a credit card. Pole paused in his phone game with Michiko and shot Wynda an inscrutable look she ignored. She fell again under the gaze of Aurelius Zane, who sang "You Are My Sunshine" in her direction, with Brad providing chalkboard-scratching harmony.

JACK BOUGHT Saffire and himself a pair of matching shot glasses from the Big Texan gift shop, imprinted with "Take Your Best Shot in Texas" in black lettering. Each wee glass was molded as if a gun were thrusting through its walls — handle on one side, barrel on the other. Classy. But they were just fine to hold tequila, easy enough to find on a Saturday night in Amarillo. The cab driver got them to Pinkie's and back to the hotel, but Saffire wasn't inclined to join him in his room. "Let's go to the pool," she said. "Meet you in five."

It was more like fifteen, but he didn't mind so much. He had on his trunks and was immersed in the pool's adjacent hot tub, with its lukewarm, anemic gurgling. The view was minimal: A dozen plastic lounge chairs surrounded the rectangular lagoon, lit by an underwater fixture whose colors were ever-changing. By the sunken tub was one sad plastic palm tree molded from illuminated green tube lights, and a couple of electric lanterns on posts washed the scene in yellow. The hotel's brick walls formed a horseshoe shape around the pool that shot up four stories, with blank windows gazing out like dead eyes. On the fourth side was a black iron fence and, judging by the faint odor, trash bins hidden behind the bushes that lined it. Yet overpowering the unpleasantness was a flowering scent. He couldn't identify it, but it was relaxing, reminiscent of his childhood and Southern summer evenings.

By the time Saffire showed up, he was almost drowsy from sipping the booze. He perked up when he saw what she was wearing: strappy red sandals with a low heel and a short, white, terry robe. He smiled and raised his eyebrows, imagining what was underneath, as she approached and lay her towel next to the hot tub.

"Better pour me one," she said. "I'm losing my buzz, and it looks like you're about to succumb to yours."

"Never give up, is what I say." He reached over to the rough cement lip where the glasses sat, hefted the clear bottle, pulled out the wooden stopper and poured her one. "Come on in. The water's fine." He handed her the glass.

She knocked it back in one swift motion, put it down, then let the robe slip away in a calculated move obviously refined by a lot of acting classes.

"Techno-babe alert," Jack quipped, but he was more moved than he let on. She lived up to her star billing, dressed in a red-and-white polka-dot bikini, high-waisted in retro style, accented by a heretofore unseen tattoo on her back left shoulder sporting a mermaid. It might have jumped directly from the arm of a World War II sailor. Her honey-blond curls were pinned up on one side, and her lips had the sheen of recently applied, candy-red lipstick. Jack cleared his throat as he took in the whole package and wasn't sorry his lower half was underwater.

She kicked off the sandals and eased in alongside him, and he felt the familiar comfort of a woman in the crook of his arm, a warm, wet, beautiful woman. Comfort and excitement, mellowed by tequila.

"Good stuff," she said as she took her turn filling the glasses.

"Nothing worse than a bad-tequila headache on a chase day."

"Spoken like a guy who's been there."

"Well, it hasn't always been tequila," he said, sipping.

"How long have you been chasing storms?"

"Depends," he said. "Do you count the time when I was eight and I rode my bicycle two miles during a tornado warning to see the tornado suck up a house?"

"You saw a tornado suck up a house?"

"That day, only in my imagination. But I did get bruised by quarter-size hail."

"I bet your parents freaked out."

"My mother kind of did. She didn't tell my father." He took a long sip.

"Why not?"

"It would have hurt worse than the hail, I'm pretty sure."

She looked concerned. "Your childhood was like that?"

"Oh, he didn't beat me, per se. He just let me know when he was disappointed. It's OK. We've kind of reached detente."

"What about your mom?"

"Dead." He strove to change the subject. "You like the tequila?"

"Smooth," she said in a stagey hoarse voice, making him laugh. "But I prefer margaritas."

"Sometimes it's better just to go for the straight liquor, unless you know a bar is making margaritas the right way."

"There's a right way?" she asked. "They're all pretty good to me."

"What we're going for is *great*," he said, topping off his shot glass; then, feeling a wave of wooziness, putting it back down so he wouldn't drop it. "Real lime juice. Agave syrup. High-quality stuff. Not that mix crap."

"My problem is, I always want nachos with my tequila," she replied.

He looked at her profile as she relaxed in the water, the elegant, straight line of her nose, and thought about a road trip with her, taco stands, no cameras, lots of tequila. He picked up his glass again and managed a sip, then eased his face closer to hers.

"Hungry?" he whispered, feeling her breath.

"Peckish." She turned her head slightly away, making him wait.

"I'm not hungry," he said, so quietly she had to lean closer to hear. "But being with you makes me ravenous."

She turned her head back toward him, a smile creeping over her face, and let him complete his move. His lips were on hers in an instant. He dropped his glass into the gurgling water as he reached out to glide his hands across her wet skin. Her mouth opened under his, and one of her arms encircled his waist. Her fingers slipped just inside his waistband, making him crazy. Slow, he thought. No need to rush. Make it inevitable. And then they could go to his room. His desire built like clouds on a day when storms were forecast, bright and white against a crystal blue sky, then darkening into a tempest of depth and power that only she could answer. God, he wanted her right now. His mind slipped in and out of a tequila haze as he kissed her. She answered his eager mouth with her tongue as she began to slide her hands slowly up his back. He lightly held her beautiful, round behind and allowed his eyes to open as they kissed, to glimpse her abandonment. He wanted that from a woman, her immersion into his yearning, making the moment complete. But even as he dreamily regarded her subtly sparkling eye shadow and decadent curls and tasted her tequila-tinged mouth, thinking of what came next, he caught a glint of something, a phantom in the corner of his eye, and he broke the spell and looked up.

"What?" she murmured, kissing his neck.

"Spies," he said.

She grudgingly pulled away and slid down so the water gurgled above her shoulders. "What do you mean?"

"Something upstairs."

"No one is up this late and is that bored," she said, laying her head on his shoulder, letting her hand ride along his thigh.

"Normally I wouldn't care, but I don't want you to find yourself on YouTube in a compromising position."

"How gallant." She laughed. "That'd be the best thing for my career so far." She grabbed the shot glass that remained by the tub and drank it down. His own glass bobbed among the bubbles near their feet.

"I want to fuck you right now," he whispered in her ear. "But I'm not going to do it for the peepers."

"Don't turn on the poetry unless you mean it." She sounded annoyed. "I thought this would be simple."

"It is. Come on. We can go upstairs."

"You're a tease, you know that? Damn your green eyes."
She let her fingers trail up his inner thigh and lightly brush his
growing bulge, as if but not quite by accident, then stepped
out of the tub and slipped on her robe.

He stifled a groan. "I can meet you in five. Your room or
mine?"

"You should have asked me that five minutes ago, before
you cut me off."

"I would never do that. I think my room has a Jacuzzi?" he
offered hopefully.

She laughed. "No, it doesn't. It's going to have to wait,
pardner," she intoned in an exaggerated Texas accent, picking
up her shot glass and aiming its tiny gun at him. "I have to
look good in the morning. Let this be a lesson to you. Never
put the chill on a lady packing heat."

And you are hot, Jack thought. *Damn it.* "Don't leave me here
to die," he twanged back, the alcohol easing him through his
disappointment.

"Bang! Bang!" She shot him with the shot glass. He
clutched his chest and let his body slip under the water,
watching her blurry form wash away. Bang, bang. *I wish.* He
stayed under for several seconds until he was sure she was
gone, contemplating the tornadoes formed by the water jets,
feeling his erection objecting to this turn of affairs. He found
his shot glass and popped his head out of the water into the
cool night, hearing the sound of traffic and a distant siren and,
after a quick scan of the windows, seeing no one. He got out
of the tub, grabbed the half-empty bottle and walked
unevenly, dripping, back into the hotel.

AURELIUS'S CELL phone rang at 4 a.m. At first it seemed less like a phone and more like a plague of vampire crickets pursuing him with chirps and fangs as he ran down a misty alley in Los Angeles and plowed right into a film crew, which told him that, to pass, he had to hold the light reflector under Helen Hunt's chin until the end of the scene. That's when he knew it was a dream, because he had no acquaintance with Helen Hunt other than his multiple viewings of the movie *Twister*. So to avoid having crickets rip into his throat, he blinked a few times, then picked up the phone from the beige bedside table in his beige hotel room.

"Zane," he announced himself as the paper he'd left on top of the phone, the habitual note that told the world traveler where he was, fluttered to the floor.

"Aurelius Zane," came the snarky voice at the other end.

He snuffled in the darkness. "Perceptive of you, given that you called me. Do you know what fucking time it is, asshole?"

"It's 10 a.m. here, but for you, time is running out, you prick. How's the production going? Where are you? Did you get your tornado yet?"

That's about the time Aurelius realized that he was not talking to just any asshole, but to Rodney Mezner, the asshole who'd lent him the money to rent the UAV and invested in his show. Rodney knew Zane's imperative: Get extraordinary tornado footage with his flying machine per his contract or lose his money. Aurelius immediately switched to charming mode, the groggy edition.

"Rodney! You should have said it was you. I'm in …" He thought for a moment. "I'm in Texas. What the hell are you, I mean, where the hell are you if it's 10 a.m.?"

"Scotland. I'm working on a documentary series about unexplained phenomena. This episode is called 'When

Animals Explode.' They have some awesome stories about mutilated cows here."

"Sounds dangerous."

"You have no idea. Terrific cheese, too. Listen, Zane, have you got your footage yet?"

"Trust me, Rodney. Have I ever not delivered?"

"You like to play it on the edge, Zane, and I like to have decent liquidity. I've just sealed a deal to fund my next movie. It's about vampire superheroes, and it's hot. I want to make sure my investment in you is going to pay off."

"They aren't crickets, are they? The vampires?" Aurelius asked, wondering if he were still dreaming.

"They have good drugs there in Texas, Zane?" Rodney asked. "What's the story?"

"I already have some excellent storm footage, and I expect we might get our tornado today," Aurelius said with an over-confidence that was pretty much his trademark. "If you can call it 'today' here."

"You're not blowing smoke up my ass, are you, Zane?"

"I wouldn't dream of it, Rodney. Anyway, the season has just started. We have weeks and weeks to get our tornado."

"You know, I caught one of your lectures once," Rodney said.

"Yes?" asked Aurelius, instantly on his guard.

"You went to great lengths to explain how nearly impossible it was to get into perfect position to get extraordinary footage of a tornado."

"Well …" Aurelius tried to clear the fog in his brain. "That was just puff talk, Rodney, to get people excited when I finally did show them the extraordinary footage of the tornado."

When Rodney responded, his voice was lower, with an uncomfortably sharp edge. "Don't 'just puff talk' me, ever,

Zane. I'll look forward to seeing your extraordinary footage and knowing you can pay up. Because if you can't pay up, I'll take it in other ways. I have friends in India who are always looking for new kidneys."

Aurelius swallowed, then forced a laugh. "Rodney, you are such a card. You've been looking at too many cow entrails. I will talk to you soon, my friend."

"Yes, I'm sure you will," was the reply the adventurer heard as he gingerly pressed the "end call" button.

He lay back on the pillow, hearing the traffic on I-40, and became simultaneously aware of his full bladder and the sound of plaintive moos through the walls. He got up, padded across the carpet and pulled back the heavy hotel curtains to see a livestock truck parked outside his window, full of presumptively smelly cows en route to their doom. The moos sounded like moans. The steak deep in his digestive system seemed to undulate in intuitive response. "When Zanes Explode," he muttered, letting the curtain drop, and headed to the bathroom.

JACK NEVER LIKED low visibility in the morning, even if he knew the clouds would clear eventually. He felt a prickling unease no matter the source of the clouds — the atmosphere or alcohol.

In this case, it was both. Again. His head hurt, and despite brushing his teeth both before and after his cereal-and-hard-boiled-egg free hotel breakfast, his tongue still felt like a pickle covered in cat hair. He coughed and lit up a cigarette on the edge of the hotel parking lot, gazed up past a couple of scrubby trees toward the high morning cirrus clouds streaming in from the northwest, and pondered his vices. He really should give one of them up. But not women. Not yet.

It was almost noon. They had started loading up the vehicles in the hotel parking lot, with plenty of time to get into position — probably a little north, into the northwest Panhandle. Upper flow was strong, and the surface low would be moving out of southeast Colorado, bringing with it mounds of instability. The winds had already strengthened out of the south-southeast. A few low, white clouds scudded across the blue sky. It was a good day for tornadoes. Maybe not so good for mornings-after.

He'd taken care of his own needs after the hot-tub debacle. It certainly wasn't the first time. And he'd had way too much tequila. This was why he used to stick to beer on the road. He was trying to remember why he had succumbed to liquor. Something to do with women, he thought. When they were around, it was just more fun to get drunk and to invite them along. Or sometimes, to forget, though it never really worked.

Women. No, Saffire. She was all he could think about, at least when he accessed the few remaining brain cells that were not preoccupied with the chance for tornadoes. As promised, she looked good this morning, filling her techno-babe role with aplomb. She wore tight jeans and a not-quite-translucent, orange, V-neck T-shirt that brought out her golden-brown eyes and hinted at a lacy bra underneath. He caught Razor giving him a knowing look and turned away in disgust. The last thing he needed was the rest of the crew getting into his business. He was just the background guy. The consultant. He had one job. Get Brad into a tornado. Not fuck the starlet. That wasn't the job. A bonus, maybe, but not the job. She definitely wanted him. She was so direct about it. Refreshing, really. And he felt more from her, a strength that intrigued

him, a sense that she was smarter than she let on with the
Hollywood act. He'd only seen her glimmering surface, and he
wanted to look into the light. But he had a job, and she was
starting to jam his radar.

When he wasn't hung over, he enjoyed these kinds of flirtations. Sometimes, they were more than flirtations. They
started to turn into relationships, and sometimes, he wanted
them to. A relationship meant even more intensity, the flame
of commitment, of mutual devotion, however illusory. But in
that strengthening bond he smelled stasis, and stasis was
death. He didn't want to get too deep. There was no point in
love. Love ended, or was taken away. There were no divine
eternities. Nothing was forever. Why wait for the cold wind of
winter? Chase while it's still spring. Feel the sun and the rush
of tumultuous change, while it's all still green.

And there she was, that temptation, a sun of her own
making, and he felt her heat.

His phone rang in his pocket with a snippet of wailing
guitars and a buzz. He glanced at the screen before he
answered. "Marcus, my friend. You're going to need that hail
helmet today."

There was a laugh on the other end. "Love the high plains
for hail," Marcus said. Marcus was still working on his doctor-
ate. A hail fiend and fellow researcher, but a few years
younger, he'd been Jack's one confidante, however rarely.
Sometimes that meant grabbing a few beers when he was back
in town and talking about football and close calls with storms
— though Marcus had seen relatively few tornadoes, given
that he was usually buried in the hail core.

"Where are you headed today?" Jack asked.

"I was going to ask you the same question."

"Probably the same place as you."

"Dumas, we're thinking," Marcus said. "This is the first outing for our mini research project this year."

"You can't go wrong starting in Dumbass." Jack didn't really think Dumas was dumb. Or at least, circumstances had not yet proven it so. It was just what chasers called it.

"I hope we aren't dumbasses today. Where did you say you were going?"

"I didn't. Maybe Dalhart."

"So who exactly are you chasing with, anyway?" Marcus asked. "I mean, you told me it was a TV crew, but does this show have a star, some chaser we know, or are they trying to do a *real* reality show?"

Jack guffawed. "Reality is overrated. Who do you think would be the perfect daredevil to star in a show about storm chasers, a hero known for surviving tornadoes by his guts and wits?"

"I would guess Aurelius Zane, except that he's not known for tornadoes."

Jack raised his eyebrows. "Funny you should mention him. He's out here doing a show, too, but not this one. I believe our producer has the hots for him."

"No shit."

"No shit." Jack coughed and took another drag.

"I thought you were going to quit."

"Goddamn it, you can hear that? I'll smoke till I'm dead."

"Famous last words." Marcus laughed, and Jack quietly dropped the cigarette and ground it into the pavement. "OK, who is it?"

"Seriously, think. Who would the great gods of television choose to be their golden boy?"

There was silence on the line for a minute, and Jack looked

around at the bustling team, which was checking gear and getting shots of Brad walking in and out of the hotel.

"Oh my god," Marcus said. "It can't be."

"Yes, the proprietor of Thor's Tours himself."

"Not after he almost killed a vanload of tourists."

"You know that. I know that. But America thinks he's awesome. America is into selective truth anyway."

"Don't start getting political, Jack."

"I'm getting psychological."

"Oh, please. Then you might actually have to think before you bang your next blonde."

"Ouch, that hurt," Jack said, almost indifferently, as he eyeballed Saffire leaning over an atlas with Brad and Devlin, hamming it up for the cameras. Her cleavage gleamed like two mounds of French vanilla ice cream.

"Who is she?"

"What makes you think —"

"There's always someone. Of course, you probably don't know her that well yet."

"Sometimes that's best," Jack said dryly.

"You ever talk to that girl in Kansas?"

That was unexpected. Jack didn't like to talk about the Kansas girl, or girls. The women of Pancake. "If you mean Judy, not since Prairie Rock … Listen, Marcus, this is not something I really have time to discuss right now."

"Just wondered," said Marcus, chastened, hearing Jack's tone. "She's been popping up on the boards lately. She and her boyfriend are doing kind of an interesting lightning project."

"Lightning?"

"An art project in a field outside Pancake."

"That's been done, right? In New Mexico?"

"This sounds different," Marcus said. "Anyway, tell your producer about it. They might get some cool shots."

"Maybe. If we're bored. After this system, we might be bored for a few days."

"Let me know if you get back to Wishwell. We'll have a few beers."

"At least," Jack said. "Where did you say you were?"

"I didn't. We're rolling west, about thirty miles out of Amarillo."

"I'll see you under the meso, Marcus."

"Don't go Hollywood on me. Bye."

Jack holstered his phone and made a resolution to think of anything but women for five minutes. It was getting brighter. The high clouds were clearing out, making way for the sun's heat and the fuel they'd need for the bigger, better clouds he expected later today.

He headed into the hotel lobby, got a cup of free coffee and idly watched the TV playing The Weather Channel's high-tech graphics, which rehashed the social posts of people who were hot in Miami and cold in Chicago. Everybody wanted to talk about the weather, but almost no one wanted to get inside it the way he did.

He wandered to the front counter, where a white board on the wall sported a colorful handwritten forecast: "83° and partly sunny, chance of storms!" next to a doodle of a happy sun wearing sunglasses. Jack contemplated its simplicity for a moment, its inherent optimism, before choosing the black pen from the handful hanging from the board. He drew a horizontal loop near the top. The loop grew into more loops, twisting upon themselves as they swirled down the page to a grim point, forming a ghastly tornado that obliterated the

happy sun in a whirlwind of ink. Satisfied, Jack walked out
into the bright, partly sunny afternoon.

WYNDA WEXCOMBE TRIED hard to strike a balance
between seething and exploding. On the whole, she preferred
exploding, because she usually channeled the scorching excess
energy that engulfed her soul into her work, and her work was
paramount.

Her work was what had gotten her out of the family dairy
farm in Wiltshire and away from her parents. Her mother was
from Scotland, as was Wynda's name; her father wasn't. They
were dear people but completely baffled by their daughter's
ambition. Wynda was fairly sure they were relieved she visited
only on major holidays.

Her first step toward a TV career had to be London, a
luminous city rich in history with almost enough energy to
match her own. She paid her dues in menial coffee-toting,
cable-carrying, button-pushing jobs before she realized that
her talents demanded more and better challenges. She was
tired of her aging-hipster male boss chatting her up at every
opportunity while steadfastly refusing to give her the gigs she
wanted. And when she saw with disgust the success of her
dear, sweet cousin Becky, another TV producer whom
everyone adored and who had cultivated enough sources with
her charm and brains to land sexy international video productions on a regular basis, Wynda knew she'd had it with
assistant-land. She used her own money to finance her first
real production, a clever documentary about lighthouse keep-
ers, and it was up from there.

Wynda's charms were not so refined as her cousin's, and her brains were so nakedly sharp as to turn off many who met her. They felt instinctively that Wynda made them look less witty or that she might eat them for lunch. She'd chewed through more than a few people in order to get the jobs she wanted. The controlled explosion that was Wynda Wexcombe subsequently began to succeed. She soared with a documentary about modern zeppelins. She froze her arse off in Greenland during a painfully esoteric shoot about snow. And then there was the bungle in the jungle with Aurelius Zane, in which he came out looking extremely good on TV, and oh so much better in person, right up until the moment when she realized she was stuck alone on a boat ramp in the rainforest of northern Brazil with eight metal cases of camera gear and a wounded black squirrel monkey.

Still, she made it work. That documentary miniseries helped clinch Zane's reputation as Adventurer Deluxe, despite the difficulties she'd had with the production company. Wynda, explosion in progress, rarely left a scene without singeing it.

She was changed by the rainforest shoot, too. It left her muddled, as she found herself at the top of her creative and administrative powers while simultaneously falling into awkward and uncontrollable lust — she daren't call it love — with the boyish, oblivious and reckless Aurelius Zane.

Her schoolmates had once tormented her with the nick-name "Wyndy," and the irony inherent in her helming a storm-chasing documentary did not escape her. Nothing came easy, she told herself, as her newest crew headed north out of Amarillo. Maybe this would be it, the breakthrough project that would make her the go-to gal when it came to fabulous and popular documentary filmmaking. Today, she lurked in the back of Van One so she could keep tabs on Brad, who looked heroic in the driver's seat after a good night's sleep; Saffire, who was lovely as always but discernibly distracted in the passenger seat; Devlin and camera-slinging Andre in the middle; and brooding Jack in the back, next to her, working his computer. Michiko and Razor followed in the support SUV to get mobile shots, while Pole drove the Bubblevan. Despite their disparities, it was a good crew, she thought, and a great concept, albeit somewhat too sci-fi even for her. But the production company had invested a great deal in the Bubble, helped along by an engineering lab, a ration of modified NASA Mars-probe technology and some possibly misplaced grants. She was sure it would make great television, even if it didn't make great science.

It was nice to ride along, and Wynda liked being able to talk to her stars without getting on the CB. Thus she could keep Zane out of the loop, though she was spending an uncomfortable amount of time wondering just where he was. "Where are the tornadoes, Jack?" she asked.

"I'm having them delivered," he joked. He was a mystery man, that one, and undeniably attractive, with his dark hair, arch expressions and come-hither green eyes. Not as brawny as she liked, but still. No wonder Saffire was interested. "Nothing to report, yet," he added, more seriously this time. "But we're headed in the right direction. We might need a few more clouds first."

As they neared Dumas, the brownness of the landscape overwhelmed her. Not unlike Mars, Wynda thought. The drought was partly to blame, locals had told her, but this barrenness was so different from the green fields and lush, chalk downlands of home. Low, rolling hills and buttes straight out of a cowboy film interrupted the horizon. Ranch gates sprouted at intervals in rusty metal geometries; worn, ancient fence posts looked as if they were ripped right from the hearts of trees and pounded into the dusty ground. Beyond them, black cows dotted tan expanses of earth, stark and serious, like cutout silhouettes.

"What's the forecast?" she asked. "Brad, what do you think? Get this, Andre."

Andre was already "getting it," with a substantial video camera almost permanently mounted to his shoulder. Only a subtle rise of an eyebrow betrayed his irritation.

"A strong storm system is moving in," Brad said over his shoulder, "and the southeast winds should really kick up by later today."

"The shear," Devlin prompted.

"Oh, yeah. There will be strong veering wind profiles in the atmosphere that should get these storms spinning. I'd say we have a good chance at seeing tornadoes."

"Excellent!" Saffire said. "As long as they don't hit any towns."

"That was great!" Devlin exclaimed.

"I'm not an idiot," Brad said.

Jack grinned.

"What, Jack?" Wynda asked, growing tired of his mockery.

Their forecaster looked up from the laptop and paused a moment before responding, as if weighing how much of a smart-ass he wanted to be.

"Tornadoes make me happy," was all he said, though the furtive glance he shared with Saffire made Wynda think that tornadoes were not all that made him happy. And that idea, that ace in the hole, made Wynda Wexcombe exquisitely

happy as they reached the Dumas city limits and passed the
Zane Films vehicles parked in a gas station lot.

JACK LOVED that moment in a chase when it became clear
that the day would not be a forgettable one, another blank box
in a black-and-white calendar. No chase was ever really a total
loss, as he loved giving himself over to the power of the sky,
no matter where it led him, no matter how thin the clouds or
soft the wind. But he wanted a date to remember. He wanted
to feel the weather's power, to lose himself in it, to see its
gears turn, to feel the trembling of the air and ground as the
great machinery rumbled into motion.

They'd dawdled a while in Dumas, debating whether to
move on to Dalhart, as they watched clouds billow on the
dryline. Showers started to appear on radar, and they decided
to investigate one of them south of town. That's how it always
started. Tornadoes didn't come from nowhere. These humble
beginnings were part of the fascination for Jack, how one
cloud at the perfect intersection of air masses, bathed in ideal
dynamics, could grow and mature and spin and become the
monster of his dreams, the one that might consume him, free
him from his otherwise tedious existence.

The crew stood on a gravel road at the apex of a gentle
slope, almost directly under the base of the growing storm.
Brad shared his contrived excitement with Razor and Michiko
as Andre filmed Devlin and Saffire standing on a tussock next
to a wire fence. The wind ruffled their hair as they cut an
attractive pose in the gentle green light. Pole was still behind
the wheel of the Bubblevan, observing through the open
driver's-side window.

Not far away, a dozen black Angus cows grazed, seemingly oblivious to the vaporous spaceship beginning to spin in the sky above them. A subtle curvature brushed the edges of the dark cloud's base, and Jack felt the motion as much as he saw it. This was when he knew the day would not be a waste of time. This storm had intentions. It was like knowing that moment when a girl wanted him as much as he wanted her. Fun was in store.

Thunder rumbled, the first of the day. Jack wandered over to where Wynda was standing, several feet from the Brad tableau. "This is where I should issue my obligatory warning that any of us could be hit and fried by lightning," he told her.

"Duly noted," she responded, wrapped up in watching Brad perform, evidently not going to do anything about it. Not that Jack intended to sit in the van, either. He'd take his chances. But he had his reasons for reconsidering a few moments later when another lightning bolt hit so close, he saw the barbed-wire fence flare and spark down its length for several yards. The flash was followed almost instantly by a much louder report of thunder and a short, startled scream from Saffire and Devlin. They jumped backward, giving the cameras a nice moment of drama as they narrowly avoided turning into lightning rods. That would make the final edit somewhere, Jack thought. He restrained his impulse to walk over to Saffire and give her the obvious advice — don't stand near a wire fence — as she and Devlin were already moving away and toward the others.

The stars instinctively coalesced to talk about their prospects for the cameras and marvel at the storm. It was developing rapidly. Jack had that sense of time being compressed that he got at the start of some of his most interesting chases. Heavier rain fell from the dark cloud, and the cows trotted off to the west, out of its way. Shreds of condensing vapor now began to unfold from the base, thread by thread, gradually forming a ragged lowering: a wall cloud, already, Jack marveled. He felt light rain on his face as the drops filled in and the storm eased in their direction. The lowering's fuzzy teeth moved slowly counter-clockwise, promising more.

"Look at the rotation!" Brad said, exhibiting a moment of genuine enthusiasm.

"Should we deploy?" Devlin asked.

"Yes!" Wynda said.

"No, I don't think so," said Jack. Already, the wall cloud was losing cohesion, being absorbed back into the storm. "It's not quite ready. The base is still too high. But I'd be thinking about our next road option. This could get very interesting."

The drone of engines caught their attention, and they turned as one to see the Zane Films vehicles roaring by, moving on to that next road option.

"We should go!" Wynda said, voicing the human instinct to follow. And the chaser instinct to wonder if the other guy really knew where the best spot was.

"Not yet," Jack said. "But another mile or two wouldn't be a bad idea. Besides, we'd be a little safer from lightning in the vans."

Wynda smirked at him, but Saffire gave him a little smile, and he let himself enjoy being the nice guy. He smiled back.

Returning to the vehicles, they advanced two miles south, turned onto a road that would take them northeast and stopped at the intersection. No one got out. The storm was already much darker, bigger and, if radar was accurate, starting to drop significant hail. Jack took a quick look at Spotter Network. The Internet map of chasers and storm spotters was filled with green dots, some streaming toward their storm, others pushing lemming-like ahead of it, determined not to be left behind. Jack wasn't ready yet. He liked the look of the storm's southern end. A new wall cloud appeared to be forming, and he didn't want to get too far east. Plus, if they could deploy the Bubble early, all the better.

On radar, the storm appeared more elongated as the rain and hail filled in — but also more beastly. Jack looked up, noting not just rotation where the new wall cloud formed but more towers growing into the back of the storm.

Lightning struck close by in a field, its channel glowing white-hot as it contacted the ground. "Tell me you got that," Wynda said to Andre.

"Of course I got that."

Brad seemed resigned to his fate as he saw the newest rotating wall cloud mature. "You say it has lightning protection?"

"The Bubble? Absolutely," Devlin said.

Brad sighed. "We'd better think about where we're going to deploy."

"COULD you believe how disgusting the hotel toilets were this morning? Half my room flooded," Ernie, in the passenger seat, said to Evie, who shared the Zane Films van's back seat with Thing One and Thing Two. The couple filmed furiously as the team worked to stay abreast of the storm and get to where Aurelius and Ernie figured the next area of rotation would be.

"The clerk said the pipes were backed up something awful," Evie agreed with Ernie. She'd started to show more interest in the young meteorology student as her crush on Aurelius faded, which was just as well, as he had no grad-school stories to share with them. And he was still thinking about Wynda. He clutched his stomach briefly at the memory of his pipe-clogging night, then picked up the radio.

"Duncan, are you two ready to launch at any time?"

"We've even set up a net in a field near here. The rancher's looking forward to his hundred bucks."

"Excellent. Ernie, how do you think the storm's doing?"

Ernie consulted the laptop on the mount in front of the dashboard and flipped through radar images showing reflectivity and velocity. "It's starting to sprawl, honestly," he said. "I think it's going HP fast."

"HP?" asked Evie, who hadn't studied weather in her journalism classes.

"High-precipitation. A rain and hail bomb."

"What are our tornado chances?" Aurelius asked.

"I wouldn't want to put a number on it," Ernie said, "but it still has a lot of potential. We're coming up on a new meso, and it's spinning hard. Even that old wall cloud we left hasn't given up the ghost. It's almost multicellular at this point."

Thanks to the rain, Aurelius couldn't see any evidence of the meso — the mesocyclone, the large area of rotation that might engender a tornado. "It's dark as hell," he said.

"Yeah. We're going to need radar to target the best spot. Even then, I'm not sure how much the plane is going to see. Or us, either."

That wasn't what Aurelius wanted to hear. He had to film a quality tornado. "Road options?"

"This is the best and really the only decent east-west road close to the storm," Ernie said. "We just have to watch out for the hail core. If this thing creeps south just a little bit, say goodbye to the windshield."

"Least of my concerns," Aurelius said. "Duncan!" he shouted over the radio. "Hang back. Let us act as a hail probe. I don't want the drone smashed to bits. Not until there's a reason, anyway." He laughed.

"I can't imagine what reason that would be," Duncan said, his voice tinged with worry. "Phil and I will definitely hang back till you say it's time to deploy."

"Thank you. Always a pleasure working with professionals." Aurelius hung up the mike. He was starting to miss volcanoes. At least they weren't a moving target, until they blew their wad and tried to kill you.

"I THINK WE SHOULD KEEP GOING," Devlin said. He stood next to the van, leaning in to look at radar on Jack's computer. Most of the crew was now outside, getting a few more shots. "That adjacent red and green to the east — that's wicked rotation, right?"

"Right," Jack said. "But this isn't done. I think it's a new updraft driving this side of the storm. We've got a cluster, or quite possibly a clusterfuck, but my instinct tells me to stay."

Wynda had wandered up to the open door to listen in. "That's one of the reasons we hired you. Your Professor Malik mentioned your instinct specifically. Well, that, and your degree. And the fact that you are not completely hideous," she joked, allowing herself a small smile.

"I'm not one to ride on my good looks," Jack said, even as he thought, that's exactly what I do, when I can get away with it. "You're the boss, but I say this mesocyclone isn't done. The wall cloud is starting to look more serious."

"That lowering thingy?" she asked, her British diction lending even more absurdity to the word.

"Yes, that's the thingy," Jack said. "At this point, I would consider deployment."

"Saffire! Brad! Van!" Wynda shouted immediately. "Devlin, plot a course with Jack's help."

"Is there a road due north?" Jack asked.

As Brad hopped into the driver's seat, Devlin jumped in the front, awakened the mounted laptop there and zoomed in on the Global Positioning System map.

"A little east, there's a dirt road north."

"No good," Brad said instantly. He'd learned the hard way that dirt roads were not necessarily good roads.

"In this case, that appears to be our only choice if we want to intercept this one," Devlin said.

Jack looked around, at Razor filming from outside Brad's window, at Andre filming from inside the van, and at Saffire, who'd been listening at the door before she bumped Devlin out of the passenger seat and back in the middle with Andre.

"What's the worst that could happen?" she asked, looking directly at Jack with a bright, innocent smile that thinly veiled a spark of mischief.

"We move fast," Devlin said. "Get in, deploy the Bubble, get out."

Jack felt the rush of Saffire's gaze and the power of the storm, whose new wall cloud was rotating with conviction, its fingers reaching toward the ground like a mammoth claw.

"What the hell," Jack said. "Gotta die of something."

AURELIUS and the Zane Films van were well ahead of the UAV truck, and it was just as well. Icy golf balls hit the roof and occasionally banged off the windshield in wince-worthy impacts. It was decision time: launch or back off.

Aurelius Zane was never one to back off. "Duncan, don't come any farther. It's hail city up here. Launch and try to circle around to meet the tornado east of us."

"Do you see a tornado?" Duncan's voice came back over the radio.

"Not yet. But there will be one. I'm sure of it."

"There's a warning," Ernie said, "but it's for the western side of this cluster. Southwest of us, actually."

"Should we go for it?"

"If storm chasing has one rule, it's never leave a rotating storm," Ernie said. "And our storm is rotating."

"Is the circulation southwest of us on the ground?" Aurelius's deep voice was grim, and he flipped the weather radio on, just a notch past silent, so they'd hear if another warning were issued.

"Radar-indicated at the moment."

"Good. Keep it that way." He grinned, his mood lifting as he pushed the accelerator. He pressed the button to roll down his window and leaned out, driving with one hand as he looked up. "Ouch!" he exclaimed as a hailstone hit him on the shoulder. He couldn't afford a hit to the head or, worse, his face. Not if he wanted to keep looking good on camera. He closed the window. "Ernie, look right. Do you see it?"

"Deployed," Duncan said over the radio at that moment.

Ernie rolled down his window and looked out and back, a little more tenuously than Aurelius had. "No, I — wait, there it is. Almost lost it against the gray. It's curving south and should be ahead of us in no time."

"How's the video?" Aurelius asked over the radio.

"Fuzzy signal, but it's OK. We'll get the high-def on the drone's memory cards," Duncan said. "We need to see enough to avoid hazards — and so far, so good. Just need the tornado."

"Working on it," Aurelius said.

The hail barrage intensified as spiky baseballs smashed on the road in front of them. *Smashed* was the operative term. If they'd been hard enough to bounce, there wouldn't be a windshield to look out of. As it was, they already had a small crack from one of the earlier golf balls. These big ones were more like snow cones. Aurelius started to feel just a tiny bit victorious. This was going to be his day, and the rest of the expedition would be gravy.

"Evie, anything to report?" Aurelius said, just to get her on Thing Two's camera.

"I'm getting beautiful shots back here," said the eager student reporter, who was using a digital SLR to grab video out the window. It was so small compared with the professional couple's gear. "It looks like a monster!"

A green monster, Aurelius thought, as a few harder hailstones hit the van with loud clunks before they thinned out and stopped. They were ahead of the core, for the moment. "Ernie, when will be in position to see the tornado?"

"Actually, if you pull off at this next road, we'll be just southeast of the meso," Ernie said. "But I'm worried about the rain."

"Unless you're a wicked witch, you won't melt," said Aurelius.

Ernie frowned. "I'm worried that the rain is going to hide our view," he explained.

Aurelius's brow furrowed as he made the left, drove up a slight rise and parked on the shoulder.

"It's in there?"

"The meso is in there," Ernie said.

"All I see is gray and green."

"Yeah. Well."

Aurelius grabbed the radio mike again. "Duncan, how's it doing?"

"Flying great," came the response. "Murky video."

The weather radio went off with a hideous screech, then mellowed into a more manageable tone before a robo-voice announced a new tornado warning for their location, indicated by radar.

"Give it time," Aurelius said. "Everybody out. Get some shots of us looking at the tornado," he directed Things One and Two.

Outside of the van, they scrutinized the curtains of rain and the gray-green mass in front of them. Black, scudding clouds lowered from the storm all around what should have been the tornado — mock funnels, the type of feature that spawned phony warnings. The drone truck pulled up, but the techies stayed inside, watching their monitors and flying the plane.

"Is that it?" Evie asked excitedly, pointing to a darker area inside the green haze.

"I think that's just a heavier rain shaft," Ernie said.

"Let's say it was a tornado," Aurelius said. "Is that the right place?"

"Sort of," Ernie said. "Honestly, I can't see a damn thing. The UAV may get a better position on it if it gets a little northeast — it might get a window."

"Tell Duncan," Aurelius said impatiently as he lifted his

chin to improve his profile for the cameras. His rakishly cut blond hair flapped nicely in the inflow, as did his tailored rain jacket. He didn't want to think about how much he needed the shot. He didn't want to think about his creeping debt, about Rodney and his exploding cows and his precarious investment. He just wanted to be awesome. And seriously, it shouldn't be this difficult.

◣

JACK HAD BEEN on worse dirt roads, but the rain hadn't hit this one yet, and he knew it wouldn't be pretty once it did. This was how Brad got in trouble near Prairie Rock, and both of them knew it. Their route took them north, but in a meandering fashion that was disorienting at best and dangerous at worst, if a tornado headed their way.

"Jack, tell us when it's time to pull over," Wynda said. "Devlin, get ready to move quickly." She was in the back of the lead van, with Michiko and Razor in the crew SUV and Pole driving the Bubblevan, bringing up the rear.

"Another half mile," Jack said. "Start looking for a good spot."

The landscape was mostly flat, but at the moment, they were climbing. "We'll get the best view at the top of the hill," Saffire said. "Not that it's much of one."

"Just enough," Brad said, "but not so much that I'll go rolling like a bowling ball again."

"The idea is to get you flying, not rolling," Devlin said as the others chuckled.

"We'll see about that," Brad said quietly. He was nervous, and for good reason, Jack thought. This quest was looking crazier all the time.

"This looks ideal," Saffire said as they crested the hill. There was a small lot next to a slowly bobbing oil pumpjack that had just enough flat, open space to work.

They were in silent agreement as Brad pulled the van into the lot, followed by the others. There was a sense that this might actually be it, that they might launch him into a tornado, and with it, the nagging idea that their TV stunt might become something more serious. They stepped out of the vehicles to face the storm.

Devlin and Pole pulled open the back doors of the Bubble-van, extended the ramp, moved the clamps and gingerly rolled the clear sphere out. Except for a few scratches, it looked pretty sharp after their buffing and tinkering in the wake of its last rough outing. Now the metal struts, airbag boxes and sensor housings had a patina that only comes from action.

"Are we a go?" Devlin asked, looking to Wynda and Jack.

Jack stepped away from them, just a few feet, to give himself a sense of being alone with the storm. His eyes swept the western horizon, blackened by the rain- and hail-filled supercell. They already felt the misty kiss of it, and he could see the wall cloud spinning slowly. It wasn't far off, and it was becoming more substantive, its fingers lifting and lowering, eager to grasp the ground. He turned back toward Wynda.

"If you're going to do it, now's the time."

"Brad?" Wynda gave him his cue.

Their star was peeing on a nearby rock, obviating any bladder issues before his second outing in the sphere. He gave a little hop and zipped up, then turned toward them, his face strangely clear, his eyebrows having assumed one of their least worried positions. He gave the impression of having entered another plane. He was another Brad now, the TV Brad, and he looked resolute, even brave. "Open it, guys. Time to see what the inside of a tornado is really like."

Wynda's expression was gleeful as Devlin and Pole unlatched the curved door and helped strap Brad in. Brad inserted his key into the manual airbag deployment control, the one that protected the clear plastic box over the button, and donned the helmet.

Jack caught movement in the corner of his eye and turned to see Saffire also looking west, her hair blowing around her face as she observed the rotating wall cloud he'd been watching. "Let's go," she whispered, concern creeping into her voice, and he knew she was talking to him. She was beautiful in her skittishness. And she was right. You didn't need to be a meteorologist to see that something wicked this way came. Their eyes met as they both pulled their gaze away from the storm. "Now?" she asked.

"That would be wise," Jack said as the rain began to intensify, dousing them, their cameras and, more to the point, the dirt road. He touched her shoulder as they turned and stepped back toward the group. Her skin was warm through the soft cotton shirt, and he felt a rush of desire. Confusion. He had to focus.

"Don't get stuck, guys," Brad said with a hint of derision as Devlin and Pole shut the Bubble's door.

"Locked and loaded," Devlin said as they closed the Bubble. They all felt the change in the air around them, a shift in pressure, an uptick in the warm inflow, and they did their radio checks in a hurry.

"Go," Jack said. "Let's go. Now."

Devlin took the wheel in Van One, and the rest piled in their vehicles. Led by Pole, they circled around the Bubble and wished Brad well, bouncing headlong back the way they had come. To the west, Jack noted, the tendrils of the wall cloud touched the ground. Dirt swirled up. It was a multivortex tornado, a spinning spider with twirling legs, and it was headed right for Brad — and, depending on its motion and this damn winding road, their caravan, too. Lightning flashed ahead of them, reflecting in the growing puddles as the dirt road started to turn into pudding.

Showtime, Brad, showtime, the star told himself. *Oh shit. Oh shit. Oh shit.*

It was a tornado. There was no mistaking it this time. But this was no classic cone. There were multiple funnels on the ground at once, lifting up and touching down like a demented merry-go-round. And it was slowly, inexorably coming his way.

His assumed calm threatened to crumble in the face of this decidedly non-theoretical tornado. He'd done a lot of painful thinking in the past few days, reasoning that this TV show was one of the easiest ways for him to make money he'd ever encountered. Or at least, it had seemed that way up until this moment. Damn Jack and his forecast.

Brad had worked hard to convince himself that despite the Bubble's obvious, uh, experimental nature, it probably wouldn't kill him. Hedging his bets, he'd sent his dad's corporate lawyers a copy of his contract to see if there was a way out, but he knew there was potential for profit here. If he could get through this — and hell, the likelihood of this device ever actually getting picked up and flung by a tornado was infinitesimal — there were so many more opportunities waiting in the wings. His recent tour of the talk shows with his Prairie Rock video had generated a lot of interest, and it had even paid off a couple of times in young women he'd met who watched too much late-night television. Just this morning, he'd had a call from a Japanese toymaker who wanted to talk with him about an action figure. For a modest sum, he'd already endorsed a brand of cheesy rain gauges that doubled as light-up plastic flowers. Even though the Bubble had been kept under wraps, the word was out that he was starring in a very cool new series, hyped more than a little by his social feeds. If he played his cards right, he could be more famous than that Aurelius Zane guy.

All of this went through his head again, a lot more rapidly than it did during his earlier deliberations, as he looked through the rain-spattered shell of the Bubble at the approaching tornado. He had to think about the long term, he told himself. And the tornado might still miss him. He clenched his teeth.

"OK in there?" Devlin's voice came over the radio wired into his helmet.

"Yes," Brad managed, then remembered his role. "Tornado is approaching. Unclear if I'll be hit, though."

"We should have put in pedals," Devlin quipped. "We won't be far. This is turning into the road from hell. Slow going. We're trying to find a spot to film. Tell us as soon as anything changes."

"Will do."

To the west, the land over which the storm churned was flat and almost featureless. Behind him was the gentle slope and the road, nothing to worry about this time, he was sure. It was the tornado that worried him, still multi-vortex, still unclear about its intentions. The center of circulation seemed ill-defined, yet the vortices picked up dirt and small debris as they did their circular dance. And they were getting closer. As the southeasterly inflow picked up, the Bubble rolled gently toward the tornado, just a few feet, just enough so Brad felt the gyroscope keeping him upright, harnessed in the seat in the inner ring. If he turned his head back and to the right, he could see the pumpjack bobbing deliberately, a senseless metal dinosaur, oblivious to the beast stalking it. And him. Brad looked back toward the tornado. Almost imperceptibly closer. Bigger.

He could unstrap himself if he had to, pop the latch and run. But there was no place to go. No house. No bridge, not that those were advisable. Not even a goddamn ditch. Just the great, flat plain, the darkness in the sky, the needles of wind stabbing the ground and spinning toward him, the swirling dust.

Oh shit. Oh shit. Oh shit.

THE WHEELS WERE NOT TURNING. Or, to be precise, the wheels were turning quite a bit, but they were no longer advancing the van.

Devlin was trying all levels of pressure on the accelerator — sustained, staccato, hard, soft — but at this bend, the puddle they hit was too deep, the mud too mucky. In the process, the van had shifted diagonally across the road. They were well and truly stuck, and since they blocked both lanes, the crew car was trapped behind them.

"Fuck," Jack said softly to himself as he pushed open the side door and hopped out, craning to see the tornado over the bank that turned the horrible road, at this low point, into a short, shallow canyon.

"We're a little farther away," Saffire said hopefully, though she didn't sound convinced.

"Andre," Wynda barked, "get up on the bank and try to film the Bubble while we work on getting unstuck. Jack, go see if you can find a tow rope in the SUV, and tell Razor and Michiko to film us. Devlin, radio Pole to keep going. We're going to need someone mobile when all this is through."

Devlin, looking pale, laid off the accelerator, shifted to park and picked up the radio. "Pole, if you can still move, keep going south. We're stuck, but we're going to see if the SUV can get us out."

"You sure? I could come back."

"No point in all three of us being stuck."

"OK. I'm just a couple miles from the main road. I'll hang out there. Be safe."

"Thanks." Devlin turned to the Bubble radio. "Brad, how is it?"

"Closer," came Brad's voice, which was equally bleak. "Still not sure it's going to hit me. It has a slight southerly component, but only slight."

"Keep us informed. I might as well tell you, we're stuck."

"*Really?*" Brad asked, or rather exclaimed with glee.

Jack, with chagrin, heard the latter part of this conversation over the radio as he sifted through the crap in the back of the crew SUV. Razor and Michiko had already hopped out to film the crew scrambling to find something, anything, they could put under Van One's tires or use to yank it out of its predicament. Getting wet as the rain spat on his back, Jack looked in vain for a tow rope. What he really wanted to do was look for the tornado. All he found were endless bags, boxes, inadequate bungee cords and video cables that were unlikely to be of much help.

He hastened back to Wynda and kept striding past her. "No luck," he said over his shoulder. "I'm going to check on our tornado."

"I was about to ask you exactly that," Wynda said, her voice more tense than usual. "Devlin, Saffire, get up on the bank and look telegenic."

"What about the van?" Devlin asked.

"Fuck it," she said. She looked up, where the dark and roiling storm overshadowed their location. "We'll be fine."

I hope to hell she's right, Jack thought, as he clambered up the bank and beheld the tornado. It was one of two reported on this multicellular cluster of storms. In the few minutes since they'd left Brad, the tornado had advanced perhaps a mile, putting it within a mile of the Bubble. It didn't look particularly strong, and that factor might be in their favor. Jack shielded his eyes against the rain and tried to be objective. It was still a multivortex twister, with a ring of multiple, narrow funnels touching the ground and lifting. At any moment it could evaporate, or it could strengthen into a large tornado.

He looked around. They were partially shielded by the bank along the road, but there were no ditches here. Just mud. He hoped it didn't come to that. He really, really did.

Devlin and Saffire moved next to him, trailed by the cameras and microphone and the hovering Wynda. Huh. Now they actually wanted him on camera?

"What do you think, Jack?" Saffire asked. She had transitioned from nervous to excited. "Are we going for a ride, or is Brad?"

"An excellent question. That's a wide tornado, and it appears to be moving east-southeast. We're slightly southeast of Brad. It might nail both of us, or it might thread the needle. Or it could lift before it reaches us."

"That might be best," Devlin said. An understatement. He was looking north. "I don't think it's going to lift before it reaches Brad."

"So the Bubble might get to bounce? This could be historic," Saffire enthused. "Brad could be the first person ever deliberately launched into a tornado."

And we might follow, Jack thought.

Brad's voice came over Devlin's portable radio. "The Bubble's starting to move around," he said. "It's rocking and rolling a little, too."

"Excellent!" Devlin said, starting to get caught up in the moment.

"Rock and roll," Jack said dryly. Wynda gave him a dirty look, but he couldn't muster enough enthusiasm for her little show. All he could see now was the tornado, his focus sharpened by imminent danger. They could be seriously fucked.

"I'm rolling!" came Brad's voice over the radio.

The tornado appeared to be slipping just south of Brad, but the northern edges of the circulation had reached the Bubble.

"Now it's spinning!" Brad said. "Oh, gah —" There was a burst of static as lightning hit nearby, cutting him off. As they watched, the tornado slowly sideswiped the ball, which gleamed briefly as it reflected the scattered lightning. They could just make out the Bubble's struts in motion. The ball was spinning, all right.

Jack stepped behind Andre's tripod to look at his camera's viewscreen. The Bubble looked like one of those tops that appears from above to be perfectly still, even as it spins like crazy. One of the dancing vortices gave it just enough of a nudge that it slammed into the base of the oil pumpjack, bounced off and rolled away, out of the worst of the advancing winds.

"Brad?" Devlin called. "Brad, you there?"

There was a moment of unnerving silence before they heard coughing over the radio. "Your turn," came Brad's tremulous voice.

The Bubble was almost instantly forgotten as they all began to fathom that the tornado was less than a mile away and moving in their direction, ready to whack its next pinball.

2

FUNDAMENTAL FORCES

Zane Films was not having its best day.

"What do you mean, the tornado looks weird?" Aurelius asked his techies as he leaned into the window of their truck, straining to see their monitors in the back. Things One and Two filmed him from multiple angles.

"The video we get off the cards might be better quality," said Duncan, his unruly red hair and unkempt beard reflecting his anxiety, "but what I'm saying is there's too much rain and stuff in the way to really see it properly from the air."

"Or the ground," Aurelius said with disgust. "They're not paying us to see it from the ground, anyway. I want an aerial view. A beautiful, clear, *National Geographic* aerial view."

"Not going to happen today," Duncan said. "Or at least, not with this tornado." His wan colleague Phil, operating the joystick in the back seat, just nodded in agreement, clearly not wanting to incur Aurelius's wrath.

"We're losing the light. This is our tornado," Aurelius said. "Ernie!" he shouted.

The meteorology grad student emerged from the van, as

did Evie with her camera, though they stayed a few feet away from the fuming adventurer. "Yes, sir?" Ernie asked.

"Give me hope. Any hope."

"Well," Ernie said. "We might not be seeing much, but judging from radar, it's actually quite a sizable tornado. That's got to count for something."

"A large tornado, exactly what we're looking for, completely wrapped in rain." Aurelius sighed. He had to salvage what he could out of the day. Maybe they weren't going to get the money shot, but he needed a lot more than this to fill the six hours of airtime he was planning to occupy. "OK, then, my friends. Look excited. And impressed." He sucked a sizable breath from the misty air and appeared to grow taller as he exhaled. In his Zane baritone, he assumed his role, looking at Thing One's camera.

"This is an extremely dangerous tornado, and we are extremely close to it," he said. Then, quietly, to Thing Two: "You're zooming in on it, right?" At the nod, he turned back to Thing One. "At this moment, our aerial probe is investigating the twister at great risk. What you are seeing is a massive wedge tornado, my friends. This is exactly the way they look — a wall of darkness. With a heart of darkness, if you will." He allowed himself to feel momentarily smug for being literary. "This is why we chase storms. We chase storms to get close to the danger so you will not have to. We chase storms to share warnings with the public and our research with the scientific community. We are out here to make you safer by putting our own lives in peril. We are here *for you.*"

The rest of the crew was entranced. Aurelius had the delivery and conviction of a preacher at his most intense. They were rapt, convinced of their higher purpose. They were converted. And then he laughed.

"Cut," he said. "Land the damn plane. Let's go get some tacos."

"WE'RE NOT JUST GOING to stand here, are we?" Saffire asked the group point-blank as the multivortex tornado began to fill the horizon.

"Too late to move the vehicles," Wynda said. "Ditch?"

Jack eyed the tornado, trying to get a sense of its track. He was not getting into a fucking ditch, even if there was one. Besides, they'd have to find a pretty big one to bury, er, save all of them. "One should never, ever take shelter in a car in a tornado," he said. "However, it's weakening, and I think it's going to miss us. I think we'll be OK. But we should get into the vehicles."

They detected his thinly veiled urgency and swarmed as one down the bank and through the mud and rain. This time, Wynda went to the crew SUV, perhaps sensing that Razor and Michiko would be little comfort to each other as they faced down the storm.

"We're not stuck. We can't get around you, but we could head north," Michiko said into her radio. "Should we?"

"No," Jack said, looking out the window, hoping he made the right call. "You'll run right into it."

"Great," she said.

"Yeah, I know," Jack answered.

"Looks like it's getting closer," Brad's voice came over the radio. "It better miss you. I need you to get me back to civilization. Right now it's just me and some very wet cows."

Devlin pressed a button on his headset. "Are you out of the Bubble? Is it OK?"

"Thanks for your concern, Dev," Brad said sarcastically. "Yes, I'm out. Nice view from here."

"Shut up," Jack said to Devlin. "Just for a minute. If you're still alive in five minutes, you can all talk as much as you want."

"Gotta go," Devlin said brightly, if hollowly, to Brad.

"I can imagine," Brad said, coughing again before he keyed off the mike.

"Of course we're going to be alive in five minutes," Saffire said to Andre's camera. "This is a big adventure."

"To die will be an awfully big adventure, or so I hear," Jack said.

"Just so, Peter Pan," she said, looking in his eyes in a way that made the hairs on his neck stand up.

He tore his gaze away and looked up and out the window, then grabbed his radio. "Make sure your windows are closed. It might help. Michiko, back off us a little if you can, just in case it starts moving us around. I don't want us banging into each other."

"No sense of fun," Saffire joked as Michiko cranked the SUV into reverse and backed up the road by several feet.

Saffire had a brave streak, or a reckless one, Jack thought, though no more crazy than his. He realized that part of him wanted to be hit by the tornado more than anything. It was a strange sensation, like the one he'd had more than once on a hike as he stood at the tallest point on a mountain trail, where nothing stood between him and eternity but a dusty ledge. The abyss beckoned.

The van was stuck at such an angle that Jack now had a nearly perfect view of the storm. The advancing tornado was close enough that he could see most of it despite the muddy bank, and the winds around them were intensifying. The tall grass on the side of the road bent toward the tornado, as if in its thrall, then whipped up and down in a feverish dance before bending again to the ground. A platoon of tumbleweeds bounced among them and up the bank, toward the storm. Swirling dirt became visible, mixed with small bushes and unidentifiable streaks of darkness, minor debris. The tornado appeared to be falling apart, but small vortices stirred up the earth. It was a still a twister, albeit a confused one. As they watched, a cracking, rushing sound accompanied by a blast of dust built around them, paired with a ghostly whistle as the wind forced itself into every channel it could find. Jack felt his ears pop.

"Brace yourselves," Wynda's voice came over the radio.

"Cover your heads," Jack responded. "Do it now!"

They obeyed quickly, ducking and covering. Andre hid his face while keeping his camera aimed toward his stars. Jack was the only one who didn't hide, feeling responsible, unable to turn away. He didn't want the lives of these people on his head. He willed the tornado to shift, even as he was drawn into its fluid, malevolent motion. It was mesmerizing. In that dark space, as all other sounds faded, he heard the siren. In his trance, he recalled the safe, the thing that let him survive the Prairie Rock tornado when so many others had not. The rotation above the road drew him in, a swirling gateway to infinity, all the circles of nature, a tunnel to the past. The funnels spun up sporadically now, and he again became aware of the sounds around him, rocks and grass hitting the van. The crew SUV rocked violently as the circulation passed overhead. Then he caught a glimpse of a finger descending from the spinning cloud above. In a mighty explosion of glass, it blew out all of the van's windows.

Saffire and the others screamed. "Stay down!" Jack said,

lowering his own head, albeit too late to avoid the sting of broken glass on his face. He touched his cheek. It felt wet. His fingers were streaked with red. The van shuddered for a few more seconds, and the tornado was past.

The radio crackled. "Andre, get out and film that bastard!" Wynda shouted.

The cameraman looked up, shook his head and grinned. "Isn't she a peach?" he asked as he moved gingerly across the glass-covered seat and got out to shoot the retreating, dissipating tornado. Saffire and Devlin unfolded themselves from their safety positions and began to pick glass out of their hair and clothes. A few pricks of blood on their arms revealed minor scratches. Devlin grabbed the radio. "Pole, we're OK, but the van is now windowless as well as stuck. I hope you have the tow rope. Come back, please."

"I have the tow rope," Pole said. "Everybody OK?"

"A little scraped up, but yes, we're OK."

"Give me ten minutes."

Devlin activated the Bubble radio. "Brad, we'll be there shortly. Smoke 'em if you got 'em."

"Did it miss you?" Brad sounded disappointed.

"Not exactly."

"Ah-ha. It was worth getting stuck for a great show, right, Jack?"

Devlin turned toward Jack with eyebrows raised behind his rocket-scientist glasses, his face a question. Bristling, annoyed with himself for getting them into this position, Jack shook his head, declining to respond. Instead, he turned to Saffire. "You OK?"

"Fine. Excellent. Worth it for a great show," she said, then laughed. "You? Looks like you landed face-first on a cactus."

"Thanks," he said, allowing himself a smile. "I'm OK."

"I'm looking forward to a warm bath and a drink."

"Now you're talking," Jack said, imagining her in that bath, and him handing her that drink, and he was a little bit more glad to be alive.

WYNDA WONDERED how these Texans endured Amarillo, the flatness, the brownness. She loved travel because it was such an integral part of her career plan, but this evening, finally settling down alone for a late meal at the all-night diner next to the hotel for a pathetic American incarnation of fish and chips and a beer, she longed for the green and pleasant land of home.

What a cock-up today had been. It had taken the better part of an hour, but with the tow rope, they'd used the Bubble's truck to get Van One unstuck so they could get the other vehicles back to Brad. As she and Jack stood around with the wounded vehicle, he silently chain-smoking, she calling the rental company and trying to explain why she needed a replacement van, the rest of the crew went to retrieve the Bubble. It was even further scarred but, miraculously, still functioning. Devlin was whining about running more tests, but she didn't have time for it to be locked up and babied in a garage in Oklahoma City, not with more storms expected tomorrow. He'd have to do what he could on the fly.

Without a windshield, there was no way they could drive Van One any distance. So they'd taken forty-five minutes more to transfer all the cameras, computers and other gear from Van One to the fortunately cavernous SUV. They finished just in time to hand over the keys to a tow-truck driver who couldn't stop laughing at their predicament. Then they crammed into the remaining vehicles and limped back to Amarillo.

She tried to find the positives as she ate and typed a few ideas and emails on her tablet, hoping to mollify her overseers at Palatable Productions, who had no idea of the ridiculous miles and hours and luck that went into getting what little they got each day. At least they had filmed extraordinary footage of the van's windows being shattered from inside and out. The rental company had finally agreed to give them a new van in the morning, though it had found nefarious ways to raise the insurance. Brad had survived unscathed, but he was jittery, and that worried her. The show needed him. And that meant she needed him. She closed her eyes for a moment and rubbed her forehead, trying to imagine a less skittish hero, a good day with a good road and a fine, cinematic tornado that would take the Bubble for a highly photographable ride.

"May I buy you dessert?"

Wynda opened her eyes to behold Aurelius Zane standing over her table, lacking his entourage but not his charm.

"No, but you may buy me another beer," she said with a cautious smile.

"A long way from your pub."

"This will do. Almost everywhere I travel, there's a spot I can get a pint, and that's all that matters."

"Long day?" Aurelius asked, sitting and flagging the waitress, pantomiming "two" as he pointed to Wynda's beer.

"Long, dreadful, but decent footage."

"And how is your — device?" he asked.

Ah. That's where he was going. "Excellent," she said.

"Good to hear," he said. "Ours is functioning quite well, too."

It was like talking about the children they didn't have. "Get some exciting shots, then?"

"We're building a decent library for our little series," he responded, his tone evasive.

"I see."

"But why talk about work? I want to talk about you." The beers had arrived, and he took a swig out of the bottle.

"Bollocks," Wynda said.

"Excuse me?"

"When do we ever talk about *me?*" she asked.

"As I recall, we were better at not talking," he said, training his gray eyes on her blue ones and reaching over for her free hand, the one that didn't have a white-knuckle grasp of her beer bottle. She allowed him to touch her briefly before executing a similar crunch on his fingers.

"Ow!" he said, withdrawing. "Wynda, I miss you, no matter how much pain you cause me."

"Pain I cause *you? *That's rich."

"We were travelers. Ships in the night."

"You were traveling. I was abandoned with all the gear and that bloody monkey."

"How'd he make out, anyway?"

"Aurelius," she said, emphasizing each syllable. "Forget the monkey. What do you want from me?"

"How about a walk under the stars?"

"You're out of your effing mind," she said, but she felt his strange magnetism again. It had been a couple of years since her last pathetic relationship, and months since her last good lay, and that was with a production assistant on a previous gig who'd been great in bed but hopeless at everything else. Aurelius Zane, at least, was good at nearly everything, except perhaps managing his money. He was a natural-born television hero, too, who was drawn to disasters like a fly to honey. Maybe that's why he was drawn to her.

No, damn it, she was not a disaster. She was getting this show right. So what if its hero was a little reluctant? Aren't those the best heroes of all?

"You know," he said, "if you need any help with your show, I'm completely available."

Was he reading her mind? "Liar. You have your own show to shoot. And we're just fine, thank you."

"There's nothing in my contract that says I can't appear in two shows. I mean, if you need help, of course."

"My show is perfectly all right," she said, "and I have planned for a variety of outcomes if the weather does not cooperate."

Aurelius got up, leaned over her side of the table and whispered in her ear. "I just want you to know I'm available for *whatever* you may need, my dear Wynda." He gently kissed her cheek.

She was stunned and, she had to admit, a bit tingly as she watched him walk away. He was out the door before she realized he'd stuck her for the two beers.

"So you've managed to hijack one of our two remaining vehicles for the sole purpose of taking me out to the middle of nowhere to see some junk cars?" Saffire asked from the passenger seat of the crew SUV as the city lights of Amarillo played across her face. "If I weren't so trusting, I'd say you have nefarious designs on me."

"*A*, it's not junk cars, it's Cadillac Ranch," Jack said as he drove. "*B*, I absolutely have nefarious designs on you." He gave her a grin before turning back to the road. It was nice to drive again. It helped clear his head.

"Where is it?"

"Barely west of town. I guess it used to be the country, but it's hardly out of the lights anymore. Just tell me when we're at the exit."

She looked it up with her smartphone and told him where to go. A U-turn later, they were on the eastbound access road, looking for the lonely gate.

"Here we are," he said as he spotted it and pulled over, shutting off the engine. An old Jeep was parked ahead of them, beyond the gate. It showed no sign of occupation.

"This is it? Where are the cars?"

"Out there," he said, gesturing over the fence. "Let your eyes adjust. You'll see them."

"And your plan is?"

"We'll check it out. Maybe shoot some star trails. Then, who knows?"

"Get eaten by bugs, is my guess," she said as they got out of the car.

"Nothing like those freaky things at the gas station. What are they again?" The black beetles had been crawling all over the gas pumps, the curb and one another.

"Ground beetles. *Carabidae*. There are so many this year, it looks like they're eating each other. I think they're kind of neat."

"It was like a horror movie. And they stink," Jack said as he pushed the turnstile gate, manhandled his backpack and tripod and helped her get through.

"Only if you step on them." She walked next to him in the near-darkness down a dirt track toward the dim shapes in the field. "Respect our bug friends, and there's no problem."

"It's them or me."

She laughed. "You'll never win."

"What's with you and bugs anyway?"

"I just think they're fascinating. I had pet tarantulas when I was a kid. I had this millipede that would ooze smelly black goo onto my hands when it got scared, and it would stick for days. I had Madagascar hissing cockroaches, too. You can't look one of them in the face without admitting it's cute."

"Oh, I think maybe I could," Jack said.

"Hey, what's that?"

Flashlights moved among the shapes in the field. "Guess we're not alone," he replied as they got closer.

The car shapes became more defined in the darkness before revealing themselves as a line of ten vintage Cadillacs, embedded nose-first in the ground at an angle.

"Now this is cool," Saffire said. "We should put this on TV."

"Oh, god, don't suggest it. Not until we're desperate."

"Today was kind of the definition of desperate," she said. "At least when we were waiting for the tornado."

"That was, I admit, a little scary. But 'desperate' is chasing under a death ridge when there are no storms for two weeks. You end up putting on a lot more miles chasing scraps than you do real storms."

The moving lights revealed themselves as three people already among the cars, one with a camera on a tripod, the other two running around with high-tech flashlights.

"What are they doing?" Saffire asked.

"Painting with light, I think," Jack said. "When you do a long exposure in the dark and add light to the equation, like a moving flashlight, you get cool effects."

"Ah, OK. Now I'm starting to see the appeal," she said. "You can make things glow."

"Something like that. Let's just step over here and watch for a minute. I'll set up my tripod, too."

Jack always enjoyed visiting this quirky art installation. One might compare it to Stonehenge, but Carhenge in Alliance, Nebraska, was a better analogue. Cadillac Ranch was especially intriguing at night, though it was hard to see its details.

The others' voices and laughter carried in the darkness as they dodged in and out, illuminating the cars and one another with their flashlights. "Oh, hi," one young fellow said as he popped out from behind a graffiti-covered Caddy and saw them. "You shooting, too? We'll be done in a few minutes." Then he was off, weaving in and out of the Cadillacs like a demented slalom skier, waving his light around in the process, switching the beam from blue to green.

Jack got the tripod set up, pulled his Nikon from his bag and popped it into the mount. Next came a blanket he'd scrounged from the hotel-room closet, which he spread on the ground, and a petite bottle of bourbon. "Care to?"

"What, the drinks at dinner weren't enough?" Saffire asked, smiling, before taking the bottle and a modest sip.

"We'll be out here a while," he said as he took the bottle. "I need to unwind after today. I'll exercise moderation."

"Sure," she said, sounding unconvinced but in good humor.

The lights had stopped dancing among the cars, and they heard the others packing up and heading back out to the road. "Good night!" they called.

"Bye!" Saffire said, then to Jack: "Another sip, please."

"Yes, m'lady." He handed her the bottle, positioned his

camera and started experimenting to get the right exposure to show off the cars and stars.

She capped the bottle and lay it on the blanket, then walked over so she was in front of the camera. "Can you paint me with light?"

He stopped playing with the camera and looked her over. Starlight, gas station lights down the road, and the faint glow of the city behind them all conspired to cast a fragile illumination on her cheeks, her wavy hair. When he looked off to his right, the northeast, he could see dim, flat flashes, what some called heat lightning. It was the storm that had tormented them earlier, retreating far to the east, now absorbed into a nasty squall line.

He turned back to Saffire. In the scant light, she was more black-and-white than color, a beautiful specter.

"Stand close to that first car," he said. "Turn on your phone. You have one of those light apps? Wave it in a pattern, like you're drawing a big picture, when I tell you to go."

She pulled her phone from her pocket and tapped it a few times until its light came on, a glowing, blue-white point. "Ready."

"OK, go," he said, hitting the remote to open the shutter. She moved her phone in big swoops and lines. "What are you drawing?"

"You'll see, I hope. OK, done!" She turned off the light.

He clicked the shutter and reviewed the image. The cars were vaguely visible in the background, with her bright doodle in the foreground, her figure a smudge behind it. "It looks like a cloud, with a squiggle. Is that a lightning bolt?"

"Yes! Let me see!" She bounded over to look. "Oh, that's pretty cool. A little off but pretty cool."

"Very cool."

"But I want you to paint *me* with light."

"I'd rather paint you with paint. All over you. Finger paints, preferably."

"Light, Jack," she said with a smile. "Please try it. I want to glow."

You already do, he thought. "OK. I don't have a flashlight, but I'll use my phone. Go stand by the car again. I'll get the camera ready."

He tweaked the camera settings and opened the shutter.

"I have to get close to you to do this in color. The phone isn't that bright," he said, walking over to her. "Hold still."

"Yes, doctor," she said, her dimples showing, even in the dark.

He breathed in her lavender scent as he stood next to her, then turned on the phone and activated the light application, choosing a red glow. He started at the ground, aiming the light at her feet, bringing it slowly up one side of her body, around her jeans-clad hips, her breasts, her arms. He hadn't reached her neck when the shutter clicked. "Damn it," he muttered. He moved to the camera and adjusted its settings so he could leave the shutter open indefinitely.

"What does it look like?"

"I wasn't done, but it's kind of interesting. Half a lit-up silhouette." He walked over to her and clicked the remote. "We're trying again."

"OK," she whispered as he brushed against her.

He stood slightly behind her and began his leisurely tour of her legs, hips and torso. He went even more slowly this time, limning her figure. As he illuminated her shoulder, he leaned toward her and pressed his lips against her neck. She gasped in response as his light moved up to her chin and he kissed it, too. Now her breathing came faster, more shallow.

He moved the light painstakingly around those delectable cheekbones and over her honey-gold hair. She closed her eyes as he painted her eyelids with the glow and touched his lips to her forehead.

As he moved the light around the other side of her face, he kissed her nape. She began to lift her arms. *"Stay still,"* he whispered. She made a small, yearning sound. He felt her impatience, her heat. He was enjoying this. His light brushed her shoulder, followed by his lips, a kiss through the soft cotton of her V-neck shirt. The mermaid tattoo was under there, he knew. As he moved the glow down over her breasts, he pulled a little on the fabric in front, just enough so he could kiss the delicious curve that led to where he really wanted to go. But he released the cloth and lit her waist and then her hips, running his hand up under her shirt and across her belly as he did so. He lightly caressed the last leg of his journey. He stopped at her feet, where he knelt like a supplicant for a moment as he clicked the shutter closed and pocketed the remote and phone. He could imagine worshipping this woman, but he had something more direct in mind. He stood and took her in his arms, pressing his mouth against her warm lips, sweet with a hint of bourbon. He always liked a cocktail of girl and bourbon. His tongue touched hers and she moaned slightly, finally releasing her stance and wrapping her arms around his neck. He pushed her backward until she bumped softly into the side of the nearest half-submerged car, then pressed his body against hers, wanting to feel all her curves with all his angles, which grew harder by the second. He felt so alone with her out here, alone with her and the ghosts of the drivers of these old, strange cars, forever pushing into the earth. He felt the motors' hum, the mystical road deep beneath them, as his and Saffire's kisses grew more urgent. He reached smoothly under her shirt with his left hand and let his palm curl around the lace cupping one lovely, round breast, then slipped his fingers under the bra's fabric to squeeze one nipple. Her tiny cry broke the kiss, and she stood panting, looking in his eyes, as he released her and let his hands come to rest on her hips.

"You're stunning," he said.

"You're a terrible painter."

"You can't say that. You haven't seen the photo yet." He leaned in and kissed her neck, gently sucking, feeling her breathing pick up again.

"Let's look at it." Her voice quavered. For a reason he couldn't discern, she wanted him to stop.

He reluctantly pulled away and cleared his throat. "Sure," he said.

Saffire moved to the blanket and sat down, opened the bourbon bottle and took a sip. Jack walked over to the camera, popped it off the mount, sat next to her and hit the preview button.

"Wow," she said.

"You're a gorgeous ghost."

"An eerie red blur. And you are my shadow."

"Enveloping you," he said, leaning in for another kiss.

She seemed reluctant to pull away, but after a few seconds, she did.

Jack watched her face for an explanation, then got up and put the camera back on the tripod. "I thought you wanted this simple. Here I am, simplicity itself," he said, as he plugged in the intervalometer and started the process of shooting a time-lapse of the stars and cars.

"Uh-huh. I think we bypassed simple when we survived death together."

"Hardly death. Just a little broken glass," he said, returning to his spot next to her.

"Still." She took another sip of the whiskey and handed it to him. "Guys used to have me on their terms. I decided a long time ago to have them on mine."

"I agree to your terms," he said with a smile, sipping the bourbon.

"You have no idea what they are."

"I don't get you. You jump in with both feet, then you jump out, teeter on the edge of the pool." He leaned closer. "The water's fine."

"I like you, but now that I know you a little better, I worry about getting involved with you."

"Thanks," he said dryly, then added: "We'll keep it as simple as you like."

"I told you. It's too late for that. And I have places to go."

"Not for the next few weeks."

"Look, I had this boyfriend once — "

"Don't tell me. I remind you of him."

"Not at all," she said. "Thank god. He was a nightmare. Of course, I didn't think so at first. It was, like, twelve years ago. I was only in high school and pretty innocent. He was good-looking, so I suppose you have that in common. But he had nowhere near your confidence. He tried to make up for it in other ways."

"Not good ways?" He heard it in her voice, which had grown quiet, without her usual sparkle and froth.

"I didn't understand at first," she said. "I liked the attention. Boys didn't go for me much in high school."

"Hard to believe. Where'd you go to high school?"

"An L.A. suburb. I was not in the 'in' crowd. Guess they didn't recognize the diamond under all that frizzy hair and braces. I didn't get the concept of glamour back then. But this boy, he treated me like a glamour girl. He bought me flowers. He took me on elaborate dates — his folks had some money. And he was so jealous of other boys, whatever acquaintance I'd be talking to in the hallway. I thought it was cute. I mean, he and I didn't do much. Just some kissing in the car, that kind of thing. But his jealousy started to get scary. He'd call the house to see where I was. He'd follow me and my friends to the mall. He accused me of sleeping with other boys; I hadn't slept with anyone yet. It was crazy. Every time he'd do something loopy and I got upset, he'd come back twice as nice, bring me presents, promise never to do it again. Then at this one homecoming dance, when I was talking with a guy who was my lab partner in biology, the boyfriend from hell comes up and starts screaming at me, calling me things I'd rather not repeat."

She paused for a moment, took the bourbon and sipped. Jack so wanted to take her hand, but he knew he shouldn't, not now. Not when she was working her way through the memory.

"He practically ripped my arm off trying to drag me out of there," she continued, looking off into the stars, following the eye of the camera. "He got me out of the gym and into the parking lot. He hit me in the face. And really, once was all it took. I didn't need any more convincing. I know the stories. I've heard a lot of stories since then as a shelter volunteer. At the time, we had these neighbors — everyone knew what he did to her, his wife. My parents called the cops a couple of times. We all wondered why she didn't leave, but I knew. She was so afraid of what he would do."

"What did this boyfriend of yours do after that?" Jack was

angry on her behalf. He wanted to step back in time with her, defend her.

"He called. He threatened. But I'd had a moment of clarity, you know? I looked into his eyes and saw his weakness and manipulation and walked away. He eventually figured out I wouldn't play his game, and I learned to trust myself. I rarely get involved with men now. There have been only a couple of serious ones, and despite the Hollywood hype, I'm even picky about my simpler entanglements."

"Do you worry about another guy doing that to you? Me?"

"Of course not," she said. "I know a lot more now. My point is that I've learned, to misquote a song, it takes a pretty good guy to be better than none at all. Especially when I have certain goals in mind. I like to have control over my life. And let's face it, charmers like you are a terrible distraction."

"I'm no charmer," Jack said.

"I see it all over you, mister," she said. "Not that there's anything wrong with that."

She had him. But it was something else she'd said that bothered him. He was trying to pinpoint it, then just as quickly pushed it away.

Too late. She'd seen it in his face. "What is it?" she asked.

There it was again. He was in another place, in Virginia, in the house of his childhood. "Nothing."

"Something," she contradicted him.

"OK. OK." He took the bottle back and sipped again. "It's just that I think my mom was always afraid of my dad. I never saw him lay a hand on her, but he said things to her I don't want to remember. He just — raged. He got into these modes when he was so angry. She'd hide me away. We'd sit in the spare room and close the door and play Monopoly and listen to him slamming stuff around.

And drinking." Jack's laugh was flat as he held up the bottle of bourbon. "When she died, I guess she found her way out."

"How?"

"Car crash."

"How old were you?"

"Thirteen."

"I'm sorry. I was a little older when my father died." She paused. "In retrospect, being a teenager kind of sucked, didn't it? I was a senior when I figured out the perfect boyfriend was a disaster."

"Nothing like your first high-school love."

"Who was yours?" she asked.

"Miss Edgehill."

"A teacher? You had a crush on her?"

"Slightly more than that," he said. "I guess I was in need of some womanly influence at the time. And she was pretty hot. Though almost every woman looks hot when you're sixteen. She was — educational. Then she moved to another district, married some businessman."

"Jack," she said. "That's pretty awful."

Her sympathy bothered him. "I enjoyed it at the time. And I soon came to realize she wasn't the only woman in the world."

"Not for someone like you."

"There have been a few," he said. "More than a few."

"So," she said, "neither of us have much reason to go to high school reunions."

"I think forgetting high school is generally a good policy for almost anyone," Jack said.

"What did she teach?"

"Chemistry. She always said we had a lot of chemistry."

Saffire let out a little chuckle, and the tension eased. "Of course."

"Just glad she didn't mess up physics and meteorology for me."

"That would be impossible," Saffire said. "You have storms in your blood."

He smiled in acknowledgment, dug into his bag and pulled out a cigarette and a lighter. A flick, a flame, the comforting first draw. Then he lay back on the blanket, smoking, as the camera did its thing.

"Why do you smoke?" she asked.

"The usual reasons. Peer pressure. It pissed off my dad. I like it."

"But you don't need it."

"Oh, yeah, and I'm addicted," he added.

"Oh, *that.* How much longer for the pictures?"

"Give it a half-hour."

"OK." She lay next to him, looking up as he did, as the stars spun around them.

"So," Jack said. "I'm not simple enough for you, but I'm not complicated enough, either?"

She laughed. "At this point, I have no idea. Maybe you should ask me tomorrow."

He did what he'd longed to do earlier. He took her hand and, with a colossal act of will, kept the rest of his aching, overheated body lying casually next to her.

"I most definitely will," he said.

VAN ONE HAD BEEN REINCARNATED. The rental company dropped off another white whale at the hotel, the same model of large minivan with all its windows and the added bonus of satellite radio. The crew spent a couple of hours by dawn's early light wiring it for cameras, sound, power and laptops. Antennas went on the roof, luggage went in the back, and soon, Devlin was driving them east on I-40 toward Oklahoma with Brad in the passenger seat, Andre and Saffire in the middle, and Jack in the back, looking over data. Wynda followed in the crew sport-utility vehicle with Michiko and Razor, while Pole brought up the rear with the scratched, hastily cleaned Bubble.

Today had potential, and Devlin had been fretting over not being able to perform more tests on the device. But after yesterday, Jack was starting to think it would never get off the ground anyway. It hadn't lofted at all when the tornado sideswiped it. It would probably take a huge tornado to lift it, and its curved surface wouldn't help the wind find purchase. Maybe the struts would be a plus, but the job seemed to get more challenging by the day, and he saw his bonus withering in the face of the technical obstacles and Brad's dithering.

"Shamrock is full of Route 66 landmarks," Saffire said for the cameras as they passed through the eastern Panhandle town, just shy of the Oklahoma border. "The Tower Service Station was built in the 1930s."

"I don't understand why people get so excited about old gas stations," said Brad, who was irritable after consuming two energy drinks and rubbery taquitos from the Fuel & Flee.

"It's the romance of the road," Saffire said. "Finding America. The idea of a more innocent time, when gas was cheap and the highway offered the promise of adventure. You're on an adventure, aren't you?"

At her words, Brad appeared to become aware that he was

being filmed and moderated his tone. "Sure I am," he said, unconvincingly.

Jack grimaced, recalling the service stations where chasers practically lived while on the road, all of which seemed to advertise something more scintillating than gas: the Pump N Pantry, the U Pump It, the Kum & Go — *pump, pant, kum,* he thought — and Hop 'n Sack with its kangaroo logo. He so badly wanted to hop in the sack with Saffire, and these carnal connotations weren't helping.

About 1 p.m., somewhere north of Weatherford, where they topped off the tanks, Wynda halted them alongside a gently sloping field undulating with young, green wheat. The gravel road here rolled over a couple of minor hills, providing a photogenic spot the caravan subsequently traversed a dozen times, raising dramatic clouds of dust, so the camera guys could get drive-by shots.

"OK, kids," Wynda said when they were done. "I want my stars lined up in front of the van, walking toward me and the cameras with the wind blowing your hair around. You're going to look like movie stars."

"Shouldn't the van explode behind them?" asked Jack, who leaned against a fence post, smoking. Devlin groaned, but he followed Saffire and Brad to a spot in front of the lead van, which was parked in the middle of the road for the shot.

"Jack, get over here," Wynda called.

He looked at her in surprise. "What do you want me for?"

"I need my on-camera personalities on camera," she said.

"Then you don't want Mr. Lack of Personality," Brad snipped.

"If only you knew," Saffire said under her breath.

"Brad's right," Jack said, never imagining that was a phrase he'd utter. "I'm not one of your personalities."

"It's one shot, damn it, Jack," Wynda said. "Get in front of the bloody van."

He was puzzled for a moment, then dropped his cigarette, ground it out and walked over to the group. "What about Pole?"

"Oh, that won't be necessary," Wynda said blithely.

"Thanks," Pole said dryly from his spot next to the Bubblevan, where he was rocking his '70s sunglasses.

"All right," Wynda said. "Jack, move over there next to Saffire. On her left. Just so. Now, all of you, look straight ahead, past the cameras, and walk with purpose down the road, like you're about to kick somebody's arse."

They all laughed, then tried to compose themselves.

"Andre, wide shot. Razor, pan, then get me some close-ups. I want the high frame rate for slow-mo later, OK?"

The camera guys fiddled with their settings, and when they were ready, Wynda said "Action!" as if this were some sort of fictional movie instead of a documentary. Which it was, Jack was beginning to realize. He walked forward, looking at Wynda as if he wanted to kick her arse, only to feel the corners of his mouth curling up at the absurd scene. He cast a sidelong glance at Saffire and saw she'd become glamour incarnate, striding forward with the grace of a lioness, her wavy hair blowing about her pink cheeks. He could almost see her in slow motion.

"Excellent," Wynda said, looking at her cameramen. Andre offered a thumbs-up; Razor gave her a nod. "You all are pros. I won't even make you do it again. Brad, now it's your turn. Get in that wheat field."

Michiko put the wireless mike on him, and he waded into the tender stalks up to his knees, talking earnestly to the camera about his deep connection to the weather. As far as

Jack could tell, they were all up to their knees in bullshit. He grabbed a soda from their snack cooler and joined the others hanging around the vehicles, waiting for Brad to shut up.

"Watch out," Saffire said quietly, leaning next to him against Van One. "You'll step on the rain bugs."

Jack gave her a glance that suggested no bug would determine where he stood, unless it stung, but he looked down anyway.

"I don't see anything."

"The red specks. Rain bugs, or velvet mites. They're doing their circle dance. They come out after a rain."

He looked closer and saw tiny scarlet creatures moving around in the brown dirt by the side of the road. "Bright little critters," he said. "Why are they doing a dance?"

"Why does anyone do a dance? To get girls," she said with a grin.

"Hey, whatever works." He moved to the other side of her so he wouldn't step on the creepy revelers.

"So do you have a taste for stardom yet?" she asked.

"I am in this for the tornadoes. And enough bucks so I can chase more tornadoes."

"It's all about the tornadoes, then? All the time?"

"Almost," he said, giving her the green-eyed stare that had melted so many. She did not dissolve, but she returned his charged look with her golden one and smiled, and then smiled a little wider.

"You make it sound so simple," she said. There was that word again.

"Oh, it is," he said, remembering his mouth on hers, wanting more. "It is."

"Quiet!" Wynda roared at them. "Brad, one more time."

But quiet was not to be. The rattle of an aged pickup truck

stopped their star in mid-sentence. The vehicle creaked to a halt a few feet from theirs, and a tan, leathery man, on the far side of sixty, stepped out and slammed the door. His jeans were worn, and his white T-shirt had holes in it.

"What the hell are you doing in my field?" he barked at the group, though his eyes were on Brad.

"Filming a TV show, sir," Brad said.

The farmer was unimpressed. "Do you know how much it costs me a year to farm this acre of wheat?"

"Um — fifty dollars?" Brad guessed.

"Try close to two hundred fifty. I'm lucky if I make thirty bucks when it's all done. And you just trampled about a hundred dollars' worth of wheat. I've a mind to call the cops, or maybe I'll just see if my shotgun's still working."

Jack suspected the man was exaggerating, but there was a gun rack in the truck. Besides, the last thing they needed to do was piss off local farmers, who had enough troubles.

"I'm so sorry, sir," Saffire piped up. "It's just that your field was so beautiful, we couldn't help ourselves." She smiled her purest dazzler, and the man's face softened.

"Well, I do enjoy your TV show, Miss Soulliere, but this young man is out of line," he said, pointing back to Brad with a scowl.

Wynda jumped into the fray before anyone could make it worse. She walked up to the farmer, wielding a pleasing expression Jack had never seen. "Please let me compensate you for your trouble, and then we'll be gone. Immediately." She turned to glare at the cast and crew, who hastened to get to their vehicles. "Will a hundred and fifty be acceptable?"

Jack chuckled to himself as she worked out the deal. Back in the van, he settled behind his workstation and hit the power button. Now Brad got in the driver's seat, with Saffire riding shotgun. The hierarchy of stardom had asserted itself, albeit on an extremely small scale.

Jack logged on to the van's mobile hotspot connection and started paging through the latest outlooks, surface charts and computer models. When Wynda hopped in next to him, he was ready.

"The data still look good. I think there's a decent chance of tornadoes today," he said. "Probably not as good as yesterday, but you can count on supercells. And since we're in Oklahoma, there'll be a ton of chasers around. Let's get across the river so we don't have to do it later, somewhere we can still get a signal and keep an eye on it."

"You're the weatherman," Wynda said, then grabbed the radio he kept next to his laptop mount. "All right, crew," she said. "You performed beautifully, you didn't get shot, and today, you're going to make Brad fly. Follow us."

"That might be overstating it," Jack murmured as Brad put the van in drive.

"Dr. Andreas," Wynda said, "overstating it is my job."

"OH FUCK ME," Aurelius said as a dozen chase cars, heavily adorned with decals, lights and antennas, zoomed past the otherwise empty gravel lot where they were parked. "Is every chaser in Oklahoma out today?"

"And all the ones from Texas and Kansas and Colorado, too, I think," said Ernie, whose head was buried in the laptop mounted against the dash of the Zane Films van. He was trying to find some subtle sign that would tell them where the best storm might pop up this afternoon. So far, the satellite image showed they were in the middle of a vast CU field that spanned much of west-central Oklahoma — cumulus clouds, fluffy and white and full of potential — somewhere in the vicinity of the stationary front. The dryline was advancing, and there were still outflow boundaries lingering from last night's convection. Something would happen. But where and when?

Through his window, Aurelius idly watched Evie blowing bubbles for the cameras, as there was really nothing else to film at the moment. "Will there be tornadoes today?" he asked.

"I've been working on the time machine, but it's not ready yet," Ernie replied.

Aurelius looked at him for a second before he realized the grad student was joking, then laughed his deep laugh. "You almost had me," he said. "Now that's a show I want to star in."

"I want to go back and see the Tri-State Tornado of 1925," Ernie said wistfully, taking a moment to look up from the computer and out the windshield at the crowd of clouds, which drifted east in their blue field like lazy sheep.

"The cars weren't nearly as fast back then," Aurelius pointed out. "Chasing would be a lot harder."

"Duh. My time machine will have wheels. It might not look much like a Tin Lizzie, but I don't plan to get caught."

"Invisibility, too?"

"Now you're just being silly," Ernie said, returning his attention to the laptop.

Aurelius sighed. He didn't have the tornado footage he needed, and he wasn't entirely sure Wynda got his broad hint about his willingness to fly in her device, which he still hadn't seen. Or maybe he did suspect she got it and was just ignoring it. They were monitoring her CB channel, just so he could keep tabs on her crew, but they had to be in range to get any intel, and at the moment, they were nowhere near. Or, at least, Wynda's crew wasn't talking.

Evie caught his attention again. Now she was twirling, the light shining on her long brown hair as it spun with her, her long brown legs lithe all the way down to her sandals, the sun glistening iridescent in the bubbles swirling in her wake. Thing One and Thing Two circled her with their cameras as she laughed. Oh, to be twenty-one again, he thought. To travel back in time, to re-experience his first typhoon, to meet again the fiery Wynda in the jungle, to buy shares of Apple stock instead of being in debt up to his eyeballs. Rodney had been sending him emails. He needed something to report. He wasn't used to being this … doubtful.

"Towering CU," Ernie said. It sounded like "cue," and it was Aurelius's cue — his cue to stop moping and start chasing.

"Where?"

"Not far. A little north. It's probably worth checking out."

Aurelius stepped out of the van and looked back toward the drone truck, where the guys were sitting on the tailgate, drinking out of enormous Fuel & Flee cups. They stood when they saw him. The camerathings also halted what they were doing, as did Evie, and turned to him, waiting expectantly for his word. He looked in the direction of the towering cumulus clouds that were depicted in satellite imagery, but they were too distant to be visible to the eye. A bluish, shadowy hue suggested their presence far beyond the nearest puffs.

"Ready?" he asked Things One and Two. They nodded. "All right, people. Storms are starting to fire on the dryline. It's time to rock and roll!"

They were all still standing there, not sure if he was done.

"All right. Let's try this again," he said caustically, and they immediately straightened up and got TV-ready looks on their faces. "Storms are starting to fire on the dryline! It's time to ROCK AND ROLL!"

They jumped, they scrambled, they rushed to their vehicles as Aurelius stood gazing nobly at the western sky for a few seconds, holding his jacket by the lapels, his profile artfully posed for the cameras as he let the wind ruffle his blond hair. Then he climbed into the van with the Things hot on his heels, started it up and thrust it into drive.

IT ALWAYS IMPRESSED Jack how a cloud, a nebulous collusion of water vapor, could look hard enough to break. Their storm had started as one of many vigorous cumulus clouds across western Oklahoma, but it had outpaced the others. It had taken root so quickly and shot up so fast, its billowing surfaces had a glossy look, like a bright white candy shell. Inside was sweet convection, a sweet confection for any storm chaser. The white soon gave way to bruised gray and green as the storm developed, just west of their position. Which was in the Oklahoma City TV market, if the helicopter flying overhead was any indication.

"They'll chase anything, won't they?" Wynda asked as she looked up. They were all standing outside their vehicles along a narrow secondary road near the top of a low hill that sloped down, toward the west, and then up, toward the growing storm.

"More to the point, they don't want to be beaten by the competition," Jack said.

"That, I understand," she replied, looking over at Brad,

who'd sported a ghastly pallor all afternoon after the energy drinks wore off.

Saffire crouched next to a nearby fence post, showing Andre something in the dirt. His lens flirted with the ground.

"Be careful," she said to the cameraman as Jack wandered over. "You don't want to scare him."

Andre pulled the lens back a little as Jack leaned in. "What is it?" Jack asked.

"A funnel weaver," Saffire said. "*Agelenopsis*, what you might call a grass spider. Isn't he cool?"

Andre abruptly stopped filming. "I got enough," he said, then walked away.

"That was odd," Jack said, standing up and back a little, not relishing the idea of a spider jumping on him. The brown-and-black striped creature crouched in a gossamer funnel of web that widened into the crunchy grass. "Is it poisonous?"

"They have one of these in Australia that's deadly, but this guy won't do you much harm."

"I am a man," he said, "but I am not going to screw around with spiders."

"Not when you have other things to screw around with," she said with a faint smile.

"You are a vixen." He held out his hand and helped her up, holding on a few seconds longer than was absolutely necessary. "Can this spider weave a funnel for me, maybe out of that cloud?"

"No, but he would catch you if you shrunk a whole lot and got anywhere near his lair. He runs really fast."

"That's a different science-fiction movie," he said. "In this one, we're about to launch Brad into outer space in a human hamster ball."

She laughed as they walked back toward the others. "We

can only hope it launches a few feet. Either way, Wynda will be thrilled."

The storm was barely moving, but it was growing. Judging by its striations and a nascent wall cloud, it had a little spin, too. Lightning sparked from its base, followed by deep and lingering thunder. Jack liked the look of it, but he wasn't convinced it was tornado material. Still, Wynda would probably want to deploy.

"Devlin, figure out where we can deploy," she said at that moment.

"Yes, boss." He walked over to the van, got in and started paging through maps on the laptop. In a moment, he re-emerged. "There's another road off this one — we go a little south, then west. Should be flatter, too, my topo software says."

"Flat is good," Brad said quietly. He'd been standing by himself, looking west as the southeast wind rippled his black golf shirt. He was an ideal subject for Razor's camera as Michiko stood in range with her boom mike and mixer. The brooding hero, Jack thought. Or the freaking-out hero. Jack couldn't blame him, really, after the Bubble's recent spin.

The helicopter roared again, high overhead, keeping a safe distance in the inflow.

"I hope they're not paying us any mind," Wynda said, looking up. "Just as well that we move."

Another quarter, Jack recalled Brad's catchphrase, *and time to play.*

❧

"LAUNCH IT!" Aurelius shouted into the ham radio. "And get close. I want my shot today, Duncan."

"I'll do what I can. Fierce winds, you know. We'll have to be careful."

"Just do it." Why didn't they snap into action, as he did? He snapped his finger to emphasize his thoughts.

"Brilliant insight?" Evie asked hopefully from the passenger seat. When she wasn't snapping photos of Aurelius, she posted updates online with her phone.

"Yes," he said, exploiting the segue. "We're going to film the tornado from as close as possible. We're going to get *inside* the rain today with our plane."

"Awesome," she said, snapping her hundredth profile shot today. He'd have to talk to her about donating a few shots of him looking rugged for his next book. And see if she wouldn't mind pumping him up online.

The other radio, the CB, crackled with a more distant transmission. "Devlin says this is where we need to deploy, guys," Wynda's voice broke in. Ah. So they were in the area. He wanted to get a closer look, but he'd have to find them first. Somewhere in the path, then. He drove a little faster north, then took a right on a rough gravel road that would put them in front of the storm. The truck hung back, and soon he heard Duncan's confirmation of launch.

A few trees peppered their path, wherever there was a homestead, but this was mostly open country — cattle land, farms, hills carved by creeks and gullies. When they topped one rise, he spotted a cluster of vehicles in a hollow down a side road. He hoped they were Wynda's and didn't belong to some tour group. Quickly, he slowed his van, pulled under a lonely tree and stopped.

"I need to take a little walk," he said to the others as he opened his door.

"We're right behind you," Thing One said, as he and his wife prepared to hop out with their cameras.

"I'd really prefer to urinate without your assistance," Aurelius said.

Ernie laughed. "I think I'll walk whichever way you aren't." The others settled in to wait, a skill they were all mastering.

Aurelius crossed the road and walked up the short slope that hid Wynda's group from casual observation. Clever girl, he thought. Clever woman, actually. She'd wallop him for calling her anything but. And oh, what a woman. She'd wrangled that jungle shoot like some sort of manic general and made him look damn good, too.

The southeast wind was gusty and humid, and he heard thunder from the storm filling the western horizon. He looked up, hoping to see the drone getting close as he'd instructed. Instead, he saw a news helicopter, but he knew his plane couldn't be far off. For now, he wanted to see what else was in the running to fly into a tornado.

As Aurelius neared the crest of the hill, he crouched along the side of the road, making his way up a gully along a fence. Then the vehicles came into view, along with — what was that? A ball?

Not just a ball. A conveyance of some kind, with a door that was open. Or was it without propulsion? He suspected the latter. It was large, big enough to hold a person, clear but lined with metal struts and boxes, with no obvious rockets or engines or wheels. Wynda's people were strapping in their star, Brad Treat, the one who'd snagged that amazing footage of the Prairie Rock tornado. Only this time, Brad would be the one inside the tornado.

Aurelius felt an intense surge of jealousy. If anyone were to fly inside of a tornado in that beautiful ball, it had to be Aurelius Zane. Brad didn't look all that happy about it. Aurelius would be ecstatic. He'd just have to figure out how to manage it.

He ducked as Wynda's eyes swept the horizon. No need to announce himself just yet. Besides, he still had a chance to get his own tornado shot today. He crept backward, turned and headed toward his van at a trot.

A few minutes later, after maneuvering farther east of the storm, Aurelius parked the Zane Films van next to the drone truck. They were in a small lot by a tall, old grain silo, a lone tower against the sky. Pouchy mammatus clouds emerged from the storm's anvil, and the light became more dreamy and blue as the storm blocked the sun. From this spot, the rolling plain afforded them an enviable view of the layered supercell. They'd seen no more chasers. Increasingly frequent thunder accentuated the quiet as most of the crew stood outside, watching and waiting.

Aurelius leaned into the truck, trying to see what the drone was seeing. In the back of the extended cab, the characteristically focused Phil sat in a specially built chair in view of four small, low-resolution camera monitors and a laptop flickering with control readings. He manipulated a joystick to fly the aircraft. Aurelius strained to see what his little plane was seeing as it circled above. Then he shouted over his shoulder. "Ernie, where is my tornado?"

Ernie poked his head in the door, too. "There's weak rotation in the storm, but I'm not sure it's enough," he said. "It sure is pretty, though."

"Pretty, my pretty ass," Aurelius said. Just what he didn't need. "Let's reposition so we can get a better look at the base. Gentlemen, get as close as you can. If it puts down even a little fart of a tornado, I need it recorded, do you understand?"

"We're doing what we can." Duncan sounded weary.

Phil grunted. "I'm fighting some tough winds up there," he said. "This is no helicopter."

❧

JACK LOOKED up at the helicopter and then at Saffire. She was helping Pole and Devlin get Brad strapped in as their star inserted his key in the manual airbag control and donned his helmet. Wynda was making Jack stand there with nothing to do, so he had plenty of time to watch Saffire work, her every movement filled with grace and purpose.

They'd found a relatively flat area along a gravel road, neatly hidden behind a stubby hill. With no other hazards to speak of, short of a wire fence that wouldn't pose much opposition, there was nothing the Bubble could easily slam into. It was as low-risk as they were likely to get, not counting all the risks that would come with flying. Jack didn't even want to think about what kind of insurance the production company had to carry in the case of a tornado actually tossing their probe.

Not that he thought a tornado was imminent. This storm was shaping up beautifully, with a striated, flying-saucer appearance, but its intermittent wall clouds were halfhearted affairs that had yet to produce a funnel. The lightning, though — the lightning was incredible, intense and more and more frequent, with percussive thunder to match.

"Look alive, now. We need to get to safety," Wynda said, apparently having learned a few lessons from their experiences so far. "Brad, what's bothering you, my lad?"

"I'm fine," he said, looking anything but.

"Are you sick?"

"Fine. I took some stuff for my stomach, and something for the motion sickness. I get a little dizzy, you know, once in a while, but I'm good." He was pale and sweating.

Saffire and Devlin exchanged glances while Pole looked on impassively. The cameramen and Michiko were getting everything.

Wynda cleared her throat. "All righty then," she said, unconvinced. "Brad, this is it. This is what this show is all about. I need you to be my star. Are you ready?"

He nodded.

"Then please say what you need to say for the cameras." She backed up, allowing a clean shot of Brad in the Bubble and the crew encircling him.

Brad did not go into hero mode. Now, he sounded as if he were stuck in a trench in World War I, about to go over the top, prepared to meet the atmosphere's deadly weapons.

"There are extraordinary things we have to do in the name of science," he said, his voice as thin as rice paper, his eyes glossy as he looked over Devlin, Saffire, Pole and Jack. "This is one of them. I am going to face my destiny today. The Bubble will take you and me where no human has gone before: inside a tornado."

Wynda looked a little stunned. "Oooookay," she said. "Nice words, nice words. You sound really heroic. I love it. But how about a little more energy this time?"

Lightning struck nearby, followed almost immediately by a tremendous blast of thunder.

Wynda flinched. "Never mind, then," she said as Brad looked around in a daze. "Close it up! Into the vans!"

Devlin and Pole got the Bubble latched shut in record time

as Jack backed out of the shot. "Locked and loaded!" Devlin said, darting toward the vehicles.

Saffire looked into Andre's camera. "I felt the surge from that one, didn't you?" she said to the imaginary audience. "Don't try this at home." She ran to the caravan with the others as big drops of rain started to fall, rapping a quickening drumbeat on the Bubble's surface.

MARIBETH LISBON LIKED FLYING news helicopters. It was far more enjoyable than her long combat days in Iraq, supporting troops around Tal Afar, but it pumped her with just enough adrenaline that she wasn't bored out of her mind. Especially when she was chasing storms from three hundred feet up.

The Bell JetRanger was a pleasure to fly, much like the Kiowa she'd flown overseas. And Roland, her photog, was a decent companion, though they didn't talk much over the engine roar, noise-canceling headsets notwithstanding. Seated in the back left, diagonally opposite her, he was a whiz with the camera joystick and was opposed to the idea of not coming home to his wife and two kids. They were out to get the best footage possible without getting killed.

They'd been in the air for ninety minutes and were about halfway through their fuel, whose odor permeated the cockpit like an old friend. Below them, the green and brown quilt that was Oklahoma in springtime spread out over an undulating bed of earth. The Canadian River stitched across it in a braided swirl, more silt than water. And to their west, a large, spinning supercell spiraled into the sky.

They hovered and looped in the storm's inflow, where it

wasn't too bumpy, despite southeast winds of about twenty knots. Maribeth could see the gray-white curtain to her north that denoted the hail, filled with nature's ice bombs. It was potential death to her heli, and she stayed well out of its way, flying *S*-turns in and around the inflow so she could get a feel for the air around her. On the belly of the helicopter below her, the antenna used GPS technology to maintain a constant transmission to their station in Oklahoma City, though there wasn't all that much to see yet — just storm chasers, creeping along the roads below them like ants.

She loved the weather, too. Most pilots did, or they at least learned enough about it to make a decent flight forecast. But she couldn't imagine being stuck in an earthbound tin can, trapped on a grid of roads that rarely took chasers into the perfect view she relished.

"Crazy lightning with this storm," she noted to Roland.

"Yeah," he said, still concentrating on his monitor as he used the joystick to maintain his image of the supercell. "At least we have something interesting to shoot. The storm is looking pretty nice."

"It's rotating, but there's not even a wall cloud. Just a severe warning. We aren't even live, are we?"

"Not at the moment," Roland said. "I think they're going to do a weather update after commercial, so at least they'll show our stuff."

"So does James still want to be a helicopter pilot?"

He laughed. "No, but Rosie does. I blame you. James has moved on to race-car driver."

"Imagine, not wanting to be a journalist in this day and age," she joked.

"Hey, there's nothing better than being an underpaid, overworked member of the evil media machine," he said wryly.

"OK, they're coming back from commercial. They're just going to show the images for now. No interview."

Maribeth was accelerating forward, looking for the best position for the shot, when she caught a flash in the corner of her eye. Lightning? It wasn't that bright, and she didn't hear the thunder.

"OK, we're live," Roland said.

"What is that?" Maribeth muttered.

Roland looked up from his screen at Maribeth, then past her. His eyebrows rose. "Oh my god," he said, just as Maribeth uttered a far more interesting oath. It was already too late.

Not far from Watonga, parked next to an old shack, its wood weathered to gray, its fissured walls leaning into a disastrous future, the Zane Films crew had a terrific, terrible view of their little plane as it careened in an unhealthy turn with a distinct downward component.

"Hail clipped it, I think," Phil told Duncan and Aurelius. "It's only responding to controls in bursts. It must have damage. I've got to try to land it."

"You're already too close to the storm," Duncan said, looking up. The rest of the crew had gathered around the UAV truck, half looking up, half trying to see the monitors in the back, where Phil had a death grip on the joystick. The tension among them crept upward, a spider crawling on their necks. "Get back. Get down."

"I'm trying. Oh, shit," Phil said.

"What?" asked Aurelius, looking up. "Goddamn it, what the hell are you doing? There's a helicopter up there!"

"It's ignoring me. I'm trying," Phil said, sounding desperate.

Aurelius was horrified, but at the same time, the producer in him took over. "Make sure you're filming it," he snapped to Things One and Two. "No matter what."

❦

ATOP A GENTLE SLOPE three miles away, Jack and the Palatable crew stood outside their vehicles, watching the storm approach Brad's location.

"I don't think this is going to be our tornado day," Jack said, his voice impassive.

"Of course not," Wynda said sarcastically. "When is it ever?"

"The hail footage could be interesting," he added.

"If it doesn't destroy the Bubble," Devlin said, looking worried.

"It's supposed to survive a tornado," Saffire said. "Why wouldn't it survive hail?"

"It'll survive, but it could be damaged in ways we haven't considered," Devlin replied. "And we don't need any more issues."

Brad's voice came over the Bubble radio Devlin carried. "The storm looks pretty amazing from here," he said. "It's rotating, and another weak wall cloud is starting to form, but no funnel or anything yet." Brad sounded relieved.

Lightning struck nearby, and Jack wondered again if they should be in the cars as the thunder reverberated around them. There was another sound, too — the buzz of the helicopter, or was it something else?

He and Saffire both looked up. "Oh, my god," she said. "Look."

It was a drone, soaring in a sick spiral straight toward the helicopter.

"That's not good," Jack said.

Lightning hit nearby, but Jack didn't see where. Devlin made an unintelligible sound before speaking into his headset. "Brad? Brad? Are you OK? Brad?"

"Tell me that did not just happen," Wynda said. "Also tell me that you got it on camera, boys."

"Got it," Andre said.

"I was filming Devlin," Razor said.

"Perfect," she answered.

"What happened?" Saffire asked. Jack, who'd also been distracted by the drama above, was glad she asked.

"The Bubble got hit by lightning," Devlin said. "Brad?" he called again into the radio. "Talk to me, man. If you can hear us, we're on our way."

"One second," Jack said, looking up again. He pointed toward the sky. "Andre?"

The cameraman instinctively pointed up as the news helicopter and the drone met their fates.

MARIBETH HEARD a loud bang almost immediately after she saw the strange object swooping toward the fast-moving helicopter. A deep vibration shuddered through the heli, and bits of debris flew past her window.

"We're hit," Roland said to their producer. "What was that? Maribeth?"

"Got it," she said, gritting her teeth as the helicopter

started to spin with a mind of its own. "It must have dinged the tail rotor." Because anything more than a ding, and they wouldn't be having this conversation, she thought. And then her training kicked in.

She loved the building whine of the JetRanger when she cranked it up, the thrilling sensation of imminent flight. Now, it sounded all wrong. She had to regain control, and a rapid descent was her only option, forcing the helicopter blades to spin via autorotation. In the precious seconds that followed, she mentally vowed to dump her flaky boyfriend, take up guitar, and chase more storms in cars.

As she rolled off the throttle, disengaging the engine from the rotor system, she did her best to maintain speed. She wanted to head into the wind and keep her nose up as she began their precipitous glide to earth, but the earth was coming up a lot faster than she'd hoped. The helicopter shook even as she fought to control its spin, and she wondered if it was more damaged than she realized. She couldn't see the tail, but one thing she knew was that when things went bad in a helicopter, they usually went bad fast.

"You can do it, Mari," Roland said. She hoped so. She had her eye on a pasture below and had just one chance to reduce their speed before the ground did it for her. She made the flare maneuver about sixty feet from the ground, tilting the helicopter back, but she was still turning, and the move didn't soften their landing enough. The helicopter slammed down, and with a hard rebound in her seat, she felt the impact as they pushed forward. She knew the skids would be spreading below them, helping take the force of the hard landing. At least she hoped so. There was a rapid succession of loud noises and shudders and the flash of broken rotor blades flying past her windows before the helicopter rolled over sideways in a cloud of dirt. Maribeth sat there, hanging by her straps, feeling it in her shoulders. She took a few breaths until her heartbeat eased back from the red zone.

"Roland?"

"OK. I'm OK. For the most part."

"Stay still for a minute." She hit the fuel switch from her awkward position, looking at the perpendicular horizon. "We made it this far. Let it wind down. We want to make sure no flying parts are going to chop our heads off."

LIKE THE OTHERS, Jack was transfixed by the rapid descent of the helicopter. The tiny plane had vanished in what appeared to be a puff of debris, but the helicopter sank with remarkable speed and grace before nosing up mid-turn and slamming into the ground just over a mile away. The rotor blades on top flexed downward, chopping off the tail boom and, in the process, breaking off and hurtling a scary distance from the machine. The helicopter rolled to a stop and was still.

He had his phone out and called 911 almost instantly. He tersely related what they'd seen and the approximate location of the crash.

"We should help them," Saffire said as he got off the line.

"Wait a bloody minute," Wynda responded. "We have to see if our star is still alive. If you recall, the Bubble was just struck by lightning."

"Pole and Devlin can go to Brad," Jack said. "You and Michiko can go, too, Wynda. Saffire and I will check out the helicopter." Saffire wanted to help, he rationalized, and he wanted her to come. Wynda thought it over and nodded.

"Razor, you're with me. Andre, go with Jack and Saffire in Van One."

"Right," Andre said, and they quickly loaded up.

It took Van One about six minutes to navigate the back roads and find a way to the spot where the helicopter had crashed. Jack drove, gingerly taking the van down what was essentially a dirt track, all too mindful of how they'd spent the previous day and what the impending rain might mean to their transit. The storm was just to their north, spinning like a top, but still without a meaningful wall cloud. Jack heard thunder as he stopped within twenty yards of the wreckage. In an adjoining field a quarter mile away, one of the rotor blades stuck out of a big, round hay bale like a knife in a loaf of bread.

They jumped out and ran over to what remained of the helicopter to find a man and woman sitting on the ground, both on cell phones. The woman — the pilot, judging from her flight suit — looked up at Jack as she wrapped up her conversation. Her eyes were wide and gray, her cheeks freckled, her long brown hair untidily tied back. Jack admired her immediately. Maybe it was that just-defied-death life force she was giving off, but it was attractive.

"I'm Jack," he said. "We saw the crash. Was it just the two of you? You OK?"

"Maribeth. And we are fabulous," she said dryly. "Right, Roland?"

He'd ended his call, too. "My back is killing me, but it could have been much worse. Our producer is both thrilled and horrified."

"So is my dad," Maribeth said. She looked at the camera with annoyance, then curiosity. "What hit us? Did you film it?"

Andre didn't want to give up his shot, so Jack answered. "I think it was a drone. A UAV."

"What, is the government spying on Oklahoma now?"

"Probably media," said Roland. "You know how we are."

They both laughed at what must have been an inside joke. "You're pretty close to the mark," Jack said. "There's a film crew chasing storms with a drone. I can only assume that's what hit you, unless there's more than one flying around out here."

Saffire stepped up. She'd produced a couple of bottles of water from the van and offered them to the survivors. "That was a hell of a landing," she said.

"Thank you," the pilot said. She took the cold bottle and held it against her forehead, closing her eyes.

Roland stood up with difficulty. "Our station wants to know who hit us. Do you?"

"I can't say for sure. We've seen Aurelius Zane with a drone," Jack said. "He's making a documentary." In the distance, they heard sirens. Help was on the way.

"Unfortunately, when we went into our descent, I don't think I got a great shot of it," Roland said. "And I definitely didn't get a good look. Maybe you guys can help us out."

Andre finally stopped filming. "I want to help you," he said, "but I'm not sure I got the collision, and I'm at the mercy of my producer. Maybe we can work out a deal. Do you feel like being interviewed?"

"Definitely not right now. I'm giving myself an exclusive," Roland said. "You want to share your footage?"

"I can't at the moment."

"At least until the NTSB gets involved," Maribeth said.

Jack pulled a card from his wallet and handed it to her. "Call us if you need us."

"We have to go now," Andre said. "We have another friend in trouble."

"Something in the air," Maribeth said, and Roland laughed. At least they still had a sense of humor.

"Good luck," Jack said warmly, then walked with the others back to their van.

"You're always working it, aren't you?" Saffire asked once they were inside and Jack was executing a precarious three-point turn in the soft dirt.

"What do you mean?"

"That thing you do. With women."

"I have no idea what you're talking about," he said blandly, but he gave her a sidelong glance.

"*You* know," she said softly, leaning closer. "And you should know you're not the only one who knows how to use one's breathless charm." All thoughts of the helicopter pilot evaporated. The urge to kiss Saffire was pressing. As he braked at the main road, he leaned toward her just a little, close enough to feel her breath on his face. Her lips were pink and moist, and he almost forgot that a storm was bearing down on them and their crew was in serious shit.

"You might do well to remember," Andre said from the middle seat, breaking the spell, "that the cameras are on. And I have to film at least a little bit of you driving, or Wynda's going to wonder what the hell I was doing back here."

"Oh, piffle," Saffire said, leaning back into her seat. "She doesn't care about a little drive between incidents. It'll never make the final cut."

Jack sighed and made the turn.

"Just saying," Andre said. "I've seen enough journalists and politicians head into the restroom or make an inappropriate remark while their mikes were hot. It's like the cameras in this van. You forget they're there."

"I never forget," Saffire affirmed. "I'm a professional. Anyway, your helicopter footage is going to be the shot of the day."

"I really only got the crash to ground. I couldn't even see what hit them through my viewfinder," Andre said. "I can't believe she landed that thing."

"They're lucky sons of bitches," Jack said, accelerating down the paved road toward where they'd left the Bubble. "We'll see if the same can be said of Brad."

THE MOST INTERESTING part of the storm was now moving to their northeast, and Jack reluctantly bade it farewell. It took them about ten minutes and the GPS to find their way to the Bubble. The rest of the crew had gathered in a circle around the back of the Bubblevan, but around what, wasn't immediately clear. Jack hoped Brad wasn't dead. He didn't like the guy much, but being barbecued in a big ball was a lousy way to go. He could feel the tension mount as he, Saffire and Andre got out and walked over in the soft rain.

Wynda gave them a nod and moved aside. Their star sat in the open back doorway of the truck, shivering in a borrowed, pink, too-small Minnie Mouse sweatshirt Jack had seen Michiko wearing. Saffire stepped in and gave Brad a hug, a heartfelt gesture Jack didn't expect, before she stepped back and joined the circle.

Brad's face was peculiarly sunburned — no, lightning-burned — in an angry, red blotch on just one side. It would be comical if it weren't so obvious a reminder of how close Brad had come to being fried. He had an almost blank look that ramped up to annoyance every time Wynda asked him what he'd seen and felt, with Razor and Michiko recording.

"Did you get video of it?" Wynda asked Brad.

"I don't know. There was a buzz, and the monitor went dead."

"What did it look like?"

"I don't know. Bright. I keep seeing the afterimage," Brad said. "Did it hit me?"

"The Bubble worked the way it was supposed to," Devlin replied. "It diverted the charge around you. It's just that you were so close, it looks like it gave you a sunburn, kind of. Flashover, maybe."

Jack took over the interrogation. "Do you feel sick? Disoriented?"

"Not any more than the Bubble already makes me with its rolling around."

"Did you pass out?"

"No."

"Does your head hurt? Are your ears ringing?"

"No, no, no," Brad said, his voice rising. "I'm OK. My face stings a little. There was this flash of light and heat and a big bang. My ears feel a little weird, but that makes sense, because it was loud. Really loud."

"Well," Jack said. "I think you lucked out."

"Oh, really," Brad said.

"Though you might've gotten a nice dose of radiation. Nothing to worry about in the near future," Jack said.

"Oh, *really*," Brad said again. "Really. Great."

"Now, now, Brad," Wynda said. "You've been a champ today. You've survived an extraordinary event, one that we filmed, and you're only the worse for wear for a bit of sunburn. Lightning burn," she corrected herself. "Razor, Michiko, get him some water and give him a little air. Devlin? Jack? Saffire? Pole?" She motioned them over to where the Bubble still sat on the side of the road. "How bad is it?" she asked, *sotto voce*.

"Brad'll be fine," Jack said.

"I don't mean Brad. I mean, all well and good, but I'm talking about the Bubble."

Devlin's look was grave. "We cannot continue in its current state. I can't even start it up. We have to get back to Oklahoma City, test it, fix it, test it again. Even if I could kick it and get it going, I wouldn't trust it."

"It's been through a lot," Saffire said.

"The hill," Devlin noted.

"It banged into that pumpjack," Pole said.

"And now struck by lightning," Jack added.

"I'm not superstitious …" Devlin said.

"I'm not either," Jack said, "but …"

"Maybe it's cursed," the men said simultaneously.

"Jinx," said Saffire.

"Rubbish," Wynda said in a furious tone. "Absolute rubbish. It just got a little power surge, that's all. I'm sure we can fix it. Devlin?"

"I'm sure we can fix it," he echoed, not sounding convinced. "But we have to take it back to Oklahoma City."

Wynda looked around at her damp team. "Damn it," she said softly. "All right. I am not going to waste another day or, god help us, another week just doing repairs. Devlin and Pole, you'll join Razor in the Bubblevan and go back to Oklahoma City to fix the Bubble and document everything. Meantime, the rest of us will take Brad and shoot a couple of extra stories I've been kicking around that will fill out our series nicely. How much weather are we going to miss, Jack?"

"Tomorrow, the action is probably in eastern Oklahoma and Arkansas," he said, "with even less chance of tornadoes, in the trees. After that, we're going to have a few down days, till we get the next trough. So your timing is pretty good for a disaster."

"This is *not* a disaster," Wynda said, glaring at all of them. She took a moment to compose herself and took a deep breath. "I happen to have been reading about a lovely art installation we're going to check out tomorrow," she said. "It's a lightning piece, believe it or not. Appropriate, don't you think?"

"Where?" Jack asked, but he already knew the answer.

"Pancake, Kansas. I do like pancakes," Wynda replied. "Have you been there?"

"Yes," Jack said flatly, then felt Saffire's impish gaze on him, seeing more than he wanted to let on. So what if he'd been to Pancake, seen one of its legendary tornadoes, dated its women? When you're a chaser, every town has a memory. Their crew would go, and then they'd move on. It was what he always did.

Saffire was still giving him the eye, and he wondered if she could read his mind. As they walked back to the vans, she leaned over and whispered in his ear. "I can't wait to hear this story," she said.

"I'm a man of the present," Jack said. Before she could say another word, he pulled her in for a quick, hot kiss, ignoring the surprised looks of Devlin and Pole, who were straggling behind the others. He released her, leaving her stunned and glistening in the rain, and climbed into his lonely back seat in Van One.

AURELIUS'S PHONE would not stop ringing. At first, he ignored the calls, and then he decided there was no such thing as bad publicity and started answering. Yes, he told the media callers, he was flying a drone this year. No, he assured them, whatever hit the helicopter wasn't his. His drone was perfectly fine. It must have been someone else's. Of course his was legal, just a toy, flown at low altitude. It posed no danger to anyone. Yes, he was delighted that the helicopter crew had survived, and he congratulated them on their courage and skill.

What he did not say was that shortly after the collision, his crew was able to track his shattered drone's GPS beacon to a fallow field three miles away from the crash, where they found bits and pieces scattered over three acres of ground. "No posting," Aurelius ordered Evie as they gathered around him.

"But I'm a journalist."

"First and foremost, you are a member of my team," Aurelius said. "I just want to remind you, all of you, that you have signed a nondisclosure agreement. If I hear one breath of what happened today outside of this circle, I have the ability to sue you for everything, your college tuition, your house, right down to your underwear. Gather every piece of debris you can, buck up, and we can continue our merry chase. Duncan, give me a second."

The techie looked pale as he surveyed the damage, but he reluctantly joined their star in the van.

"You know we can't tell anyone," Aurelius said.

"The NTSB is going to be all over this."

"Chances are, nobody got us on camera, and even if they

did, they don't know it's ours. Everybody's got a goddamn drone these days."

"We hit a TV helicopter," Duncan said. "Don't you think they filmed it?"

"We'll know soon enough. I don't want to go to court. I don't want to go to prison. And I don't even own the plane. You know who's going to take the heat, don't you?"

Duncan turned a whiter shade of pale behind his reddish eyebrows, scruffy beard and doubtful mouth. "Shit," he said.

"It's your company. It's your plane. And we have a spare, which our little insurance arrangement should pay for."

"Our agreement covers the loss of one," Duncan said. "You lose another one, you're going to owe me a lot of money."

"You mean, if *you* lose another one."

"The agreement is specific," the techie said, rallying.

"Well, we won't lose another one," Aurelius said. "I need it as much as you do."

And thus began the great drone charade, terse interviews with investigators and studious denial of everything. Drones still flew in a gray area where the rules were concerned. Aurelius knew these kinds of cases were driving the feds crazy, and he didn't feel like being made an example. The headlines so far said "Unknown object brings down helicopter" and "Suspected drone never found in chopper crash." He'd unearthed only one video on YouTube, from a storm chaser who hadn't been anywhere close, so it was hard to see exactly what had caused the accident. No one seemed particularly outraged, though the reporter from the TV station that lost its helicopter seemed a little more worked up. Understandable, since he'd been on board.

Two days after the incident, as he awaited the storms' return and poked at some oatmeal and raisin toast in a diner near his Oklahoma City hotel, the one number he'd been dreading popped up on his phone.

"Rodney," he answered. "How are those British cows?"

"I'm with my crew in Mexico now, looking for the Chupacabra," the producer said. "Did you fry that plane?"

"Of course not," Aurelius said. "That wasn't mine."

"Is that so?" Rodney sounded skeptical, but then again, he didn't know that his investment had also paid for a spare. "Whoever it was, they could have killed those people."

"Absolutely not," Aurelius said, refusing even to consider the thought. "It barely touched the helicopter. That's what they're saying, anyway."

"Have you seen the TV station's footage?"

"It wasn't much to look at. A blurry object flies by, and then they go into a spin and head for ground. People are much more excited about the crash than the blurry object."

"Did you get footage of the crash?"

"I was nowhere nearby, so no, regrettably not," he lied.

"I see," Rodney said. Aurelius wondered if he really did see, and the idea made him nervous. "Did you shoot a tornado yet?" the producer asked.

Aurelius took a sip of coffee. "We shot a wedge tornado with the drone the other day," he said. "A big, dark, nasty thing."

"Dark, huh? So you couldn't really see anything?"

"That's not what I said."

"I know what you said, you prick," Rodney answered. "And I know what you're not saying. Zane, there is no compromise on the tornado shot. You have to get it, or you don't get paid. It's that simple. And don't crash into anything."

"Not a problem," Aurelius said. "Trust me."

"You always say that, Zane," said Rodney. "And I'm starting to wonder why."

JACK WAS BACK IN KANSAS, a dreamland for storms, a nightmare for almost everything else. But, he acknowledged to himself, he might have been biased by past events.

It was a sunny afternoon behind the front. He was with most of the TV crew on the far western outskirts of Pancake, watching Wynda and company film Brad and Saffire getting a tour of a peculiar former baseball field from Judy Hale and her boyfriend. It sat at the end of a narrow gravel road that extended almost two miles off a rural highway, remote enough to avoid terrorizing the locals, he presumed. A blue and gold sign at the gate said "LIGHTNING IN A BOTTLE" in a font that evoked circuses and, in smaller type, asked "PLEASE, NO VIDEO OR PHOTOGRAPHS WITHOUT PERMISSION." Another yellow sign with a thunderbolt icon declared "EXTREME LIGHTNING DANGER. SEEK SHELTER IMME-DIATELY IF YOU HEAR THUNDER."

The bleachers, if there had been any, were gone. The field's green turf was rough and dotted with wildflowers. On it, two dozen bright blue plastic barrels spiraled out from the pitch-er's mound. With few exceptions, the barrels each sported a long, metal pole that grew from the middle and reached for the sky. The poles were adorned with long sky-blue and yellow pennants snapping in the wind, as if they were advertising a medieval joust. More complicated contraptions topped the remaining barrels.

Jack watched the action unfold from inside the van, where he pretended to look through data on the laptop. He just didn't see an immediate need to get out there and get into what was going on, and to meet Judy again. But even from here, he could see she looked well, a little softer, smiling in her straw-colored braids, comfortable in her blue blouse and denim shorts, relaxed, which is something he couldn't say any other time he saw her. And she looked even less like her sister now, whose loss he didn't like to think about, ever.

He mentally slapped himself around and decided he wanted a cigarette, no matter who was outside. He grabbed one from his backpack, slipped out the side door and quietly lit up. Then he sidled over to a yellow SUV parked under a metal carport next to the gate, just within earshot. Jack noticed the car's open windows and a scratched-up area on the hatchback. He was still trying to figure it out when he heard Brad talking.

"So do you trigger the lightning or just wait for it?" the star asked. The side of his face still glowed pink from yesterday's Bubble strike.

"We have a handful of small rockets we can set off when conditions are good," Judy said, gesturing to the barrels with the contraptions on top. "Each unreels a copper wire that helps direct the lightning where we want it, if it's lucky enough to trigger a strike. But for the most part, we just wait for it. Cameras are running all the time when there's any chance of storms. The barrels each have their own lightning rod, and we hope they'll catch a bolt and, at the same time, create a fulgurite."

"A fulgurite," Brad said, nodding earnestly but blankly.

"It's a lumpy glass tube created by the lightning channel in the sand," said the boyfriend, who looked familiar — oh, yeah. The guy in Prairie Rock that day. "The lightning melts and fuses the silica. Each barrel is filled with sand."

"Ingenious," Saffire said. "Lightning in a bottle. Or a barrel."

"We hope," Judy said. "We haven't actually caught one yet."

"And the dugout?" Saffire asked.

"Because we've enclosed it and included lightning protection, we're confident it will act as a shelter," the boyfriend said. "And it gives us a place to set off rockets if we're actually here during a thunderstorm. We've buried a control system that connects us to the launchers. And we installed a carport outside the fence, in case of hail." He and Judy exchanged knowing glances.

"How does one pay for all of this?" Brad asked.

"The barrels are donated," Judy said. "I got a deal on the sand from my uncle's hardware store, and I was able to lease this field from the town for next to nothing, since no one used it anymore. We worked with the university at Wishwell to include a couple of their experiments, including a high-speed camera, so they helped us get the permission we needed to do this and some of the gear. Plus we got an arts grant to take care of some of the more technical stuff, like our cameras and the rocket system. Robinson's our rocket scientist."

The boyfriend laughed. "Hardly," Robinson said. "But I had good advice from a few engineers."

The stars thanked Judy and Robinson, ending the interview. As Wynda enlisted Judy to point out details of the launch system for close-ups, Robinson wandered toward the yellow car and noticed Jack.

"Oh. Hey, I know you." Robinson didn't sound thrilled, but he held out his hand and smiled. "Jack, right?"

"You got it," Jack said, shaking Robinson's hand. "Quite a setup you have here."

"Only from an artist's mind," Robinson said, nodding his head at Judy. "I never could have dreamed this up."

"It sounds like it'll be pretty cool if it works."

"Even if it doesn't, it's been a hell of a lot of fun to build. And it's getting a lot of attention. It seems the media never tire of reporting on mildly crazy people. Excuse me a minute." Robinson peered in the open passenger window. "CG!" he said. "Wake up!"

"CG?" Jack reflexively looked around for a cloud-to-ground bolt. Then he heard a happy bark and saw a wiggly, curly, golden-brown mutt jump through the window into Robinson's arms.

"Our dog. Hey, buddy." Robinson rubbed the little pooch's head, which was only slightly more curly than his master's. "He always sleeps in the car. He's a good boy. But now he'll want to run." He put CG down, and the dog tore across the field in a wide, joyous circle, stopping to pee on the barrel at what used to be second base. He ran back toward Judy and jumped up to her waist.

"Whoa, baby," Judy said, picking him up, giving him a squeeze and putting him down again. He immediately ran to Saffire and demanded equal treatment, and she seemed only too happy to oblige. Then he spotted Michiko's fuzzy mike and leapt up repeatedly, trying to catch it on the end of the boom.

"Dog fishing," Brad remarked.

"Sorry," Judy said to Wynda. "He's brimming with enthusiasm."

"Every TV show needs a dog," Wynda said with a genuine smile, then waved at Andre to film the little guy romping around the barrels.

Jack felt an awkward silence settle between him and

Robinson as they watched this tableau, so he pointed to the scratches on the back of the car. "What happened there?"

"Oh, it's Kansas, you know," Robinson said. "I had this Darwin fish. You know, the Jesus fish, only it says 'Darwin' and has feet? Anyway, I've had two of them whittled off, I presume with screwdrivers. I'm debating whether it's worth trying again."

Jack couldn't help but laugh at this philosophical crime, and Robinson joined in. Jack ground out his cigarette under his foot, and they both leaned against the car, more at ease, and watched the crew finish its filming. When they were done, CG seemed to know, and he ran over to lie at Robinson's feet, panting, his face between his paws, his ears perked up. The others came over, too.

"Jack, I see you decided to join us," Wynda said. "This is Judy."

"We've met." He reached out his hand. A fleeting memory of her touch, less charged now, manifested itself as Judy grasped his fingers briefly, offering him a nod and a flash of those blue eyes he remembered so well. Saffire looked on with interest.

"You just keep turning up, don't you?" Judy said.

"The proverbial bad penny, at your service," he said with a determined smile. "You doing OK?"

"A whole lot better." She smiled back and hooked her arm in Robinson's. For his part, Robinson's gaze was filled with pride and love as he looked down at Judy. No mistaking it. So that was what happiness looked like. To Jack, their devotion was an exotic condition, but it was also strangely enticing.

He'd never wanted what they had. He wasn't sure he did now. His needs had always been more primal, more immediate, simple to satisfy. He liked it that way. But he felt the darkness within him open up, asking to be filled, as he saw their emotion, their energy. His instincts were askew, he thought. His memories were messing with his mind.

Wynda was a welcome interruption.

"Well, lads and ladies, it's been lovely, but we have to move on to our next location," she said. "Thank you so much, Judy and Robinson, and I'll be in touch about purchasing some footage when you catch one of those bolts."

"I hope we have something to report sooner rather than later," Judy said. "At least it's finally storm season."

Yes, Jack thought to himself, storm season. And once again, they were without storms. That was always when he got into trouble. He smiled and nodded as they said their goodbyes, and he took an extra second to watch Judy walk back toward the dugout with Robinson, their arms around each other, with CG cavorting at their feet. Then he turned and walked over to Van One. Saffire was waiting.

"You really do know her," she said.

"I did."

"I like her."

"So did I. For a while." A short while, he remembered.

"I bet." Saffire smiled. Jack looked for a hint of jealousy, but it wasn't there. Just that playful expression. Maybe he wanted her to be jealous. Just a little.

"Attention, my friends," Wynda called out. "I want to talk about our plans." They gathered around her on the far side of the van, next to the crew SUV: Jack, Saffire, Brad, Andre and Michiko. "I've decided that we could all use a break." A sigh broke out like a breeze among them. "However, Brad is not getting one, and that means neither am I, nor is Michiko." A wee groan followed. "Saffire, you're lovely, darling, but it just looks strange to have you in a bunch of scenes without Devlin, so I've decided to take Michiko and get some shots of Brad visiting a few of Kansas's unusual tourist attractions. You know, the Garden of Eden, and the big ball of twine, and the geographical center of the United States. And then we're going back to Oklahoma City to get shots with the Bubble, which Devlin says is coming along nicely."

"You'll want me, right, boss?" Andre asked.

"I'll be shooting Brad," she said. "Andre, I want you to accompany Jack and Saffire and get some atmospheric footage of wind farms during your little break. Don't disappoint me." She gave him a significant look and handed him a marked-up paper map of western Kansas. "We didn't get nearly enough wind farms when we were shooting B-roll in March. I want anything that says wind. And also some clouds and cows, while you're at it. And someplace with tumbleweeds."

"So ... who's actually getting a break?" Saffire asked.

"You are, dear. Unless you'd like to appear on camera now and then, which would be spectacular. And Jack will drive. Everyone clear?"

"Not really," Jack said. "When are we meeting up?"

"You expect storms when?"

"Today's Tuesday? We probably have three or four more down days after today," he said, seeing in his mind's eye the storm system oozing in from the west coast, as the latest computer models depicted it.

"Then we'll meet on Saturday, at the storm chaser picnic at Stone Pickett's house. It's somewhere in southeast Kansas. I'll shoot you the address."

"In McPherson," Jack said. "You really have been following online."

"I do my homework, Dr. Andreas," Wynda said. "For now,

we're booked in Dodge City. I hear there are steaks there. Onward!"

There were no opportunities for Jack to kidnap Saffire in Dodge City. They arrived just in time for a late dinner at Casey's Cowtown, within mooing distance of the abattoirs where cows became steaks. Then everyone pleaded fatigue and retired to their rooms in their low-end chain motel. Maybe he was tired, too, Jack thought, but he didn't want to admit it. He stayed up for a while, paging through the cable TV, hoping the pay channels might show a little skin to lull him into sweet dreams. He was disappointed to find only a mediocre high-school comedy and a middle-aged relationship movie. He'd graduated from one and might never be ready for the other, but the desire to see tits was eternal.

The next day, they split up, with Wynda, Brad and Michiko heading east in the crew SUV to the oddball tourist attractions of central Kansas, and Jack, Saffire and Andre heading west in Van One to find wind farms, cows and tumbleweeds.

"I feel like this is a break, even though she basically asked us to work the whole time," Saffire said from the passenger seat.

"That's what she wants you to think," said Andre, seated behind her. He was working harder than any of them, having already filmed several turbines, cows and abandoned farmhouses during stops as they meandered west, sometimes with Saffire in front of them. She'd expounded on landmarks, native plants and, once, the dark and light forms of the Question Mark Butterfly, as a handful of the orange-winged creatures fluttered about her in a small, wooded picnic area.

"I'm just the driver," Jack said. "So this really is a vacation for me." For a storm chaser, driving through the Plains was like a history buff taking a bus tour of battlefields. Everywhere there were names that meant something, sites of historic tornadoes: Greensburg, Kansas. Wichita Falls, Texas. Moore, Oklahoma. And other towns too numerous to name. For Jack, each held a moment of reverence and sometimes a memory. Like Prairie Rock.

"We could take a little side trip. Have a little fun. I have a place in mind," Saffire said.

"It better have wind farms or cows." Andre's tone was sarcastic.

"Well, there are lots of tumbleweeds," Saffire said.

"That'll work," Andre said. "Where?"

"Oklahoma Panhandle. We'll get there late afternoon, have an easy night, sleep late, then film some more stuff tomorrow and Friday as we wend back east."

"An easy night," Jack said, raising his eyebrows at Saffire. "I like that."

"Fine," Andre said. "I'll bow to your star status and take a little nap back here while you guys get us there. Wake me up if you see a tornado."

"Maybe in a few days," Jack said. "OK, Saffire. Tell me where."

"Just head south at the next highway," she said. "And we'll be there in an hour and a half or so."

The mostly flat landscape rolled by them, green and gold and bright in the sun, as high pressure ruled the atmosphere above their heads. Hopelessly flat clouds dotted the blue sky. Despite the dull weather, even Jack had to acknowledge it was pretty and made all the more pleasant by Saffire in the seat next to him. With the cameras off, they found an alternative rock channel they both liked on the van's satellite radio, noted roadside curiosities and chatted about the worst disaster movies they'd ever seen, most of which were on cable TV. It turned out Saffire had even played a cameo in one, though she was gobbled early in the film by a giant snake.

"Look," she said as they passed through another small town whose business district consisted of two gas stations, a few stores and a Dairy Queen. "The billboard."

"Gross. Is that supposed to be lungs?"

"1-800-QUIT NOW," she said. "I dare you."

"Right. I'll quit when I'm dead."

"I triple-dog dare you."

"What is this, high school? Let's get serious. I can't just quit. A man has to have hobbies."

She laughed. "I'll make it worth your while."

Now he was interested. "How long do I have to go without smoking?"

"Forever. Or until I let you know."

"There better be material benefits to this," he said.

"Besides living longer? Oh, yes," she said, teasing him again. "Palpable benefits."

He gave her a look and lowered his voice, though judging from the gentle snoring behind them, Andre had been asleep for some time. "You're making me crazy, you know."

"That's my evil plan." She gave him a starry smile, and he almost ran off the road.

The Oklahoma Panhandle crept up on them, but there was no mistaking its desolation. Flat, a mix of brown and green flecked with yellow, it seemed to defy human habitation. But along with the cows, there were people, too, and soon, a town showed up ahead of them. Saffire grew visibly excited.

"What is it about this place?" Jack asked.

"You'll see."

As they got closer, the traditional, wind-pocked city-limits sign greeted them:

WELCOME TO POSSUM BOTTOM
PROUD HOMETOWN OF SAFFIRE SOULLIERE!

Jack did a double-take as they drove by. "What the hell was that?" he exclaimed.

Andre shot up from where he'd been reclining in the back. "What? What?"

"That will be telling," Jack said, then to Saffire: "I thought you grew up in California."

"I did. I spent the first few years of my life here."

"I didn't know you were that famous."

"It's a small town." She shrugged.

"Where are we again?" Andre asked Saffire.

"Possum Bottom."

"Seriously?" With a resonant laugh, he pulled out his smartphone and started surfing for details.

"My mom just moved back here last year," Saffire said. "She has a bed and breakfast. I'm going to stay there, and she might have rooms for you guys, too."

"Hmmm," was all Jack said.

"Not tonight," Andre said after another minute of web surfing. "B&Bs are fine, but I want a dull, clean, well-lit hotel with wi-fi and cable and fancy beds. There's a hotel in town that this app says has whirly tubs and a coffee bar. I haven't had a real cup of coffee in days."

"Even Possum Bottom has coffee bars," Jack mused as he drove through the compact downtown's tree-dotted intersections of Branches and Avenues. It was quaint and well-kept, despite the dusty patina that seemed inevitable in these Panhandle cities, with half a dozen boutiques, a grocery store, a red-brick courthouse, a non-chain ice cream shop and a couple of cafes. Signs pointed to a library, churches, schools and other signs of life off the main drag, and he caught glimpses of inviting residential streets. A large statue of a possum wearing a cowboy hat looked over a small park in the center of town.

"It's on the west end. You can drop me off. Take the next right," Andre said, and Jack took the turn. "Wynda doesn't know it, but she's paying for a fancy dinner tonight, too, if I can find one. Any recommendations?"

"I don't know the town that well," Saffire said. "There's probably something good. Since there's not much for miles around, Possum Bottom is kind of an oasis."

"Clearly so." Jack laughed as they found themselves among a couple of newer hotels, chain restaurants and discount stores.

"There!" Andre pointed to a gleaming, new, three-story hotel.

"Well, I'll be damned," Jack said, pulling in. Andre hopped out and grabbed his bags out of the back, then tapped on the driver's window. Jack opened it.

"Call me when you're coming to get me in the morning," Andre said, then added with a grin: "And don't get into too much trouble."

"Now we go to the east end of town," Saffire said cheerfully after he'd gone. "You're going to meet my mama."

Jack wasn't terrified of many things, but one of them was meeting any woman's mama. His face must have given him away.

"Don't worry," Saffire said. "You'll love her. She likes to

talk, but she's the sweetest person you'll ever meet. She lives with her lawyer boyfriend. Oh, come on. I can't really be hanging around at the B&B with my *co-worker*" — she emphasized the word — "and not introduce you, now, can I?"

Jack sighed and turned east onto the road to head back through town. "OK, co-worker," he said. "But I would like you to know that I could really use a cigarette right now. And I am only resisting because I value our *working relationship.*"

She lifted her hand and slowly traced one finger along his cheekbone, his rough stubble, and lightly touched his lips. Never taking his eyes off the road, he took the finger in his mouth and sucked on it for a few seconds until she withdrew.

"That's some oral fixation you have there," she said, her voice husky. "Wait till you get a load of mine."

He hoped the swelling in his jeans subsided before he had to meet the dreaded matriarch.

IN TRUTH, Saffire's mother was anything but matriarchal. Tiny, friendly and enthusiastic, with a highlighted brown bob, a ready smile and a casual outfit of jeans and a loose white blouse, she was walking out onto the porch of the graceful, two-story house when they pulled up.

"I guess she got my text," Saffire said, then jumped out without closing the van door. Jack got out, too. He walked around to close the passenger door and held back for a moment, admiring the home's fresh, white paint and the light-green shingles that covered the roofs over the porch and the gables above. The house was all interesting Victorian angles and not much like anything else he'd seen in town.

Donna rushed off the porch, grabbed her slightly taller

daughter with a strength that belied her size and lifted Saffire a few inches off the ground with a squeal of delight. "Sandy, I didn't think I'd see you till Christmas," she said in a brisk twang. "Oh, it is so wonderful to have you here!"

"Sandy?" Jack said, mostly to himself.

"And who's this?" Donna asked with a keen mother's curiosity, quickly scanning Jack.

"Jack works on the TV show we're doing, mama. He's a meteorologist."

"You mean he's one of those storm chasers? Oh, I don't like storms," Donna said, her face darkening. "We get way too many around here. You don't bring them with you, do you?"

"If I did, you probably wouldn't be seeing me right now, Mrs. Soulliere. I'd be off chasing a tornado."

"You can call me Donna. But it's going to be Mrs. Dover soon," she said.

Saffire's face changed from shocked to delighted in a moment. "You got engaged to Barry?" she almost shrieked.

"Yes," her mother said. "You don't mind?"

"I'm glad," Saffire said, hugging her again. "You deserve to be happy."

"I'd hoped you would be."

"Did you get your storm shelter fixed up?" Saffire asked. Was it Jack's imagination, or did she sound more like a cowgirl around her mom?

"Now, there's nothing to fix up. It's a hole in the ground. It'll work."

"The door's broken, and the last time I was here, it was full of black widows."

"Oh, it'll be just fine," her mother said. "If a tornado's coming, I have bigger problems than black widows." As Saffire shook her head, Donna ignored her and smiled at both of them. "Come on in, and I'll give you the tour."

Jack followed Saffire onto the porch and through the door, putting his hand lightly on her back for a moment so he could touch her while her mother wasn't looking. All he could think of since their little dance in the van was getting her alone.

"The house was built in 1909," Donna said, "by one of Texas's first oilmen. Apparently, he lived in Possum Bottom as a boy, the dirt-poor son of a fur trader. He wanted to bring his family back here to Oklahoma to live. And show off. That's why it's bigger than anything else in town. I keep expecting a tornado to blow it down. The Dust Bowl years nearly scoured out this town, but the house remained, and people came back eventually. When I was a kid, I used to ride my bike by here and wonder what it was like when real people lived here. It was a dentist's office then. When I decided to come back home, I looked into buying it. I was shocked at how cheap it was. It hadn't been lived in for years. Of course, the bargain soon turned into a money pit, but it's a pretty money pit."

"You've done a lot since I've been here," Saffire said, nodding appreciatively at the polished wood floors and all the little details — fabrics, knickknacks — that brought the place together. There were way too many stimuli for Jack, but he appreciated the idea. There were a couple of elaborately furnished sitting rooms, a small office, a large kitchen whose dark wooden door sported a brass plate that said "Staff Only," and an elegant dining room with a handsome stone fireplace, opposite a long table and a huge sideboard for serving meals. The art ranged from paintings of Plains landscapes to an old photo of a Dust Bowl storm, its billowing black wall of dirt menacing the town.

"I've fixed up the cottage out back, too," Donna said.

"That's where Barry and I are staying. It's better for us. Living in this house is like living at work. Despite all the romance about running a B&B, it's mostly washing sheets and towels, cooking and cleaning and fixing broken pipes. Though I enjoy making it hospitable, and we're just a courtesy phone away. So are you two staying here?"

Jack couldn't help but notice the questioning look in her eye. "We'd like a couple of rooms if you have them," he said.

"A couple of rooms? No problem," she said, shooting Saffire a little sideways grin that had Saffire — or was it Sandy? — rolling her eyes. "No one's here this week. In a couple of weeks, that's high school graduation, we'll be full up. The bedrooms are upstairs, each with a nice little bathroom. That was a project, I'll tell you. I'll get you a couple of keys." She led them to the neatly appointed office, which suffered from an excess of cherub-covered wallpaper. On the desk were a few old photos in ornate frames. One, of a good-looking man in his thirties, was fading a little; he had his arms around a little girl. Then there was the same girl, about high school age, with brown, frizzy hair and braces. Saffire's sister? Jack realized, no, it was *Saffire*: gawky and cute, with no idea of what was ahead of her.

"Make sure you give us a bill," Saffire said. "The production company will pay."

"I couldn't charge my own daughter," Donna said, fishing around in a drawer for the keys.

"You won't be, mama. Take the business."

"Well, if you think it's OK," Donna said, "I'll give you an invoice in the morning." Finally, she found the keys she wanted and handed them to her daughter. "They're right next to each other," she said pointedly.

"Thanks, mom." Saffire gave Jack a tight smile.

"Hey," Jack said. "Why don't I take a little nap while you two catch up? Then maybe we can get dinner or something."

"Great idea. Barry and I already have dinner plans with another couple. I mean, if I'd only known you were coming … but I'd love an hour with my girl." Donna beamed.

Jack held out his hand, and Saffire took a moment to realize what he wanted. She handed him one of the keys, attached to a two-inch-square piece of wood burned with a number "8."

"Oh, good, the infinity room," he said, turning the square sideways, and she laughed.

"Maybe it leads to another dimension," Saffire said. He admired all three of her dimensions as she walked down the hallway with her mother toward a back door embedded with stained glass that gleamed like gems in the late afternoon sun.

"IT FEELS weird to be the only ones rattling around in this old house," Jack said later in one of the parlors, the one with an old record player, piles of board games, well-stocked bookshelves and ornate, dim floor lamps. They'd had a decent dinner at the Tiptop Cafe: Saffire satisfied her fishatarian urgings with catfish, while he enjoyed some real country fried chicken. Now, they were drinking a nice syrah, and he was sifting through the records, admiring the jazz collection and playing whatever suited his fancy. He'd changed into baggy shorts, a black T-shirt and his favorite black high-tops; she was in brown sandals and a casual, dusky-green linen sundress that buttoned up the front, leaving just a hint of cleavage. She looked adorable curled up in an old-fashioned comfy chair, the kind of chair with flowers and fringe that did not do anything so crass as to fold out.

"Mama says this place is haunted," Saffire said.

"Every old house is haunted," Jack said, his tone indicating he thought anything but.

"Well, it makes a lot of noises at night."

"It's probably the air-conditioning, the creaky wooden walls and those cast-iron radiators."

"Just wait till you hear a ghost yourself," Saffire said in a teasing tone. "Then you'll believe."

"Maybe when I actually see one. Oh, look, this is one of my favorites," Jack said, pulling out *Ella Fitzgerald Sings the Irving Berlin Songbook*.

"You don't strike me as a vinyl kind of guy," Saffire remarked.

"Are you kidding? I was raised on this stuff. There's this one song I want you to hear. The perfect little ballad for storm geeks."

"I didn't know Ella was a storm chaser."

"Come on, you'll like it. It's sexy." He put the second disc on the turntable and set the needle down at "Isn't This a Lovely Day?"

"Oh, she has the warmest voice ever," Saffire said, sipping her wine, looking content, as Ella sang about the delights of a thunderstorm that forces her lover to stay with her.

"She's the best, bar none," Jack said. "At least, when I'm not rocking out."

Saffire laughed.

"Want to dance?" he asked, holding out his hand.

She didn't hesitate. She set down her wineglass on one of the doily-covered tables and let him pull her up from the chair and into his arms. He led her carefully amid the ornate furniture, recalling a few swing dance moves he'd learned in college and executing them at half-speed.

"You're a man of hidden talents," she said.

"Oh, you know, dancing impresses the girls."

"We're so easily impressed," she said with a touch of sarcasm. "You're no red velvet mite, you know."

"And you're no Saffire," he said. "What's your name, anyway?"

"Oh, that. 'Sandy' just wasn't going to fly on my acting resume. And since I was born in September, I thought Saffire might be cool. With a little twist on the spelling."

"Sparkly and blue," he murmured in her ear, then swung her out and reeled her back in. The old floor creaked agreeably below their feet, and he lost himself for a moment in the feel of her, her grace and ease, as their bodies moved together.

"I'm glad mama bought this old place," Saffire said as they danced. "Though I worry about the storms."

"Why'd she — you — move to California in the first place?"

"My dad wanted to. He always wanted to work in the movies. He was good-looking. Everyone told him so, I guess. But when he got to dreamland, all he could get was work painting sets. Watching other people do what he wanted to do. I think he died young of old age. Heart attack at forty-two."

"How long ago?"

"Well, I'm twenty-nine now — so about eleven years? I'd just started college. It was tough. I think it all just illustrated to me that there wasn't any time to waste. I was starting to dabble in theater and broadcast, and I decided I wasn't going to settle for an ordinary life."

Jack softened more toward her, the child in her that

wanted to do what her dad couldn't. "You're a star already," he said.

"A very small one."

"Burning brighter all the time. You light up every room you're in." Jack pulled her closer as they danced. "Anyone you see, anyplace you go. You must know the effect you have." He spun her once, held her close again and whispered in her ear. "Dazzling."

The song wrapped up, and she stepped back as "Change Partners" came on, her eyes shining.

"Another turn?" he asked, holding his arms open.

An enigmatic smile crossed her face, and he felt his skin tingle. "Let's go for a walk," she said. "You haven't really seen the grounds."

"It's dark now."

"There are stars."

"And I like stars," he said. He let the record play, and they walked through the house and out the back door. Here, another porch looked out on a modestly landscaped garden, with pavers surrounding a small, bubbling fountain. Potted flowers and solar lights lined a meandering walkway. Trees surrounded the property — about an acre and a half back here — and through them, at the far end of the lot, he could make out the lights of what must be her mother's cottage. In the darkness, it was easy to imagine this being someplace other than western Oklahoma, a lush land far from the scrubby plain. Even at night, though, he could see the subtle lean of the trees, trained by the ever-present wind. Nothing grew out here without struggling against it.

"There's something sweet back here I want you to see," Saffire said, leading him literally down the garden path. Her loose curls tumbled around her bare shoulders. Her hips swayed under her dress. Right now, all he wanted to see was her.

In a moment, they were amid a dense clump of trees, and within it lay the shape of a structure.

"What is it?" he asked.

"Come and see," Saffire said, opening the door to a greenhouse. She fumbled inside the doorway and came up with a match, which she used to light a candle lantern that hung inside. He followed her in and closed the door.

The walls were glass panels, and they subtly reflected the lantern. The space was about the size of a two-car garage, but taller and elegantly framed with ironwork that reached up to a two-tier metal roof — some protection from hail, Jack couldn't help but think. It was warmer and more humid than outside. In the dimly flickering light, he could see that he and Saffire were surrounded by an entangled assortment of tropical plants, organized around a narrow, winding walkway, including potted palms and a profusion of hanging orchids. It was like walking into a terrarium.

"Mama showed me this today. She renovated it. It's original to the house. A private place to think, to relax. A nice spot to read a book."

"Have a smoke," Jack joked. He was surprised he wasn't more irritable, given his nicotine-free afternoon, but that would come soon enough.

"Now, Jack," Saffire said, teasing, "there are all kinds of things you can do in here, but smoking isn't one of them." He had followed her into the center, where a curvy wicker couch with big orange cushions and two matching chairs waited at the heart of the genteel jungle.

"I won't smoke," he said. He walked slowly up to her and put his hands on her waist. Her butterscotch eyes sparkled, reflecting the lantern's flame. He leaned in to kiss her neck with gentle deliberation. "But I need something to distract me." He blew softly in her ear and felt her shiver.

"It's the other way around. I told you. You're a terrible distraction," she said, her cheek against his.

"Too simple? Or too complicated?"

She looked up at him, her face shadowed in the wavering light. "I don't care," she said, and she reached up to pull him toward her, pressing her lips on his. He felt her hunger and matched it. He'd been waiting for this. He ran his hands over her back, feeling the rough linen of the dress, the bra underneath, then skimmed her bottom, pulling up lightly on the fabric. But he didn't want to rush. He stopped kissing her for a moment, long enough to lay his hands on her shoulders and run his fingers lightly down her arms, her waist, taking in her figure, her warmth. He reached for the buttons that ran down the front of her green dress. He kissed her again as he began unfastening them, devouring her more intensely with each button. He released the last one, and the dress fell open, revealing a lustrous pink and white bra, prettily laced in front, mimicking a corset as it pushed up the smooth mounds of her breasts. She wore satin underpants to match, their sumptuous style suited to this strangely Victorian setting. He stepped back so he could observe every detail of her curves and trappings. He wondered how much she had planned this encounter, and he wanted her all the more for her artful preparation, for her desire.

The corner of her mouth turned up with pleasure at his admiration, and she stepped out of her sandals and shrugged off the dress, letting it fall to the floor. "Jack." She breathed his name as if she were casting a spell. "*Jack.*"

He wasn't inclined to answer. He wasn't sure if he could.

He was already hard, looking at her, and he stepped forward. Now, he wanted to go even more slowly. He wanted to unwrap this beautiful present with care.

He pulled off his shirt so he could feel her against him as he pressed his lips against her chest, kissing the pale skin there, licking it. The bra barely contained her full breasts, and it was easy enough to lift them above the cups so her nipples were revealed, dark in the candlelight. He licked one, then the other, teasing the tips with his tongue until they were wet and firm. She unbuttoned his shorts, and they fell to his feet. He yanked off his sneakers and socks, stepped out of his briefs and half-pushed, half-carried her to the couch, where he lay her against the cushions. He was fully erect now, and his skin was slick with sweat in the heat of the greenhouse and the moment.

"Come here," she whispered. She put her arms around his legs and drew him closer. He rested one knee on the edge of the couch. She took him into her mouth with a hard suck that made him gasp, then built a slow and painstaking rhythm. He squeezed his eyes shut in delicious agony. She stopped before he could finish, and he looked down to see a last flick of her tongue.

Saffire lifted her smoky gaze to his. He needed no more encouragement. The pressure was unbearable. Jack reached down and swiftly removed her underpants. He ran one hand over her tiny, manicured triangle of brown curls and knelt to kiss her there, to lick her bud until she lifted herself toward him. He pushed two fingers inside her, feeling the tide of her arousal, and caressed her inner walls until she moaned. With his other hand, he reached for his shorts on the floor, his wallet, and retrieved a condom.

She helped him roll it on, and he paused for a heartbeat

to behold her in the gossamer light, in the palm-frond shadows. Her lips were still moist. Her breasts were round above the bra, the pale skin and nipples well-defined in the dimness, and they rose with her rapid breathing. She opened her legs for him, and he lay against her and pushed himself hard inside her. She cried out, holding on to the back of the couch with one arm, wrapping her legs around him as he thrust again and again, as he neared the dissolution into oblivion he craved. She arched her back with a low cry, and he felt her climax around him. He fell into her, engulfed in his own release, a searing explosion of stars and night and Saffire.

"*Saffire,*" he whispered, agitated by an emotion he couldn't identify.

He touched her cheek. As he kissed her, the candle guttered, bowing to an unseen wind.

BEING on the road so much, Jack was used to not knowing where he was when he awoke. But this morning, he was especially confused. Emerging from a dream of a swirling supercell that overpowered him with wind and rain, he smelled bacon, coffee and bread, the traces of a home mostly forgotten. He was wrapped around a naked woman, soft and warm. He felt the stirrings of desire before he even remembered that this was Saffire, before he began to think about how awkward their work was going to be, before he decided he didn't want to think about that right now. He opened his eyes and there she was, looking at him. He kissed her, and she giggled.

"Someone's perky this morning," she whispered as she rubbed a knee against his crotch. Her golden eyes were full of morning light, and their dark and heated union of last night seemed like a dream.

He kissed her again, wondering whether he wanted to leave or stay. The brass bed creaked as she pulled him closer. OK, stay. "We could do something about that," he said.

"That's my mom downstairs, you know. You're supposed to be in the room next door."

"I don't think she cares, do you?"

This time, she initiated the kiss, her tongue lightly exploring his mouth. "Quietly," she said as she released him.

He fumbled on the nightstand for his wallet and found a condom.

"Quiet as mice," he said, tearing it open and rolling it on.

She pushed the quilt and sheets aside and eased on top of him. He stifled a groan as he filled her. He closed his eyes and rocked her slowly, slowly, until he was back among the storms of his dreams, flying, rising until the stinging rain and wind consumed him.

Not too much later, he'd showered in his own bathroom, dressed and taken a few minutes to look at data using his laptop and the inn's wi-fi. Nothing worth chasing, really; might be something way up in Montana tomorrow and maybe upslope Saturday, but he couldn't chase in Colorado when they had to meet the rest of the crew in eastern Kansas. He had a little headache and was already missing his cigarettes. He'd have to stop somewhere and stock up on whatever there was to curb his need — gum. Patch. Lollipops. Right now, in lieu of nicotine, he'd take Saffire.

He went downstairs to find her helping her mother dish up eggs and bacon; warm chocolate-stuffed croissants; crisp, round waffles topped with melting pats of butter; and bowls of strawberries with cream. A steaming coffeepot, sugar and cream, glasses of orange juice and a pitcher of syrup were already on the table.

"I figured since it was just us, we'd forgo the buffet," Donna said. "Will this be enough? I can whip up some oatmeal."

"Oh, uh, this will be fine," Jack said. "Really nice."

Saffire looked amused. She turned to her mother. "Is Barry joining us?"

"He already took off for the courthouse. Got a big case today. Well, big for Possum Bottom."

There was something about that name that made Jack grin. He poured a cup of coffee into one of the hand-glazed ceramic mugs on the table and sipped it gingerly. Just right.

"Did you hear the ghosts last night?" Donna asked as they sat at the dark antique table, which was decorated with linen placemats and a crystal bowl stuffed with multicolored blooms. "You know, if we document enough sightings, we might get on one of those TV shows. It'd be good for business."

"I didn't hear anything. Did you, Jack?" Saffire asked.

"Me? No. I sleep hard." Saffire smiled a secret smile as Jack took another sip of coffee and dug into the food.

"I swear I hear them in the garden sometimes. Like last night. Though I'm sure you'd just say it was the wind," Donna said innocently, taking a bite of eggs.

"Definitely the wind," Jack said without hesitation, pouring syrup on his waffles.

They ate for a few moments in silence. The ticking of a clock on the fireplace mantel told Jack their time here was running out.

Donna seemed to have the same thought. "When will you be coming back, honey?" she asked Saffire.

"I'm still coming at Christmas. Maybe before," she said. "But I might have a cool new job soon." Now this was news. "My agent and I are talking with some people about a new science show. It's exactly what I was hoping for when I quit *Star Beat.* I want to do a project that really means something to me, since I'm getting on in age and all." She grinned.

"Bugs?" Donna asked, shaking her head, but her smile belied her feigned disapproval.

"Bugs and more. But I don't want to count my chickens," Saffire said.

"I'm proud of you, sweetie. I just like seeing you. Come back as soon as you can." Donna looked at Jack. "You come, too," she said slyly, and he wondered if she knew more than she let on. Mothers often did.

Jack's phone buzzed, and he pulled it from his jeans pocket. "Text from Andre," he said. "He's wondering when we're coming to get him."

Saffire released a melancholy sigh. "Tell him an hour," she said. "I guess it's time to get back to work."

WYNDA WASN'T sure what to do with her hero, but she was working on him, trying to get him feeling happy and secure and ready for another go in the Bubble. She figured a couple of days of shooting fluff footage at Kansas's tourist attractions would restore Brad's confidence and give him a chance to rest up and get all that self-medication out of his system. Instead, he was having kittens. Among the eccentric cement sculptures at the Garden of Eden, he freaked out when he saw S.P. Dinsmoor in his crypt and wouldn't talk for the hour it took them to get to Cawker City and the World's Largest Ball of

Twine. He seemed even more disgusted to be there, but he did a robotic standup as Michiko kept asking him to talk louder, at least until he screamed. Wynda bought them lunch and hoped he hadn't completely lost it. Forty minutes later, they were in the middle of nowhere, or rather, the exact middle of the continental United States, where she finally got Brad to settle down and wax rhapsodic about being in the heart of the heartland and how wonderful it was. At this point, it was Wynda's turn to consider suicide, but she got through it by imagining the speech combined with rolling shots of waving wheat and all the wind farms, cows, tumbleweeds and, especially, crew interaction she hoped Andre was getting.

When they were done shooting, it was off to Wichita for the night, with Michiko driving, Wynda in the passenger seat and Brad in the back, texting furiously.

"How are you feeling, Brad?" Wynda finally ventured. "Your sunburn — er, burn has faded quite a bit. You're looking fit."

He looked up from his smartphone. "Thanks," he said. "I'm feeling better."

"That's wonderful news. You did a marvelous job on the tourist trail today. We'll get some shots with the Bubble and get a day or so of rest, and we'll be good to go."

He blanched a little at the mention of the Bubble, but he recovered quickly. "I'm up for it," he said. "Whatever you need."

"You're our star, Brad," Wynda said soothingly, "and you are our priority. We want you to be happy. If, I mean, *when* we get you and the Bubble inside a tornado, you're going to be the most famous man in America. It will be terrific for your career."

"I've thought about that. I know this is a good opportunity.

And it's the only one I have right now, right?" He said it as if it were a joke, but Wynda heard an edge.

"One thing I've learned in my career is that a *completed project* always looks better on the resume," she said as convincingly as she could, recalling the jungle documentary and Aurelius and how she'd pulled it out of the crapper. It really had been a valuable step on the ladder, even if the climb was hell.

"I'm doing my part," Brad said. "I keep getting in the thing. It's not my fault the tornadoes keep missing us."

"Ah, but they've been so close. It's a matter of time." Ironically, she thought, Van One had been more of a tornado probe than the Bubble. "We have first-rate forecasting, at least."

"Oh, sure. As if you have to be Dr. Weather to find storms."

"Of course, you were very successful with your tour, Brad, but expert help is always desirable," Wynda said. What she was thinking was altogether different. Her quiet background check on her star had revealed that not all his tourists had been happy, and in fact, they hadn't seen much of anything until the Prairie Rock tornado. She hadn't been able to ken much of that day, but Brad had the footage and the fame, and that was all that mattered for her show. That, and keeping him in the Bubble until they got their shot.

Michiko spoke up. "Can we get sushi in Wichita tonight? I'm dying for sushi."

"Absolutely," Wynda said.

Brad made a face. "You know, it's never good to eat raw fish in a landlocked state," he said.

"It's a big city," said Michiko. "Or at least, close enough. It'll be fine."

"My stomach can't take another incident," Brad said. "And

I don't think anyone wants me throwing up in the Bubble. There are a lot of gadgets in there."

"They're not going to serve bad food," said Michiko, whose epic patience had eroded at last. "They have regulations for that."

"You can get a Kansas roll. Raw cow wrapped in bacon with wheat sprinkled on top."

"Ridiculous."

"Enough," Wynda interrupted. "We'll find a Japanese steakhouse so everyone can order what his or her little heart desires." And this, she thought, is why I'm never having children.

IN THE CHARMING town of McPherson, Kansas, a pillar of the Rock Island railroad, there was a low din in Stone Pickett's funky 1920s house. Chasers milled about exchanging stories, watching tornado videos and eating from paper plates. The old Formica kitchen table and tiled countertops were lined with party food — dips, bread, chips, cheese, salads, cookies, and platters of hot dogs, chicken and burgers that Stone brought in from the grill.

Despite the noise, Aurelius couldn't help hearing his phone ring again. He heard it the way a mother can distinguish her baby's cry from any other in a loud room. He withdrew it from one of the many pockets in his khakis and glanced at the number before declining the call, and then he turned it off. He needed a break. His recent spate of publicity had not just set the media on his trail; creditors were calling, too. So far, it wasn't anything serious, just a few ancient utility bills one would think would have gone away by now, but the calls were interfering with his public-relations effort. He was actually getting favorable buzz from some of the chasers here, especially the younger ones who were easily impressed by television and brand names, of which he liked to consider himself one. The older, more revered chasers studiously avoided him, but he was used to that. Anyone who dared run their cherished hobby through pop culture's brain shredder was looked upon about as favorably as an intestinal virus on a cruise ship. Still, the gadget freaks couldn't help but ask him about his drone, and he conspiratorially informed them that it was ready to get some killer shots during tomorrow's chase.

The word "tornadoes" was on everyone's lips. So was the word "outbreak." When these words were uttered, they evoked nervous anticipation or caustic skepticism, but the forecast had the attention of every storm geek in the room.

Today, Duncan and Phil were out testing the spare UAV, making sure it was ready. Aurelius's techies had extracted the memory cards from the debris, but they'd had no luck recovering video. Fortunately, they'd lost data only from that day, and it might be just as well, given that the books weren't entirely closed on the helicopter incident. No data meant no evidence, especially since they'd disposed of the pieces.

Aurelius had asked the rest of his crew to get shots of him hobnobbing at the party, and then he set them free for an hour. Tomorrow would be demanding enough. For now, Things One and Two drank beer on the back deck. Ernie and Evie shared a stuffed chair in a crowd of about twenty chasers perched on every available square inch of floor and furniture in the living room. They watched Brad Treat's tornado video from last year's encounter outside Prairie Rock with rapt attention. It still got that kind of attention, even now. Aurelius felt a pinch of jealousy. And now Treat had the Bubble. Did the boy realize how lucky he was?

Aurelius scanned the crowd and picked out members of Wynda's crew, but no Wynda, and no — wait, there he was. Brad was chatting up a pretty storm tourist, one of several at the party, judging from the number of large vans outside. He seemed to be doing quite well. Aurelius didn't care. With Wynda absent, this was his chance. He drifted into earshot and cleared his throat. Brad glanced up, his expression shifting from confused to annoyed to resigned before he wrote down a number on a piece of paper and handed it to the young woman with a suggestive smile. She wandered off, and his face turned sour at Aurelius's approach.

"Mr. Treat," Aurelius said. "So nice to see you again."

"Zane, you have to stop texting me."

"I have no idea what you're talking about."

"You know, I am trying to film a TV show," Brad said.

"Exactly. Opportunity's knocking, sir. Come into my office. We have matters to discuss." Then he dragged Brad into the laundry room and shut the door.

JACK WAS on the house's back deck in the shade of an oak tree, leaning against the railing, alternating beers with nicotine gum, trying to maintain something between a buzz and a freak-out. He was also temporarily avoiding Saffire to let her mingle and be photographed with the other chasers and Devlin and Brad, in hopes that Wynda would be less likely to tear out all their throats. Their producer had already eviscerated Andre in a not-so-private conversation in Stone's driveway, accusing him of not getting the footage she needed, when

Jack knew very well he'd filmed pretty much every cow and wind turbine in western Kansas.

Jack didn't want to make things worse by cavorting with Saffire in that party crowd. He felt like such a cliché, falling under the celebrity's spell. Though he hardly thought of her as that anymore — now she was the bug expert, the awkward brown-haired teenager in the photo at her mother's house, the amusing traveling companion. The girl whose smile wouldn't quit, whose essential optimism was, to him, like an alien language. The seductress in the greenhouse. And the woman of the last two nights, when they made languorous love in his hotel room after long days on the road. Saffire was under his skin, all right, and with his nicotine withdrawal in full swing and his anticipation rising for tomorrow's storms — and tonight with her — his skin was on fire.

"So where are you going tomorrow?" a voice said behind him. He turned.

"Marcus!" Jack greeted his long-haired, rumpled, bespectacled friend with a hearty handshake. "Where are *you* going tomorrow? How's the hail research going?"

"We've already busted two windshields, so I'd say it's going OK. Lots of good measurements. Where did you say you were going tomorrow?"

"I didn't say. North-central Kansas, maybe. And you?"

"I didn't say. Maybe central-central."

"Central-central-central."

"Yeah, there." Marcus sipped his beer. "How's Hollywood?"

"Oh, you know. The glitz. The glamour. The girls."

Marcus raised his eyebrows. "I got a load of that Saffire Soulliere. Surely she isn't your blonde du jour."

"Too rich for my blood," Jack said innocently.

Marcus looked him dead in the eye for a full three seconds. "You sly bastard."

"I know. Keep it quiet, OK? She's got a career to think about. It wouldn't do her any good to be seen on the arm of the likes of me."

"I'm sure that's true," Marcus said with a smile.

Jack glowered and took a sip of beer. "She confuses me. She's like magnetic north. My compass doesn't work when she's around."

"You falling for her?"

"Impossible," Jack said, but the idea unsettled him. "I think I'm having a midlife crisis."

"What, at thirty-one? You have to grow up before you can have a midlife crisis."

"No hurry to do that."

"Amen," Marcus said, taking another sip.

"So, high risk for tomorrow," Jack said.

"That's what they're saying. High bust, more like it."

"Oh, there will be tornadoes. The question is whether they'll run you over and leave you for dead. That's if you catch them in the first place."

"I know," Marcus said. "I don't like the storm speeds at all. And it looks like it'll be one of those one-day systems. Either get it tomorrow where we can see it or chase it in the jungle on Monday, and nobody wants that. Hey, look who's here."

They turned to see Professor Malik, Jack's university mentor, approaching with a cola in hand, and they exchanged more congenial greetings.

"Where's your beer, professor? I know you're a connoisseur," Jack said.

"They only have light beer at this party," the neatly dressed, ever-tan research meteorologist whispered conspiratorially. "Might as well drink Coke."

"I'll take what I can get," Jack said.

"Speaking of which," Malik said, "how's the TV job?"

"Every day's an adventure in waiting."

"Sounds a lot like chasing," the professor said. "I tried to get a look in your truck out there — I assume that's where you're keeping the choice equipment — but there's a guy sleeping in it."

"Pole," Jack said. "That's his version of 'on guard.' "

"Wise man," Malik said, "with all the insatiably curious around here. I met one of your hosts on the front porch — Saffire? I've never seen her on TV, but she assures me she's semi-famous. She pulled a katydid out of a plant that I didn't even see. You know, the leaf bugs? Then she made the sound it makes. Absolutely uncanny. She's a live one."

Jack just nodded. Geez, she'd even impressed Professor Malik. He put down his empty bottle and dug the pack of nicotine gum out of a pocket in his baggy shorts. As he unwrapped a piece and popped it into his mouth, the others watched with interest.

"You quit?" Marcus asked in disbelief.

"It's too early to tell." Jack chewed a few times and tasted the peppery tingle as he waited anxiously for the stuff to take the edge off his craving.

"Well done," Malik said. "What pushed you over the edge?"

"I'm not over the edge yet."

Marcus looked amused. "I bet I know."

"You know nothing," Jack growled. "Get me a beer." The

guys laughed at him. Or with him. It was hard to tell. He wasn't used to it, either way. And then he saw Saffire in the doorway, looking at him, her cleavage gleaming against the V-neck of her jade-green shirt. A smile crept across her pink lips and her softly sculpted face before it lit up her eyes. The world seemed to tilt. He grasped the railing and smiled back, chewing once again on the gum, feeling the fool. The happy fool. Tingling and drunk.

He was in so much goddamn trouble.

JACK RELUCTANTLY LEFT Saffire's room at 2 a.m., wanting a few hours of solitude and sleep before what promised to be an intense day of storm chasing. They maintained the illusion that they weren't involved while the others were around, though he guessed from the looks they got from the crew that no one really bought their charade. He tried not to think about it. It was time to live in the moment, and to chase storms.

He'd slowed down on the nicotine gum, but for the most part, he felt ill and cranky. He couldn't for the life of him figure out why focusing was so difficult right now, and this day would require all of his concentration.

He got perhaps five hours of fitful sleep before he couldn't stand it anymore. He sat at the desk, flipped open his laptop and looked at the early outlooks and model runs. A deep low was pushing into central Kansas, along with screaming upper- and mid-level winds that would propel any supercells that formed northeast at fifty to sixty miles per hour. It was a perfect storm situation and a horrible chasing situation. Plus, as alarmist as the media forecasts were, if his crew didn't see something, he'd never live it down.

After an hour of looking at data, he lay again in bed and drifted into a twilight sleep, the realm of the siren. He heard it getting louder but couldn't see the tornado. A musical voice called to him in the darkness, but he was inside the safe, and the door wouldn't open. He was wrenched from the dream with a start, sweating, his heart racing, by the ringing of the room phone.

"Jack, wakey wakey." Wynda's crisp British consonants cut into his sleep. "Your services are required at breakfast. We need a briefing and a plan. See you in twenty minutes."

"Unh." He hung up, listening to the traffic and the maids chattering in Spanish in the hallway. Wynda was so bossy. Then again, she was his boss. If he were chasing on his own today, he'd be delighted. But having to guide this pack of amateurs into a phalanx of storms moving at light speed did not ignite his enthusiasm.

He reached to the nightstand for his cigarettes before cursing their absence. First, he'd shower and brush his teeth. He'd have coffee. And then he would see how long he could stand it before chewing more of that nasty gum.

There was a diner attached to their economy hotel here in McPherson, and that's where he found the crew eating breakfast. "Ugh," Jack teased when he saw Saffire's oatmeal and fruit. "So healthy."

They exchanged what he thought was a subtle glance before he grew uncomfortably certain that everyone was looking at him. He sat, flipped his coffee cup right-side-up and caught the eye of the waitress. "Toast and coffee, please," he said when she came by. "And a hard-boiled egg." She filled the cup immediately and left him to his first, blissful sip as Wynda addressed them.

"It's been a while since we've all started the day in the same place, so I wanted to get everyone's temperature before we hit the road. Devlin, tell us about the Bubble."

Their geek looked tired, the shadows under his eyes almost darker than his black-rimmed glasses. "It's working, at least as far as we can tell. It's responding pretty well to tests. I talked to the lab, and we found one flaw in the electronics shielding that probably caused it to conk out when the lightning hit. It's fixed, but I'm not a hundred percent confident there's no transient damage. I'd like to test it for one more day."

"Not possible," Wynda said, giving him no chance to respond. "Brad?"

"Excellent," Brad said, a glint in his eye, lifting his yogurt as if he were making a toast.

"Good to hear." Wynda looked pleased. "Cameras? Sound?"

Razor and Andre offered simultaneous thumbs-up.

"One mike crapped out," Michiko said. "Rain got in it, I think. We have a replacement."

"Vehicles?"

"All working nominally," Pole said. "I made sure the Bubblevan and the SUV got an oil change."

"And we haven't had the new Van One long enough to need one," Wynda said. "Saffire?"

"Never better," she said. She wore a white blouse today with a low neckline, trimmed with eyelet lace, that brought out her peachy skin and that honey-blond hair. Jack was so wrapped up in looking at her that it took him a moment to realize Wynda was speaking to him.

"Hullo? Weather?"

Jack turned his gaze back to the producer. "We are definitely going to have weather today."

"Details, please."

He took another sip of coffee. "The good news is, there will be tornadoes."

"Oh," Brad said.

"You're that sure?" Wynda asked.

"Yes. Everything points to it. The bad news is, they'll be moving so fast, they may be difficult to intercept."

Wynda beamed at all of them. "I like our chances better on a day with guaranteed tornadoes than on an iffy one."

"There are no guarantees. It's the weather. I'm just trying to tell you that storms like these may be dangerous to chase, at least with a three-vehicle caravan and an unwieldy manned probe."

"I already like it," she said.

AFTER FAR TOO MUCH time in the Great Bend Subway and its parking lot, Aurelius Zane and company headed north to I-70 and Russell to sit in another parking lot, this one at a gas station. As it filled with storm-chasing vehicles, he ordered his caravan to a quiet spot on the edge of town so his drone wouldn't be under the scrutiny of fifty storm chasers. Everyone was chasing — even a helicopter, he noted with chagrin — but they would take care to avoid it. He couldn't afford another incident, and he still needed his tornado footage.

"What's the timing today?" he asked Ernie, who sat in the passenger seat.

"We already have convection on the dryline," the meteorology student said. "See those clouds just west of us? We're close to the triple point. This is where the action is supposed to happen. I think once those towers break the cap, they'll go crazy fast."

"So you really haven't answered my question."

Ernie looked at his watch. It was just after 2 p.m. "How about 3:17?"

"If that can be arranged," Aurelius said, not appreciating the joke. "Evie?"

"I'm posting lots of updates today, and everyone's excited about it," she said from the back, where one of the Things was shooting. The other was outside, interviewing the techies. "Apparently, the TV stations are predicting the wrath of God, so all my followers want to know about the tornadoes."

"Assuming there are some," Aurelius said. He sighed. In his heart, he felt there would be tornadoes, but he was already tired of his troublesome drone. He wanted to be in the Bubble, flying to Oz.

WHEN THE FIRST storm popped at 2:48 p.m., only a handful of chasers were on it. It was a good deal south of the triple point, far from that intersection of low and cold front and dryline, and Jack and friends were far east of it. They had waited in McPherson a little too long, grabbing a fast-food lunch while Jack refined his forecast. Even now, he wasn't sure they were headed for the best storm. While he was confident that there would be tornadoes, he was not altogether confident in the best location in an almost comically large risk area. At first he favored the north, but he saw multiple targets with potential. If in doubt, go for the storm that exists, he told himself as they headed west. They could always try to catch another one later.

It was weirdly overcast, and not just because of the large anvil blown off the top of the storm. It was hard to see any distinct features in the gray light and drifting mist and showers. Dewpoints were in the low 70s. That meant a lot of moisture for storms, but visibility sucked.

"Why aren't we there yet?" Wynda radioed impatiently from the crew SUV.

"I don't want to push the speed limit too much," Brad radioed back. "Every cop in Kansas is out storm-spotting and looking for chasers to pull over."

"Just get there," she said, and keyed off.

Jack picked up his radio. "I wouldn't worry. It's going to meet us halfway. It looks like it's moving fifty miles per hour or so. And it's developing a tornado signature on radar."

Just then, their weather radio alert screeched, and his fears were confirmed: Storm spotters had already reported a tornado.

"That was fast," Devlin said from the middle seat, next to Andre. "Did Wynda hear that?"

"Did you hear that?" Wynda was back on the radio. "We missed a tornado. Figure out our next opportunity to deploy."

"I love her so much." Andre's voice was heavy with sarcasm as he filmed his stars in Van One.

"There's always another storm and another tornado," said Saffire, the Pollyanna of storm chasers.

Jack's head was starting to spin with the surrealism of living in what was becoming an absurd sitcom. He needed to see a tornado again to convince himself they existed in real life, not just on TV. But with all the gray, the junk convection, it was going to be hard to see anything.

"I don't like this," he said under his breath.

"What?" Saffire asked. She was tuned in to his frequency now. He gave her a quick, intimate glance before addressing all of them.

"The visibility. We should be seeing some structure. We're close enough. There's all this rain around it. It's not going to be good for deployment or for video, either. I'm not sure it's safe."

"Maybe we should listen to Jack," said Brad.

Jack smiled at this small irony. "I don't mean not safe for you. The Bubble is built to withstand a tornado. I mean the rest of us. This storm is moving crazy fast, and now I'm seeing more development along the dryline. Rapid development. They're rotating right out of the box. All that's good, but I'm just saying we need to be careful."

"Like we were on that dirt road?"

Brad's dig did nothing for Jack's mood. "More careful," he said. "I just have a bad feeling about today. If it were just me, it'd be a different story, trust me." He imagined taking his old, green station wagon, still parked at his apartment in Wishwell, and driving into the storm's heart, blasting through the walls of rain to find the tornado he sought.

"Well?" Wynda's voice came over the radio.

"I was just saying we should pick our battles today," Jack replied. "We need to make sure we have ample time to deploy with storm speeds the way they are."

"Get close," Wynda said, "and then we'll decide when to deploy."

They were definitely getting close. The sky was much darker now, especially to the west, and radar indicated a hook echo, a likely tornado, developing not far from their position. But still, all they could see was rain.

"It's not more than two miles away," Jack said.

"Then let's deploy," Wynda came back.

"I don't recommend deployment unless we can see it."

Devlin held out his hand and took the CB mike from Jack. "I concur, Wynda. It's bad enough that we have to find the perfect spot of ground. If we can't actually see the tornado, the cameras aren't going to see the Bubble, either."

The camera argument must have sunk in. "All right," Wynda said. "Then get close enough so I can see the bugger."

"We're going to have to angle northwest," Devlin said. "I'm hoping they're not dirt roads."

They took a turn and then two more, finding themselves on a grid of rough, gravel roads that would take them to where radar suggested the mesocyclone should be. *Should* be. Jack still couldn't see shit. "Just hang tight at the next intersection," he suggested. "We should get a visual in a moment."

"Why can't we see anything?" Brad asked nervously as he paused the van, facing north. The other two vehicles stopped behind them.

"Status?" Wynda's voice came over the radio.

Pole's rarely heard voice keyed in. "Has anyone considered looking up?"

There was a scramble to the windows in Van One as everyone craned their necks to see above their heads. "Funnel directly overhead," Jack said into the radio. "Turn right. Turn right. Get down the road."

Brad nearly tipped the van in his hurry to make the corner, kicking out rocks and dirt in the process. The others followed until they were a half mile east and Jack had said "Stop!" half a dozen times.

"Nothing like keeping it exciting," Saffire said. "Why don't we get out and take a look?"

"Just be ready to get back in fast," Jack said into the radio, making sure everyone heard, and they scrambled outside to get their shots. He slipped out the side door and looked west into the gray soup. A funnel was snaking down from a blocky wall cloud that protruded from the amorphous base of the storm. The storm itself was a cottony castle of soft edges, vaguely round, melting into the gray around it, its rotation not nearly as obvious visually as what he'd seen on radar. Only the light leaking from under the base suggested the mesocyclone, the area of rotation from which the funnel descended. Debris swirled under its tip as the funnel widened.

"Tornado," Brad said, beating Jack to it. Andre focused on their star, and Razor aimed at the twister as the condensation funnel connected with the ground, darkening and widening, getting closer, moving far too quickly for them to consider deploying the Bubble. They all stood, mesmerized, as the tornado churned up the dirt. Dust blew past them and into the storm, and for a few seconds, they could barely stand in the inflow. Rain began to lash them, shifting directions, indicating the influence of the rotation. Wynda came up behind Jack. "Do we need to move?" she asked quietly.

"I think it will stay north of us," he said. "But if we want any hope of keeping up with these storms, we're going to have to move soon. The whole line is developing fast and advancing east at highway speeds."

"And we'll have to get on a paved road," Devlin said, stepping next to them. "We're too slow on these farm roads."

Andre turned to film Saffire, with the menacing tornado over her shoulder.

"Being this close to a tornado takes my breath away," she said softly to the lens as scattered raindrops glimmered on her skin and hair. Her voice rose and fell like a hypnotic song, captured by Michiko's boom mike. "You can't understand the power of it until you're this close. Can you hear it? It's a rushing sound. The wind is swirling all around us. It's touching us. The rain is enfolding us. It's like we're part of the storm." The others gasped as the tornado hit a clump of trees and tossed them easily into the air. She looked over her shoulder as the pines spun around the tornado and crashed to the ground. "My heart is with anyone in the path of this storm," she continued, turning back to the camera. "I'm humbled to see the power of nature today. I think we all feel small when we see something like this. It's frightening, but I have to tell you, it's also magnificent. Nature is powerful, sometimes even deadly, but it's also beautiful." She earnestly held the camera's gaze for a moment, then spun around to watch.

"She's good," Wynda said, sounding just a bit surprised.

"I think she really meant it," Devlin said.

"It's getting away from us," Jack said, though he, too, was moved by Saffire's intensity. For a moment, he'd thought she was talking to him. He shook off the feeling and assessed their position. "We're going to have to circumnavigate, get east and north."

The tornado had already moved far enough away that visibility was noticeably poorer. "Get in the vans!" Wynda shouted. "We're going to try to get in front of it! Michiko, you drive the crew car. Razor, join her and get the tornado and drive-bys." The producer ran to the right side of Van One and hopped in the side door, taking a seat next to Jack as the others grabbed their positions.

"Keep going east, then north at the next crossroads," Devlin said from the middle seat, tapping on the laptop. He'd moved its mount to a spot between the front seats so he could navigate without displacing Saffire. "Jack?"

"Sounds good. We need to get up to that paved east-west road and then to the north option. I think this storm is heading to the Interstate."

"We might lose it with all this stairstepping," Devlin said.

"Can't be helped," Jack said, "if you want to see what it's going to do next."

Already, the wide funnel was fading into the gray to their north, to the point where they couldn't tell if it was still in contact with the ground.

"The important thing is to stay in front of the tornado," Brad said, with the authority of someone who'd been caught by one.

"If we can see it," Jack murmured, trying to figure out what was happening as he scanned different radar images on his laptop. This tornado appeared to be weakening, but a new meso was forming to the northeast.

"I still want to deploy," Wynda said, but her tone was less resolute.

"We can't make that decision now," Jack said. "We just have to haul ass."

Brad did his best. The van ripped and bounced through the gravel and dirt roads, which, fortunately, were rocky enough that the rain hadn't made them impassible. He still had to slow down for potholes and sudden turns, but he handled the whale with aplomb. Occasionally, Michiko pulled ahead so Razor could get shots of the van and Bubblevan flying by.

Jack indulged in a quick glance at Spotter Network. The moving dots showed chasers on the roads all over central Kansas. Half were on the Interstates, half on the gravel roads, trying to get in line to intercept their storm and three other potent supercells to the south. One cell to the north of their target had already crossed the front and died.

As Wynda's crew got closer to the paved road, they encountered more chase cars rushing through the grid, rats in a maze, trying to get their teeth into a highly potent wedge of cheese. The drivers paused at stop signs but otherwise attacked the roads with an almost comical aggression, moving far faster than any speed limit would possibly recommend. Their crew saw two chase cars and a van that had skidded into ditches, and like everyone else, the Palatable convoy kept going, letting the fallen pay their own price for reckless driving. The tow trucks would be busy.

"Here it is!" Saffire said excitedly as they approached the first paved road.

"Thank god," Wynda said. "Brad's a terrifying driver."

"I thought he did pretty well," Devlin said. "Turn right!"

Finally eastbound, and despite the almost entirely flat landscape, they could now make out no features of the storm they were trying to catch. The sky remained gray and dense. The road bent hard northeast. "Where is it, Jack?" Wynda asked.

"Almost due north. We have a couple of stair-steps to do, but we should catch it somewhere west of Salina on I-70. The first tornado occluded, but there's a monster hook developing. This thing is going to be huge."

"And?"

They knew what she was asking. Devlin leaned into the back seat and looked over Jack's shoulder. Jack drew a line on the screen showing their position and the storm's.

"I can't see how we can deploy," Devlin said. "We're going to be lucky to catch it. But we can make that call when we get a visual."

"That's all I ask," Wynda said.

AURELIUS and his team had raced east and then northeast from their post in Russell, chasing the northernmost storm with high hopes. They got on it relatively quickly. It had formed near the triple point, as Ernie had predicted, but when it crossed the cold front, it weakened and lost most of its rotation.

After Ernie explained the situation, Aurelius allowed himself forty seconds of unfettered cursing before resuming camera-friendly dialogue. "We're heading south to catch the next storm in the line," Aurelius said over the radio so the techies would hear. "But we have to go west first."

So they backtracked, heading west again to Russell and then south, trying to get on the next storm. The sky was beginning to clear.

"What the hell is going on?" Aurelius demanded.

"The dryline is catching up to us. The storm we wanted is east of us," said Ernie, "and it's moving northeast, about fifty-five miles an hour."

"So we should retrace our steps?"

"No point. We'll never catch it."

"That is not what I want to hear," Aurelius said, pulling off on the shoulder, looking for a way out of this aggravating situation.

"Everyone online is sad we haven't seen any tornadoes yet," Evie reported from the back seat.

"How sweet of them," Aurelius said. "What the fuck. We have a plane. Duncan!" he roared into the radio.

"Yes, sir?"

"We can't catch it on wheels. Launch the plane. See what you can get. Stay high and dry and get in front of it."

There was silence for a minute, and Aurelius wondered what they were discussing.

"OK," Duncan finally said. "From our view, these storms look cheek to jowl on radar, but we think we can slip through. And maybe we'll catch it. Stand by."

Aurelius jumped out, followed by the rest of his crew, cameras at the ready. The techies prepared the plane, and while Thing One filmed Aurelius, Thing Two captured the graceful launch of the UAV as it catapulted off the rail on the back of the truck.

"I never get tired of watching it," Aurelius told the camera with almost convincing enthusiasm. "The plane is going after a storm that has already produced two tornadoes. It's a plucky little flying robot, and we wish it well," he added solemnly. A little anthropomorphizing never hurt.

JACK HAD A BAD FEELING BEFORE. He had a worse feeling now. They were within ten miles of I-70, and the storm was again in their view, if one could call it that. It was a dark mass to their west. Uneven light shone dimly around it, suggesting a base, or rain, or a tornado. It was all suggestion, tricks of the eyes. Radar images indicated a large and intense circulation, with massive shear. They couldn't see a damn thing.

"The updraft should be just to our west," he said as they got within five miles of I-70. "Still moving northeast, fast."

"Should I get on the Interstate?" Brad asked. He sounded

more tired than worried. Everyone in the van felt the tension of chasing something they couldn't see.

"I'd stop," Jack said. "Devlin?"

"Yeah. I can't see it in there, can you?"

"Stop, then," Wynda said. "Let's get out and get a good look." She picked up the radio. "Everyone, we're going to pull over up here and try to see the tornado. If we have time, we'll deploy."

At least she said "if," Jack thought. No point in obsessing over the radar. If a tornado was to be seen, he was going to see it. He tried to shake off his withdrawal headache and sense of foreboding as he got out of the van with the others, grabbing his Nikon just in case. He scrutinized the western horizon and tried to understand what he was seeing. In these highly unstable conditions, there was convection everywhere, deceptive towers and wannabe storms and rain-cooled scud hanging low to the ground. Rain and mist spat at them. But the storm they wanted seemed to erase every telltale visual feature as if it were an atmospheric black hole. It was dark. Fucking *dark*.

"Is there a tornado in there?" Saffire was at his side, and she sounded uneasy.

"I can't tell, honestly, but I think so," he said. "The radar can't look like that without there being a tornado. There's just no way."

"Why can't we see it?"

He looked around. The others were enrapt by the storm, and Pole was still in the truck that held the Bubble. Pole rarely got out, but he seemed to pay attention. He'd saved their asses earlier by spotting the developing tornado overhead.

Jack put an arm around Saffire's shoulders and kissed her cheek. "It's wrapped in rain. I want to see it more than anybody," he said. "But I think maybe it knows."

She chuckled. "You shouldn't have come. Darth Vader knows you're on board."

"Exactly." He released her as he saw Razor's camera panning the group. "Tornado's that way," he said, a little too scornfully, and the cameraman pointed back toward the storm without acknowledging him.

"Easy," Saffire whispered, kissing his earlobe once. He got a whiff of lavender as she moved toward the front of the group to chat with Brad and Devlin for the cameras, and his headache inexplicably eased.

The wind picked up around them, and Jack could hear their weather radio screeching again in the van. As the storm neared, it seemed to suck the light out of the sky. Dim rain curtains moved around it now. The whole thing gave the impression of grinding across the landscape, shifting and turning like a great and dismal machine obscured by black veils. The inflow intensified, and so did the rain. The grass around them bent toward the presumed tornado, and the vans shook. The darkness passed just to their north, and Jack felt a creeping sensation on his skin as the wind shifted.

"Are we safe?" Devlin asked.

"We're out of its way, at least," Jack said. "We should follow it north, go east on the highway. We might get a look at it from a different angle, see what's really in there."

They loaded up and started north at a more cautious pace until they saw the overpass in front of them. This was a desolate intersection, with just one tiny gas station to mark the exit to the Interstate. They took the right and ramped onto I-70, keeping the blackest part of the storm in front of them. Maybe it was just rain, after all, Jack mused. No funnel, no debris field. Trucks came up beside them, heedless of the storm, just another day hauling cargo from one end of

America to the other. While drizzle spattered their windows, and the wind remained intense, the darkness was already retreating to the northeast.

They approached a slight rise and crested the hill, and the picture changed in an instant. With a click of the gods' remote, they were looking at hell. In the rain and mist, the terrible aftermath of a giant's rampage lay strewn across their path.

3

FALLING UP

B rad's first instinct was to slam on the brakes, and Jack heard the SUV's tires screech behind them as Michiko tried to stop. She did, just.

"Pull over," Jack snapped. "As far off the highway as you can get. We don't want a pileup along with this mess."

Brad said nothing but accelerated lightly and parked the van well off the shoulder. The other vehicles followed.

Wynda grabbed the radio. "Get out and shoot this. And —" Her voice quavered for a moment. "Help them. If you aren't shooting, see if you can help them."

Jack stepped out of the van. He didn't know where to start, so he called 911 and the Weather Service, just to make sure they knew. Then he pocketed his phone and did a quick survey of the scene.

Gray swaths of rain enshrouded this blighted patch of highway. Perhaps most eerie was the quiet; no vehicles were moving, and any that came upon the scene stopped at its fringes, unwilling to broach the nightmare's borders. Debris was strewn over at least a quarter mile. Half a dozen tractor-trailers were on their side, most of them blown off the road. Passenger cars, ten or more, were tossed every which way, some more crumpled than others. A yellow school bus lay on its side in the eastbound lane, with most of its windows smashed or bent. Girls in maroon and white soccer uniforms were struggling to climb out the open back door.

"We'll help the girls," Saffire said, pulling on Devlin's arm and heading for the bus. Wynda and Brad followed with the camera crew.

Pole appeared at Jack's elbow in a yellow rain jacket, carrying a medical bag.

"Do you know what to do with that?" Jack asked.

"I dropped out of a lot of things after I dropped out of meteorology. I was an EMT for six months. Come on."

They stopped at the nearest big rig that lay on its side. Jack peered in the partially smashed front window. "Somebody's in there," he said. He rapped on the metal frame. "Can you hear me?"

The driver, an older man, was suspended in his seat belt, and he looked up and around as if he were just becoming aware of his surroundings. "Yeah, I'm all right," the man said. He unbuckled the belt and struggled to push open the driver's door, which now pointed to the sky. Small cuts bled in his weathered face, framed by thin, gray hair. "I didn't see it coming," he told them, sounding embarrassed. "Was it a tornado?"

"Sure was," Pole said as he and Jack helped him out, settling him on the grass of the median. "I'll come back to make sure you're OK, but there are a lot of other people here we need to check out."

"Go," the man said. He reached up to his neck and a silver cross pendant there, hand trembling, and rubbed it between forefinger and thumb as Pole and Jack walked farther up the road.

"I think we should split up," Pole said. "Yell if you find something really bad."

"OK," Jack said. He felt jittery and angry, a rage he immediately acknowledged as foolish. Was he angry at the storm? Angry he hadn't seen more? He didn't know. He glanced over at the school bus, where his companions had the situation in hand. Then he started moving from one vehicle to the next to see if he could help. The truckers seemed to have fared best. Most were merely stunned. One driver appeared to have a neck injury. The ambulances began to arrive, and Jack flagged down medics as he came across problems he couldn't solve. Tow trucks crept up on the shoulders. Traffic began to stack up on either side of the damage path, though a couple of cars tried to pick their way through until police came and blocked the site. The officers started the painstaking process of turning the Interstate traffic back the way it had come.

The cars hit by the tornado ranged from wildly mangled to barely dented; some had simply been spun or lifted a bit, and the drivers were on their cell phones, breathlessly calling their loved ones to express the joy of being alive and the misery of the aftermath. A few were much less lucky, and there was one tableau — a half-crushed car with a bloodied couple in the front — that gave Jack chills. The young woman who'd been driving looked at him and extended a pale hand through her broken-out window. She wore just one ring, a gold band with a small diamond. An engagement ring? She couldn't speak. Her blue eyes were wild, her black pupils wide. Her male companion wasn't moving. Jack lightly held her hand, muttered a reassurance he didn't feel and flagged down an ambulance that had just arrived from Salina. As the medical technicians ran up, he released the woman's hand and got out of their way, at a loss.

He was used to the violence of tornadoes but not to seeing their effects up close. He always thought of storms as a spectacle, a scientific puzzle, a thrill. Not this instrument of carnage. He watched himself withdraw to the empty room in his head with blank walls and no windows, the place he always went when emotions threatened his equilibrium. Then he looked down and saw a drop of blood on his hand. That spot of scarlet, so vivid in the dreary devastation around him, dragged him back. In a puddle on the side of the road, he carefully washed it off.

Jack stood and covered his ears and closed his eyes. He breathed deeply, pulling the chilly, damp air into his lungs, abruptly noticing how wet his hair and jeans and T-shirt had become. He was starting to find the cool core inside him when he heard the siren. He snapped his eyes open, dropped his arms and looked around. The sound was gone. "Damn it," he murmured.

A buzzing overhead prompted him to look up. A plane? No. A UAV. It had to be Aurelius Zane's flying machine, circling the scene. At least there were no helicopters in sight. Jack looked over to where an ambulance crew was checking out the soccer team. One girl was laid out on a stretcher, but she was talking. Saffire had her arms around two others, chatting with them as if she were a teenager herself, and one of the girls laughed. Saffire, so light of heart. She looked up for a moment. Jack tried to catch her eye but couldn't. He had the impulse he felt before, to run to her, to grab her by the hand and take her away from here, to make their own journey. But right now, there was only the ruin that surrounded them. Maybe that was all there ever would be. He mentally smacked himself for his mawkish ruminations and started walking again, relieved to note the drizzle was thinning to an occasional raindrop. He saw light in the west. The dryline was moving east, slowly clearing out the sky.

A young man, college age, sat on the grassy fringe of the shoulder, smoking, his clothes disheveled. Jack sat next to him. "You OK?"

"Yeah. My car's not." He gestured toward a compact car that lay on its roof. "Good airbags."

"Let me see that a minute." Jack reached toward the cigarette. The young man handed it over, and Jack took one long, sweet drag. "Thanks. I just quit," he said, handing it back with a hint of a grin. "Good luck."

Jack stood, feeling a slight rush from the cigarette, and looked around again, spotting a van he hadn't seen before lying on its side in the grassy median. It took him just an instant to recognize the warped, metal-frame basket hanging from its roof and the decals on the bumper. He broke into a run, fighting the clawing weight of dread.

"Marcus!" he shouted as he ran. "Marcus!" It was undoubtedly the hail-catcher, his friend's research vehicle. He saw the windshield smashed and the driver's-door window broken and moved around the front so he could look inside.

"I'm here, asshole." Marcus's voice floated up to him — not from inside but out. Jack looked around and saw his friend sitting well beyond the banged-up van, in the grass with two other young men. Marcus's head was wrapped with a bandage that held a pad in place over his forehead, but still, a little blood seeped through. His dark curls stuck out every which way, and he held his glasses in his hand. They were broken.

Jack felt a swoon of relief as he walked over to them. "You OK?"

"My wrist hurts like hell, and so does my head, but I'm OK. Renny was wearing his seat belt, and he's fine, but Frank's the worst. He was in the back."

Frank, the redhead, patted an arm that was already in a sling. "Broken, they think," he said in a raspy voice. "No big deal. I'll get a ride to the hospital when they have one."

"We can give you a ride," Jack said. "We can give you all a ride to Salina."

"I have to wait to get the van taken care of," Marcus said, his face lined with woe. "My poor van."

"The university's poor van," Jack said, trying to elicit a smile. "It'll be OK. You've fixed it before. How'd you get caught out here, anyway?"

Marcus looked even more chagrined. "I thought we were ahead of it. It was moving so fast, and we couldn't see a fucking thing. It was totally rain-wrapped. Did you see where it went from here?"

Jack had a split-second thought: Like Marcus, they'd almost tried to beat it, too. "I'm pretty sure it went north of Salina, at least."

"That's something," Marcus said. "Jack, sometimes I wonder what I'm doing out here."

"You're chasing storms," Jack said, feeling some of his assurance return in the realization that his friend was OK, and so was he. "What else are you going to do?"

WHEN THEY HAD DONE ALL that seemed reasonable, when the ambulances had taken away the most badly hurt, when the police had reopened the shoulder and half a lane on each side, and when another bus had come to transport the schoolgirls, Jack and the crew shifted out of first-responder mode. They boarded their vehicles and began to make their way eastbound through thickening traffic. Frank rode in the crew vehicle with Wynda, Michiko and Razor, who would drop him at the nearest hospital. Pole brought up the rear with the Bubblevan. And in Van One, where the mood was somber, Devlin drove, chatting with Brad in the front. Andre lay on the middle seat, staring at the ceiling, and Saffire sat in the back with Jack. He'd looked at data only long enough to ensure they weren't in the path of more severe weather; the line of tornado-producing supercells was east of them, speeding toward the Missouri border and congealing into a slightly less terrifying cluster of storms. The FM radio played at low volume, rattling off a stream of weather warnings.

Jack put his arm around Saffire, and she lay her head against his shoulder. "Have you chased many days like this?" she asked.

"A few," he said. "I never had to deal with anything like what we just saw. When I was in — I've seen what a tornado does to a town, but I never got that close to what it does." He knew what it had done in Prairie Rock, the lives it took. But he'd been able to walk away. He'd left right after it hit. Today, he couldn't look away from the aftermath. He looked into the bloody face of the woman in the car and what was, he was sure, her dying companion and felt as if he couldn't handle it.

"I keep thinking of Mama out there in the Panhandle with her rotten old storm cellar, and I worry," Saffire said. "I worry all the time."

"It'll do," Jack whispered, kissing her hair. "She grew up out there. She knows what she's doing. Anyway, the chance that she'll see anything like this in her lifetime is extremely low."

"I hope so."

"You looked like a pro with those girls today."

"Good, strong kids," she said. "They told me they were coming back from a tournament and didn't even know there were supposed to be storms. I have to wonder whether the bus driver had any idea. They get warnings, don't they? Was he not paying attention?"

"People think they're immune, I guess," Jack said. "They don't take precautions. It would be so simple. A weather radio, or even a regular radio, could have tipped him and the others off. Assuming they'd listened to the warning."

"They can't all be you."

"I wasn't much help today, either," he said. "I almost had us drive into it."

She looked up at him. "But you didn't."

"No, I didn't. I guess I — we were lucky, too." Incredibly lucky, he thought, as he recalled his almost casual decision to let the storm pass, his feeble ministrations afterward. He thought about what Marcus had said and wondered, too, why he was here. And why did he want to be so close to this particular woman in this particular moment? Typically any woman would do, any body to take him out of his thoughts. He leaned in and kissed her, not caring who saw or knew. Saffire's warmth, her life energized him. He brushed her hair from her forehead, and she snuggled up against him as Devlin drove them to their hotel in Salina.

WYNDA WONDERED how many more awful days they would have, but she had to acknowledge that today could have been a whole lot worse. They'd filmed a dramatic tornado and avoided being smashed by another one. To think, though, that they'd been so close and not deployed the Bubble was particularly frustrating. Especially as she felt more and more unsure of Brad. She couldn't put her finger on why, exactly, but he'd been on the phone a lot and texting and generally acting peculiar. More to the point, he'd been brimming with enthusiasm, which was definitely odd.

After the crew had dropped off Frank at the hospital and they'd checked into their hotel, she took the SUV and sought out a restaurant where she could get a few minutes' peace and a bowl of pasta. She ended up at an Italian place downtown with checkered tablecloths and battery-operated candles. The restaurant was about half full, and she requested a booth in a dark corner so she could isolate herself as much as possible. She was halfway through her spaghetti and meatballs, a glass of pinot noir and a steamy e-book on her smartphone when she heard a noisy group enter the restaurant. She looked up to see Aurelius Zane and his people, who got a table for seven near the front of the dining room. Was he actually following her? No, that was paranoia, surely. But he did seem to have a knack for ending up where she was, and she wasn't sure she minded. At least he hadn't been sucked up by a tornado today. As much trouble as he'd been, she didn't like the idea of a world without Aurelius Zane. Few men had gotten to her the way he had, and even though she had no intention of becoming emotionally involved with him again, the memory of certain nights in the jungle was a pleasant one she felt content to preserve in her mental album of Not Altogether Horrible Experiences.

She ordered another glass of pinot and took her time finishing her meal as she observed Aurelius and his crew. He was in his congenial mode, telling stories, laughing at others' jokes, putting everyone at ease. Wynda remembered that about him, just as she remembered his tyrannical and demanding moods when he felt he wasn't being portrayed as grandly as he required, or when things weren't going quite right. Perhaps he was having a good day, then. She supposed he needed one after the helicopter debacle, though he'd admitted nothing in the interviews she saw.

He didn't discover her until several minutes later. He'd excused himself from his party and headed for the restroom, which happened to be tucked in a hallway behind Wynda's booth.

"Ms. Wexcombe!" he said with genuine pleasure, his cheeks pink from the beer that had been flowing at his table. "I'm so happy to find you here. Please don't leave. I need to see a man about a horse, but I'll be right back." He vanished around the corner, and she debated whether to make a run for it. She decided if he could tolerate further conversation, so could she.

He reappeared. "Just a moment," he said, then headed back to his table and, to her shock, paid the check. Aurelius slapped the backs of the guys and squeezed the shoulders of the women and sent them on their way before returning to her booth and sitting on the bench opposite. Now she was curious.

"Aurelius," she said cordially. "Aren't you missing your coach?"

"Oh, I told them I'd get a ride," he said. "I couldn't let you drink alone." He flagged down the server and ordered a bottle of what Wynda was drinking, preemptively pressing a fifty-dollar bill into the server's hand. She cleared Wynda's plates, left a folder with the check and hurried off to retrieve the wine.

"Did you have a flutter on the horses or something?" Wynda asked. "Win a few?"

"Hardly," he said. "I did, however, get a modest royalty from one of my volcano videos deposited into my account, so I thought I'd treat my team. They work incredibly hard, and it hasn't been an easy week."

"But it wasn't your drone that got into trouble, was it?" she asked with a cheeky smile.

"Of course not," Aurelius said. "But they're feeling the pressure." The waitress arrived with another glass and the bottle, opened it and poured them each a generous ration. "In fact, my drone shot remarkable video of the carnage today on the highway."

Wynda sat up. "Did you film the tornado?"

He sighed. "No. We got there too late. Did you?"

"We couldn't see the bloody thing. So no." She drank more of the wine. Complex and mellow, from California. California sounded nice about now.

He rubbed the rim of his glass until it sang, then clutched the stem and quaffed a fair gulp. "So you didn't deploy your device?"

Why did he keep asking about that? "No, we did not. Logistics," she said, by way of not-too-detailed explanation.

"I see." He took another deep drink. "Wynda, have you ever considered working together?"

"We already have worked together," she said in an innocent tone, matching him sip for sip.

"Working together again. Perhaps even now. Couldn't your documentary benefit from the Zane brand?"

The question irritated her. Perhaps he was a brand, but she was working on a little branding of her own. "What role could you possibly have in my documentary? Especially when you're starring in your own?"

"You know what I could do for you," he said.

Feeling a little buzz from the wine, she decided to allow herself a deflection. "I know what you could do *to* me," she said, her tone neutral.

Aurelius raised his eyebrows. His perfectly cut blond bangs framed his widening eyes as he took a healthy gulp of his wine. "Ms. Wexcombe, I wonder if we are talking about the same thing."

"I know you could make my life completely miserable," she went on. "Or you could make my life a bit more interesting, at least for the near future."

"How near?" he asked, leaning closer, sounding confused.

"Very near," she said, drinking a little more wine and running her tongue over her lips. She loved teasing him like this. It was too easy.

"Wynda, would you like me to fly in your machine?"

At least he was being direct, finally. But she didn't plan to be. "My motor could use a good run, now that you mention it," she said, her tone silky. Truth was, she might be teasing him, but the wine and his charismatic if dopey presence had her feeling that, perhaps, she wasn't just kidding.

"It has a motor?" Aurelius asked, perplexed.

"I have a motor, and it could use a tune-up," Wynda said, refilling their glasses.

"You're flirting with me!"

"My god, you are daft," she said crossly.

The look on his face transformed as he reached out a hand for hers, cautiously, obviously remembering the wrenching he got at the diner in Amarillo. He switched modes now that he knew what game he was playing. "You're so beautiful in this candlelight."

"Fake candlelight." She showed her dimples. Let him try. She might let him do more.

"Your hair is a red flame. You set me afire."

"Not likely, considering the candles really are fake."

"Oh, don't tease me," he said, squeezing her hand and quaffing his glass of wine in one go.

She matched his movement, draining her glass. "I thought you liked to be teased," she said. "And I remember exactly how."

"Oh, you vex me," he cried, leaning over to grab her by the chin and plant a kiss on her mouth. She closed her eyes and melted into it, remembering hot nights long ago and thinking there might be a spot in her mental album where she could add one more page. He really was quite a good kisser. And she was getting quite drunk.

"We'd better get a cab," she said. "Your hotel or mine?"

"We're in the same one," he said, his voice still excited. "Waitress? Could you please call us a cab?"

"The same one? Are you following me?"

"Of course not," Aurelius said. "Just because I consistently act on a strong need to be near you doesn't mean I'm following you."

This argument did not make much sense to Wynda after four glasses of wine, but she tucked a wad of cash into the bill folder, grabbed her bag and stood up, a bit unsteadily. "All right, jungle boy," she said. "Remind me why I used to like you so much."

He took her by the arm, led her outside to the nearly deserted street, and nibbled on her neck until the taxi came.

JACK TOOK a shower to wash the bleak day off him, dressed and went to the hotel lobby to see if anyone else from the crew was ready. They'd agreed to meet at a sports bar down the street for a late dinner.

The lobby was quiet and softly lit. This was one of the nicer generic hotels, the kind whose decorative tables were topped with enormous modern vases filled with a few stalks of whatever gigantic flower was in season. Some kind of lily, it looked like.

He sat on one of the couches to wait for a familiar face and grabbed a magazine, but he didn't open it. He lay his head back against the cushions and slipped almost immediately into a doze. A hand on his shoulder interrupted the siren; he'd only just been aware of it before it vanished. Again.

"Sorry to wake you," Pole said. Andre was with him.

"I'm glad you did."

"Listen," Andre said. "We think there's something you should know. Have you seen any of the stuff we've shot so far?"

"No," Jack said, wondering where this was going.

"Wynda's been hoarding the footage," Andre said, "but she's out, and we were talking about some stuff she's been asking about, and stuff she's asked us to shoot, and we decided to take a look. She has her laptop and prime drives locked up in her room, but the backup drive was in the van. So we looked. And I just don't feel right about it."

"About what?"

"Just come up to my room for a second," Andre said. "We'll give you a quick idea."

Mystified, Jack followed them to Andre's room on the

second floor. The cameraman had a laptop open on the desk. "I found this clip reel on the drive," he said, double-clicking a movie icon on the screen.

"And why are you here?" Jack asked Pole.

"I overheard something Wynda said to Razor back in Oklahoma City and then in Amarillo. I wasn't sure what they were doing, but now I am."

The image flickered and settled on the Bubble in its hangar, its base in OKC. A few of their crew walked by the camera. In another minute, the video incarnation of Jack walked up to the Bubble, looked it over and got in. Then he beckoned someone off-camera, and Saffire entered the frame. Jack wasn't used to seeing himself on camera, let alone seeing himself make out with a girl. He didn't like it. "What the hell is this?" he asked.

"There's more. She has this whole collection," Andre said, fast-forwarding through window-cam shots of Jack and Saffire interacting in the van; a few seconds of that deliriously drunken kiss in the hot tub in Amarillo, shot from one of the rooms; a close-up of Jack gazing raptly at Saffire when they were doing the walking shot on the dirt road; and little moments between the two of them he hadn't even been aware of. "She yelled at me for not getting more footage of you two on that little break we had," Andre continued, "but I'd already made it clear I was not playing her game."

"What the fuck would she want with this?" Jack asked.

"It is a reality show," Pole said. "Perhaps she feels it has to have prurient content."

"Oh, come on. We're here to shoot tornadoes and the Bubble."

"But the Bubble hasn't flown yet," Andre pointed out.

"This is stupid. Does Saffire know about this?" And then a

vile thought occurred to Jack as he watched Andre and Pole exchange glances.

"We don't know," Andre said.

Jack remembered Saffire's offhand remark about always knowing the cameras were on. About how a hot tub shot might be the best thing for her career. He couldn't wrap his head around the idea that she might deliberately put their affair in front of the lens. Would she?

"Turn that shit off," Jack said as a clip came up of their kiss after the helicopter crash. "I need a drink."

JACK WAS ALREADY WELL into his fourth bourbon at the bar at The Outfield when Saffire and Michiko walked in. Razor was notably absent, but it was just as well, because Jack needed a little time to consider whether he was going to punch his face in.

Brad and Devlin played pool. Michiko wandered over to where Andre and Pole sampled the place's collection of pinball machines. This bar even had the old *Twister* movie pinball, with its fan on top, Van Halen riffs and Bill Paxton shouting "Everybody underground now!" Jack heard it dimly on occasion amid the racket of the bar, where people flirted, fed the jukebox, ate fried food and watched at least a dozen TVs showing a variety of ball-related activities. The flat-screen in front of him, unfortunately, featured an evangelist's earnest pleas for money, and none of the busy bartenders seemed inclined to change it. He held up his drink and swirled it, trying to make a tornado around its diminishing orb of ice.

Saffire walked over to Jack, smiling that dazzling smile. "I was hoping we'd catch you," she said. "We grabbed some food at the buffet down the road first. At least they have a salad bar there." She leaned in to kiss his cheek. He didn't return the favor, though his body wanted to. That was one response he couldn't control.

"You didn't miss much," Jack said, pointing at the TV with his glass. "Jesus saves and the devil spends. Let me buy you a drink."

"Is that a country song?" she asked, nonplussed.

"No, but it should be."

"Looks like you have a considerable head start." She took the stool next to his and dropped her tiny, sparkly purse on the wooden bar top.

"I'm just getting started."

"That's too bad." Her eyes twinkled. She wore a new, eye-catching outfit — snug jeans, a white tank top and a checked blue-and-white blouse half-open over it. She leaned in to whisper in his ear. "I thought maybe we'd have a drink and then head back to the hotel."

"Better make sure a camera's around first," Jack said. So that's how he was going to bring it up. The liquor was doing the talking.

"What are you talking about? It's nice to have a break from the cameras," she said.

"They're always watching, though. You said it yourself."

A barman came up to them, scanned Saffire appreciatively and asked her what she wanted. She ordered a split of champagne, a brave choice in a joint like this.

"I said I'm aware when they're watching. Everyone on television is." She took a sip from the glass that arrived with the tiny bottle. "Is there a reason we're talking about this? Idle drunken chatter, maybe?"

"Never idle. But quite possibly drunken." He drained his drink. "So you aren't aware of Wynda's little movie project?"

"You mean filming Brad in the Bubble? Yes, I am well acquainted with that project," she said with a chuckle. "I think you need another one of those just to make sense."

"Good idea," he said. "Bourbon!" He was a little too loud, but the same bartender came over, wearing a small frown, and brought him a fresh glass with an ice ball gleaming like a mountain in the middle of the caramel-brown elixir. He took a sweet, long sip, savoring the burn before the ice melted and opened and tamed the whiskey.

Saffire looked him over for several seconds before touching his arm. "Jack," she said, "what's wrong?"

"So you're not familiar with Wynda's little movie project. The one with all the clips of you and me making googly eyes at each other and sticking our tongues down each other's throats."

Saffire drew back as if she'd been slapped. "What? She's done what?"

"It could be the best thing for your career," he said, knowing it was ugly even as he said it.

"She's — she has clips of us? How bad is it? It would be the worst thing for me right now, for the new show …" She looked away, her voice trailing off as her face revealed a terrible anxiety, a fleeting expression Jack had never seen her wear before. She recovered herself. "How could you — you're suggesting I knew about this? That I encouraged this in some way? What is wrong with you?"

The conversation had gone downhill fast from her gentle "What's wrong?" to "What's wrong with you?" Jack felt a wave of vertigo as he spun on the stool to face her. "You didn't know?" Even as he asked it, he understood that she didn't.

Saffire shook her head in a mixture of disbelief and disgust. "I can't talk to you right now," she said. "To think you thought what's between us is so low, so mean. I really can't talk to you right now."

Jack was flummoxed for a moment as she grabbed her purse and walked swiftly toward the door. He didn't want her to go. He was thinking and moving in slow motion. He fumbled in his wallet and slapped down enough money to cover their drinks, then half-stumbled past the pool tables and pinball machines to the door.

"Saffire!" he called as he got outside. The dark parking lot, like the bar, was full for a Sunday night, and there was a fresh breeze with the passage of the front. He looked around and didn't see her. "Saffire!" he shouted again. He caught a brief movement under a streetlamp and a glimpse of her across the road, walking fast toward the hotel. "You shouldn't walk alone!" He put his feet in motion, but they weren't working too well. A brief acceleration to a run almost brought him to his knees. There was no way he could match her pace. So he walked after her, only more slowly, keeping her in sight for the next five minutes as he followed her.

By the time he reached the lobby, she'd vanished into her room. He tried to remember what number it was. She'd told him at check-in. Three hundred something. Three hundred thirty-something. He took the elevator, leaning his forehead against the cool metal door. When it opened, it sent him stumbling into the corridor. He deciphered the sign with the room numbers and took a right. When he reached three-thirty, he started knocking. Turns out, people aren't real thrilled with their doors being pummeled late at night in a hotel, and the few who answered theirs told him to get lost. Only about half of the ten rooms in the three-thirties offered a response. It was at the last of these that he heard Saffire when she said, "Go away."

"Please let me in."

There was silence.

"Please."

"You've got to be kidding."

He tried to see something, anything through the security peephole. "Please."

"You're going to wake up the whole hotel."

"They can sleep when they're dead. Let me in."

"I told you, I can't talk to you right now. Get out." She sounded more tired than angry. Well, tired *and* angry. And sad.

"I'm not in. Let me in, and then you can tell me to get out."

"No."

Jack placed his palms against the door and lay his cheek against the varnished wood surface. "I have to talk to you," he pleaded, knowing he was drunk, knowing he had no leash for his emotions, and knowing that he needed to talk to her more than he needed to do anything else in the world right now. "Saffire, I can't go through life without talking to you."

The silence was a lot longer this time before she responded. "We'll talk tomorrow," she said. "But only if you go away now."

He hung his head, feeling as if he'd let some crucial part of his self-control go and would never get it back. He hugged the door for a few minutes, mentally willing her to open it before he let go and walked unsteadily down the hallway. He found the stairs, letting gravity bring him down to the second floor and his room and his big, empty bed.

HANGOVERS for a few and accumulated exhaustion for the others muted the crew's morning as they drifted into the autumn-hued breakfast room. They piled their plates with free hotel eggs and waffles, sat at the tables and flipped through newspapers and computer tablets. Jack filled his foam cup with coffee and claimed a table with his laptop, looking for any of the players he'd have to confront before he could get his head back in order: Saffire, Wynda or Razor.

He'd just finished a quick data analysis suggesting tomorrow might offer a good chance of storms when Wynda appeared. She looked exhausted but cheerful, and she had the nerve to sit at Jack's table after she'd cooked her self-serve waffle and garnished it with butter and syrup. She settled in with her foam plate, plastic utensils and pale orange juice and looked over his shoulder at the computer model he'd been perusing.

"Is that for tomorrow? Western Kansas, then? That's what that squiggle is, isn't it? A low? I saw something about it on The Weather Channel this morning." She popped a bite of waffle in her mouth.

"Yes, a low," Jack said. "And I hope your plan is to film the tornadoes and not me and Saffire."

Wynda's chewing slowed almost imperceptibly. She swallowed and raised her bright blue eyes to his. "Jack, we film everyone on this crew. That's part of the agreement we all signed. We are all part of the show, and no one is excluded." She clearly knew what he was talking about, but she seemed undisturbed by his concern as she took another bite.

"I saw your little collection," he said. "Don't tell me everyone is getting equal treatment."

"I have clips of everyone organized for editing," she said smoothly. "Razor puts them together for me in case we have to develop alternate storylines for the documentary. It's standard procedure."

"This is not standard." Jack's voice was low and angry. "This show is supposed to be about tornadoes and Brad and the Bubble."

"Then we had better get him up in the Bubble, hadn't we?" She stood. "So nice to have breakfast with you."

She left her half-eaten waffle and walked away, saying hello to the others and telling them they'd hit the road in an hour. Jack felt as if he'd accomplished nothing. Wynda was a brick wall. He still had no idea of her intentions, other than the *prima facie* evidence of the video itself. And she'd managed to lay on an extra layer of pressure to launch the Bubble, a more and more ludicrous task.

Saffire still hadn't appeared. He popped a piece of nicotine gum into his mouth, closed his laptop and walked out, almost colliding with Razor in the process. "Excuse me," the tattooed cameraman said.

"Listen," Jack said without thinking. "If I catch your camera anywhere near me, I'll shove it so far down your throat you'll be filming your intestines."

As Jack walked away, he thought he heard Razor chuckle. He took a deep breath and kept walking. Walking and chewing his nasty gum at the same time. Maybe he needed to take up running, like Michiko, or some sort of sport that involved kicking things. Because if he didn't do something, he was going to explode.

JACK DIDN'T SEE Saffire until just before their departure. She tossed her bags in the back of Van One and assumed her preferred spot in the front seat, smiling and chatting with Devlin, who was driving again. Today, she wore an olive-green V-neck T-shirt and camouflage capri pants only she could make cute. Brad and Andre were in the second seat. Wynda, Michiko and Razor drove the crew SUV — apparently they'd had to retrieve it from downtown that morning, making Jack wonder just what Wynda had been up to last night — and Pole brought up the rear in the Bubble's transport. The caravan headed west on I-70, on the way to survey tornado damage and set up for tomorrow's chase in southwest Kansas. As they drove, they noted how much debris had been cleared from the path of the tornado they'd dodged the day before.

Jack observed Saffire's profile from his post in the third seat and tried not to think about how he was going to apologize for last night. To distract himself, he turned his gaze to the landscape, here cluttered with futuristic hulks: wind turbines, more revealed by each rise, spinning in a stout west wind that he knew would soon be shifting to the south. These white titans had sprouted up everywhere, chopping up the horizon, the clean, blank sky that served as a virginal canvas for Tornado Alley's storms. The turbines had their own grace, but to Jack, they were blights on nature's pure expanse. Energy versus beauty. Everything was a compromise. He didn't welcome this one.

As they dropped south, they spotted a farm that had been hit by one of yesterday's tornadoes. The crew found the homeowners sifting through the debris of what used to be the barn. The house was missing a small piece of roof, the hole already covered with a blue tarp. With a little convincing, the couple agreed to an interview, and Saffire did the honors, asking them what they'd seen and felt and heard. Jack had an impulse to rip Razor's camera away, but that was ridiculous.

This was Saffire's job, her profession, and she was good at it. As Razor and Wynda filmed Brad's thoughts on the mess, Jack began wandering through the site, looking for the little signatures of a tornado. He soon found one — a piece of straw pushed into a blasted tree trunk. So many leaves had been stripped off the tree, he had trouble identifying it, but it might have been a maple. He was marveling at this minute sign of the twister's power when he was startled by the snap of a twig behind him. He whirled to see a camera and was about to wreak damage when he focused and saw Andre.

"Whoa, man, it's just me," the shooter said. "What do you have there?"

Jack took a deep breath. "The wind forced this piece of straw into the tree. I'm always amazed by that."

Andre got in close with his shot, not asking Jack for an on-camera explanation, not filming him at all. Jack was grateful. Maybe another day he'd play Dr. Tornado on TV, but not today.

As he made his way through the scattered debris — wood from the barn, broken tools, a flowery gardening hat — Wynda approached him. "We need a good location to stay tonight so we can be in position for tomorrow," she said. "Recommendations?"

Jack thought for a moment about resuming their breakfast conversation but decided against it. There would be time later. "Garden City," he said. "We can drop south and west from there in the morning with no problem."

"Consider it done," she said cheerfully, as if nothing had happened, and walked off to gather the rest of the crew.

Jack lingered in the yard, hoping he might have a moment with Saffire, who was talking with the couple who'd lost their barn. His body ached, not just from the booze, not just from withdrawal, but from missing her. He could not casually lay a hand on her back, kiss her neck. He couldn't get that close to her until she spoke with him, and if anything, she was avoiding him. He felt as if he were withdrawing from more than the cigarettes.

When she broke away, he walked to the van ahead of her to open her door.

"Thank you, Dr. Andreas," she said pleasantly as she got in, but he heard another note in her voice. She was still hurt. An emotional woman was not a creature Jack enjoyed being around, but he took it as a sign of his growing irrationality that he wanted to be near her anyway, to make up for last night. He gave her a look of pure contrition as he closed her door.

When they got underway again, he pulled out his phone and texted her. That was one means of communication the cameras were unlikely to pick up.

"Dinner tonight?" he typed.

She picked up her phone from where it sat in one of the dashboard cubbies and shot him a quick glance before focusing on the device. "I may not be hungry," she sent back.

"All you eat is salad. You have to be hungry."

He saw a little smile at the corner of her mouth. "Give me one reason."

"Because I think you enjoy seeing a man beg."

"True. Another reason," she typed.

"Because I want to say I am sorry. Very very very very sorry."

She cocked her head and looked out the windshield for a moment as the van cruised across the plain. The skeleton of a cottonwood tree slipped by their windows, stark against the cloud-streaked blue sky.

"OK," she messaged.

He didn't type any more for fear of losing the ground he'd gained. But he felt the beginnings of a smile as he looked at the curls cascading toward her shoulders, a smile that grew bigger when she turned her head slightly, just enough to acknowledge him. At least two-thirds of him cursed his weakness, his ability to be captivated by so small a gesture. And a third of him told the rest to fuck off. He was having dinner with Saffire. She was talking to him again.

❧

AURELIUS WAS nothing short of giddy after his night with Wynda. He never dreamed approaching her again would lead him to such a delectable evening and, more to the point, cement his hopes that he might get a chance to ride in the Bubble.

She didn't tell him a whole lot about it, but he got enough detail to assure him that it was going to be the adventure of a lifetime — to ride inside a tornado, to see everything, to bounce to a landing like some kind of super ball! Awesome. And he was so good at awesome.

He'd been trying to reach her all day as he and his team traveled to Dodge City to get ready for tomorrow's chase. She wasn't answering phone calls. He'd gambled that she'd end up in Kansas's most famous cow town simply because there weren't that many big towns out here, and he'd promised to buy her a steak after her tornado catch of the day before.

Sometime after 5 p.m., when his two vehicles rolled into Dodge, she finally called him back. He was just about to check in to their hotel, but he stepped back from the counter and let the others go first so he could take the call.

"Is this the famous Aurelius Zane?" she asked coyly once he said hello.

"This is his secretary," he teased in his deep voice. "May I take a message for Mr. Zane? He's very busy."

"Well, in that case, I shall ring off and try again later," she said.

"No! Wynda!" Even to his ears, he sounded desperate. He tried to get back to awesome. "My dear, it is I. I want to see you again. Where are you staying?"

"I believe it's a Festival Inn. We're just checking in."

"You are? But so are we! I don't see you." He looked around. "Are you in the parking lot?"

"We're at the desk," she said. "Are you in Garden City as well?"

"Oh." He sighed. "I'm in Dodge City. At a different Festival Inn. If only you'd called me sooner."

"It wouldn't have changed a thing," she said, cool as marble. "This is where we need to be for tomorrow. But if I want you, Aurelius, I'll know how to get you. And I have a feeling I may want you."

"You know I want you," he said softly, so his crew wouldn't hear.

"You never know what I mean, do you?" she asked, sounding amused.

"Do you mean for the Bubble? Wynda, I am ready at any time. I will make myself available tomorrow. I will find you."

"I think you'd better take care of your little plane," she said. "I'm making no promises."

Was she leading him on? "How far is it to Dodge City?"

"Um, not sure. An hour plus, I think. Why do you want to know?" Her tone was flirtatious again.

"Because I want to go there. Right now."

"We're not deploying right now."

"You know why I want to come to you, Wynda, my redheaded tiger."

"Oh, please," she said. "Just what I want to be known as. The tiger lady."

He didn't want to tell her she already was. And it didn't matter. He was hot for her. "I'm coming anyway. I'm driving over there right now."

"As long as you realize that this is not about the Bubble," she said.

"Tomorrow, I'll worry about the Bubble. Tonight, I want you."

"Well," she said. "That can be arranged." And she disconnected the line.

Aurelius made sure the others were checked in, then got himself a room just in case. He'd need an hour or two of sleep, at least, and he'd have to be back by morning. But right now, he had the fever bad, and its only cure was Wynda.

ONCE THE CREW got to the hotel lobby in Garden City and started making plans to hit a Mexican restaurant, Jack texted Saffire again.

"Pizza? On me. So we can talk."

She didn't reply to Jack, but she gave him a nod before she told Wynda she'd order in so she could get some rest and catch up on phone calls. Jack said he had a craving for a burger, when his craving was for something else entirely, so he wouldn't be joining them, either. He caught Andre trying to hide a smile and knew he wasn't fooling everybody, but the effort seemed worthwhile nonetheless. Wynda was distracted by a phone call, and the others' minds were elsewhere. They'd been on the road for just over two weeks, and they were getting antsy, missing their significant others, their pets, their own beds. Short of a miracle or a disaster, either of which could occur with actual deployment, they could be traveling together for another week or more. Jack was looking forward to the end of their assignment and some personal chase time, a chance to be alone with the storms, but not as avidly as he had before. He wasn't done chasing Saffire yet.

Forty-five minutes later, with just-delivered pizza and paper plates in hand, he knocked lightly on her door, recalling dimly how well he'd gotten to know her door the night before. It took a minute, but she opened this one. She wore a half smile, along with the olive-green shirt from earlier and a long, black gauze skirt instead of the camo pants. Her feet were bare.

"You look nice," he said, hoping for a better start this evening. He stepped inside, finding a clone of his room, with burgundy and gray walls and dull floral engravings hanging above a pair of queen beds.

"Just trying to get comfortable," she said. "I like loose clothes after a day folded up in that van. If I don't ride in a car again for a month after this is over, I'll be happy."

"Thanks for agreeing to have dinner with me."

She nodded, retreating to the table by the shaded window, where she had a bottle of champagne chilling in the ice bucket. "Don't read anything into this," she said, pouring it into paper cups. "I just need my champagne."

He laughed. "More fruit of the van cooler?"

"Nothing but the best," she said with a reluctant smile, then sat in one of the chairs and assumed a more sober mien. "So. Are you going to tell me what this is all about? I've been worried about it all day. Is Wynda going to turn this into some kind of dating show?"

"I hope to hell not," Jack said, setting the box on the table and flipping it open. The steaming mushroom pizza smelled delicious. He sat and helped himself to a slice. It tasted as good as its garlicky aroma. "All I know is she has a collection of clips that, viewed all at once, suggest we do much more than chase storms together."

She picked up a slice and nibbled at it. "Mmm," she said. "Did you confront her?"

"I tried. She's like Rain-X. It just all rolled off. She also made it sound like this was nothing unusual and that she wouldn't need to pursue 'alternate story lines' if we got the Bubble into a tornado."

"Well, that's the trick, isn't it?" Saffire asked between bites.

"The Bubble is, frankly, just a hair this side of stupid," Jack said. "I don't think it'll ever do anything but roll around, even if we found the perfect storm. And that makes this stunt even more difficult."

"I'll talk to her. I can't afford to let her turn this into something sleazy."

"What if she did? This will probably air after you get that job you mentioned," Jack said. "You should be fine."

"Not at all," Saffire said. "The new show wouldn't be on the air yet. If I get the job, which is still a big 'if,' they could replace me any time if I appear to violate what is essentially a morals clause in the contract. They're going for a family audience. I don't want that hanging over my head. And everybody knows everybody in my business; they'd know the gist of the Bubble show before it ever hit TV. I can't believe Wynda's employers want a seedy science show, either, but everybody knows these reality shows are more about characters than substance these days. I suppose she can justify a soapy 'story line,' as she calls it, to juice things up."

"Are we soapy?" he asked in mock innocence, finishing his slice.

"We were last night," she said darkly.

Jack didn't like seeing her upset. "I'm sorry about that," he said. "I'm really sorry. I — I jumped to conclusions. I just assumed, I mean, I shouldn't have assumed anything. It was just that you had said a couple of things that made me wonder."

"I also wonder," she said, taking a sip from her cup. "I wonder if you're someone who will always see the world as divided into two sides. You and everyone else."

"Where do you get that?"

"Your distrust. Your cynicism. Do you care about anything?"

Whoa. Where was she going now? "I do. I care about things. At the least, you have to admit I care about storms."

"You may think you love storms that much, but maybe you chase them out of fear. They say people do things out of love or fear."

"Fear of what? What would I be afraid of?" he scoffed, taking a gulp of the champagne. "And yes, I love storms that much."

"Maybe you fear the vacuum," she said. "Or maybe you fear what could fill it. I don't think tornadoes can fill it."

"You haven't chased enough tornadoes." What did she mean, the vacuum? He started on another slice of pizza, not wanting to have this conversation.

Saffire watched him, calmly analyzing him. "What fills

your empty spaces, Jack? I think maybe you need to have a little faith."

"Definitely not my department," he said.

"Not that kind of faith. Faith in the future. Faith in people."

"You mean like Wynda? What's the point?"

"I mean like me."

He stopped eating and put down the pizza. He took a sip of the champagne and felt his walls breaking down. "I do have faith in you," he said softly. "I do now. I should have before."

"Do you?" Now she sat casually, done with the pizza, regarding him as if he were a specimen, one of her bugs, not the man she'd been sleeping with.

"I don't want to crowd you," he said. "Just like I don't want to be crowded. I think it's the way we are, both of us."

"Granted." She nodded. "You don't want to fence me in, and maybe that works for me. But is that how you always deal with women?"

He tried to explain. "Everyone's in motion. Women leave. It's not my place to stop them."

"It's just that you leave first."

Her conclusion shocked him a little, though he knew she was right. Still, he felt differently about Saffire, and her proximity meant his body had little time for his brain's thoughts on the matter. He reached out for her hand, and she let him hold it. "I don't want to go anywhere," he said, looking her in the eye.

"Maybe not now," she said.

"I can't imagine feeling differently tomorrow."

"You will."

"I won't," he said, getting up and pulling her up, too. Jack ran his hands through her hair, now tousled, more appealing in its lack of perfection. She closed her eyes, letting him trace his fingers along her eyelids, her cheekbones. He held her waist and kissed her neck, his favorite place to start kissing her. Kiss by kiss, his lips migrated to her mouth, consuming her with a passion that came from some foreign place inside him, from a door that had just opened, that she had opened. He pulled back, and she opened her eyes. He wanted her to accept him the way he was, right now, and to hell with tomorrow, but he meant it: This feeling was about more than tonight. "Well?" he asked.

"Who am I to argue?" The alluring husky note was back in her voice.

"You're Saffire. We can argue all night if you want."

"Arguing just wastes time. And I don't know how much time we have." She placed her hands against his chest, his black T-shirt, and pushed a little. He thought she was pushing him away until she pushed him again and he landed on the nearest bed. She walked over to a light switch and flicked off the lamp that hung over the table, leaving only the entryway light on. Her face was half in shadow, devilishly pretty. "I have decided to forgive you," she said, "as long as you're still ready to grovel."

Jack heard the teasing note in her voice. The actress on stage. At least she was done analyzing him. "Whatever you say," he said with a smile.

She considered him for several seconds as he sat on the bed. He started to wonder whether she would make him beg or kick him out when she said: "OK, doctor. Take 'em off."

He laughed out loud. "Are you serious?"

"Indulge me." She crossed her arms. "What, you don't like a woman in charge?"

"I love it, baby," he said with a wicked grin, relieved that the playful Saffire was back as he removed his T-shirt and tossed it onto the other bed. He got up and stood within a few inches of her, kicked off his sneakers and took off his socks. He slowly unbuttoned and unzipped his jeans, pushing them down around his ankles and off, watching her the whole time. Standing as close as he could without touching her, he placed his hands on his hips. "Want to help?"

"You're doing fine," she said, but her voice was lower now, breathy.

He stood before her in his dark blue briefs for a few seconds, feeling the strain in them as she watched, and hooked his thumbs in the waistband. He stretched the elastic a little, this way and that, before pulling the briefs off, too. He got harder as he watched her looking him over. She circled him slowly. He waited for her to speak, feeling his desire outgrow his patience.

"You know what my favorite part of the male anatomy is?" Saffire asked.

"I can guess."

"You'd guess wrong. A man as adroit with women as you are should know it isn't that obvious."

"The eyes? The windows to my soul?"

"They're pretty, but no."

"Lips, then." He smirked.

She walked slowly toward him, sucked on one of her fingers and rubbed it against his bottom lip. His body responded, and he didn't feel like such a smart-ass now.

"No," she said. "It's this." She lay her warm hand against the place where his hip met his leg, just above his groin. Her touch was electrifying. He began to breathe faster. She moved her hand across his buttocks, circling him again before standing before him. She traced her fingers lightly along his shaft before grasping it and building a rhythmic movement that quickly detached all thought from sensation. He took a shuddering breath, on the edge of losing control, and she smiled, a superior little smile that he wanted to devour.

Jack pushed her hand away, not ready to come, and drew her close. He breathed in her scent, then placed a hand behind her neck and pulled her even closer, putting his mouth on hers, touching her tongue with his. He kissed her and kissed her again, each taste deeper, more fervent, until she wrapped her arms tightly around his waist. But he pushed her away. "No," he said. "My turn."

He spun her quickly so he was spooned against her back, his naked body against her clothed one. She inhaled sharply as he reached under her shirt and tugged it off over her head. He unhooked her black cotton bra, pushed it off her shoulders and tossed it aside, then tenderly kissed the mermaid tattoo on her shoulder. As he teased her neck and her ears with his tongue, he cupped her naked breasts, massaging them, tugging at her hardening nipples until she made a little cry of pained pleasure.

Now he guided her. Gently, he pushed her onto the bed from behind. "Don't lie down," he whispered as she started to roll. "Stay right there. Knees on the edge of the bed. Just like that." On all fours, she gave him a sideways glance over her shoulder, sighing as he touched her back, admiring her. He reached under her soft skirt, moving his hands up her thighs until he found her silky underwear. He pushed aside the damp sliver of fabric and inserted a finger inside her, stroking her until he felt her quiver. "Are you ready for me?"

"Mmmm," she said.

"Tell me," he said. He released her, reaching for his jeans

on the floor and the condom he'd put in his pocket, and she groaned at his absence as he put it on.

"Don't stop," she said.

"Tell me what you want." He ran his fingers over her back, wanting her to say it. "Are you ready for me?"

"I'm ready for you," she breathed.

"And what do you want?"

"I want you inside me."

"As you wish, my lady," he whispered. "You're in charge."

He reached between her legs again and yanked the thong down, hearing it rip, and pushed her skirt up over the sweet curve of her bottom. He let his tip touch her, tease her before he plunged into her wet cleft.

"Oh, yes," she murmured, moving with him as he drove deeper. "*Yes.*" He felt himself expanding inside her as his cadence intensified. In his state of heightened awareness, he noticed their shadows on the wall, the silhouette of his form melting into the lovely curve of her back, her swinging breasts as she pushed back against him. The pressure built inside him to a wrenching, ecstatic detonation as he came. She echoed his release with a stuttering sigh of pleasure. She collapsed against the mattress as he made his final push into her, and he lay on top of her, still inside her, kissing her hair, her shoulders. He eased himself off so he could lie next to her and look into her lovely face, now glowing with perspiration. He kissed her with sweet languor, caressing her curves. He wasn't used to the intoxicating feeling of sex lingering so long that he not only wanted to stay the night; he wanted many more nights. And many more days. For the first time in a long time, he felt lucky to be with a woman, this woman.

"I can't imagine feeling differently tomorrow," he said again, kissing her.

"I guess we'll see tomorrow," she said, and she kissed him back.

JACK LEFT Saffire's room just before dawn so he could get a head start on the forecast for the day. But his mind was divided. It was as if he were two Jacks now — the familiar one who would do anything to chase a storm, and the other one who just wanted to be with Saffire. Or did he just want to fuck her? He didn't have time for the self-analysis, and it wasn't his strong suit, anyway. Meteorological analysis was another story.

The jet stream was bringing them another dip, less deep than the last but a storm system nonetheless. A lifting warm front would intersect with the dryline pushing into western Oklahoma and Kansas by midafternoon. The spiraling wind profile favored rotating storms. All those factors meant they had a real chance to deploy the Bubble, even if it never took off. He was pretty sure footage of a tornado intercept on the ground would satisfy Wynda as much as airborne footage, and he was also pretty sure that was all they were going to get.

On his way down to meet the crew, Jack ran into Saffire on the stairs, between floors. He dropped his bags immediately and pressed her against the wall, making her drop her bags, too, as he laid a kiss on her that would melt a mountain. She whimpered a little when he let her go, and then, not saying anything, she touched her hair, smoothed her flowy black top and clingy jeans, picked up her luggage and headed down the stairs. He smiled, grabbed his bags, waited a minute for decency's sake, then followed.

Most of the others were already in the lobby. Michiko

arrived a minute behind Jack, looking flustered, dark hair wet. "Got lost on my run this morning," she said, shaking her head. "Quickest shower ever."

"Where's our fearless leader?" Brad asked.

"You mean you?" Devlin teased.

"No, I mean our fearless leader with red hair and a bad temper," he said. "Where is she?"

They looked around at one another. "Not that I was spying on her or anything," Pole said, "but I was looking out my window early this morning and saw her in the parking lot in the company of someone very interesting."

Now the crew was more awake. "Do tell," Saffire said.

"She was saying goodbye to someone in a silver van," Pole said. "A familiar silver van."

"Not a van that belongs to a certain documentary filmmaker?" Michiko asked.

"Zane?" Jack didn't believe it. Maybe this hotel had a sex vortex around it. Then again, the way he saw it, most of them did.

"So it appeared," Pole said. "Do you want to see the picture?"

He was immediately surrounded by his curious crewmates, all straining to get a look at a crappy, hopelessly dark smartphone photo taken before dawn, from too far away, of a redhead on tiptoe who appeared to be planting a big one on the face of Aurelius Zane, adventurer. At least, his identity was suggested by the Zane Films van under the parking lot light and a flash of blond hair.

"Now I feel dirty," Jack joked, exchanging looks with Andre and Pole.

"Well, everyone's up bright and early!" Wynda's voice broke up their huddle as she strode into the middle of the group, bags in hand. "Forgive me for being the last. Boys, have you loaded up the cameras?" Razor and Andre nodded. "Jack, do we have a forecast, and more importantly, do we have time for breakfast? I'm famished."

More knowing glances all around. "We have time," he said. "I'd guess we're within two hours of the target area."

"Excellent," she said, much more cheerful than usual. "Then it's off to the pancake house. There's something about being in Kansas that makes me feel as if I simply must eat pancakes."

THE DRYLINE WAS ADVANCING. That's what the surface map said. Jack could see the change in wind direction, in dewpoints as he surfed the laptop in the parked van. There were no storms, not yet, but puffy white clouds ahead of the boundary were dense and cottony, with just enough bubbling convection to give him hope.

The Palatable Productions chasers loitered at a convenience store and gas station in Hugoton, Kansas. They'd just about run out of reasons to consume more junk food and visit the store, where a few of them had bought small tornado snow globes labeled "Kansas" to take back to their respective homes. Jack would not be satisfied with anything less than the real thing. Chewing again on nicotine gum and seriously missing the cigarettes that helped fill the endless waiting, he dreamed of a classic, visible and photographable tempest that didn't blow out their windows or rip through any highways or towns. A tall order. He stopped short of wishing for tornadoes built to spec. Somehow, a perfect tornado that didn't require a chase would be too dull.

A handful of other storm chasers passed through town, but it seemed fewer were out today, especially compared with the weekend's outbreak chase. Jack was relieved. Chasing was complex enough without sharing every storm with fifty geared-out teams, half a dozen mini research projects and Myrtle and Earl with their cell-phone cameras. Mercifully, visibility was a lot better today, too, so at least they were likely to see whatever the sky stirred up.

Saffire kept her distance, unwilling to court more unwanted photography. Brad talked to the cameras about today's possibilities for deployment and wandered off to the far end of the parking lot to take mysterious phone calls. Wynda drifted among them, looking for shots to direct, furtively texting and, finally, sitting at a plastic picnic table and eating an ice cream sandwich.

Devlin wandered over to the van's open door, bottle of iced tea in hand, and peered over the seat at Jack's laptop. "Any news?"

"I hear the Earth is getting warmer," Jack said.

"That's just a vast media conspiracy," Devlin responded, equally deadpan. "Any storms?"

"I'm interested in what may be happening a little south of here. Satellite is showing brighter puffs on the dryline — see? Towers. Better than what we've got here." Jack's repeated glances to the west had failed to elicit much alacrity from the cumulus clouds loitering there. He felt a buzz in his pocket and pulled out his phone. "Marcus, is that you? How you doing, buddy?"

"Better," Marcus said. "What's your target today?"

"Wait a minute. You're chasing?"

"I couldn't resist." His friend's voice was sheepish. "But not for research, except for whatever hail I can pick up and measure on the road. I'm in my own car. Van's out for at least a week. I had to get professionals to work on it."

"The horror."

"I know," Marcus responded gravely to Jack's joke. "What did you say your target was?"

"I didn't. Hugoton. Reconsidering. Yours?"

"Where the towers are breaking the cap right now. South of you. And I beat you to it."

"Bastard," Jack said. "Thanks."

Marcus laughed. "No problem. See you under the meso."

"Visual confirmation," Jack explained to Devlin as he disconnected the call. "Tell Wynda the chase is afoot."

AURELIUS ZANE HAD a feeling that everything rode on what happened today. He had a chance to get in the Bubble, and he had a chance to get the footage he needed with the drone. He felt he had to get something to justify his efforts, inflate his reputation and, more to the point, break even. But he wasn't ready to tell his team about his nebulous plan, part of which was waiting for Wynda's word. And that might be a long time coming. He had another feeling: that a personal visit to Wynda would be in order to seal the deal.

First, he had to get to the storms. The towers started breaking the cap well west of Ernie's target, and the Zane Films van and truck were busting toward them on a highway that swung south of the town of Pancake. He could see the line of bubbling clouds, and they were starting to look meaty.

"Pardon, but I need to pee," Thing One said from the back seat, where he sat to next Evie. She typed madly on a thin keyboard linked to her tablet computer, working on a story about their quest for her college newspaper. Thing Two was assigned to the drone truck today, and Ernie sat in the front.

"We just left a gas station, didn't we?" Aurelius said from behind the wheel.

"Half an hour ago. It's the coffee. Please, just for a minute. Any tree will do."

"Ernie? What are we going to miss?"

"It's still just showers," the student meteorologist said. "I think we have a minute. Anyway, it's all going to be moving this way as it develops."

There weren't a whole lot of trees to choose from, but Aurelius spotted a couple of them near a shabby cluster of tiny buildings far up a gravel side road. From this distance, it was hard to tell, but maybe it was a gas station. He turned north, and as he got closer, he recognized an old baseball scoreboard that lay outside what had been an outfield fence. Whether humans or the wind had put it there, he couldn't discern. But he did note that this was no ordinary baseball diamond. Flags — no, pennants snapped in the strong southeast wind, sticking out of blue barrels placed all over the field. He couldn't make out all the details, but the first-base dugout appeared to be built up with cement-block walls.

"I don't care if there's no bathroom," Thing One asked. "Please just stop."

"Yes, let's stop for a moment," Aurelius said, a new curiosity in his voice. "We're stopping," he radioed back to the truck. "Take five, everybody."

They pulled up in the small parking lot and got out to stretch their legs. Aurelius walked up to the fence, evaluated the signs and their lightning language and tried to figure out what the barrels were all about. Then he remembered Wynda mentioning something in passing about filming a lightning art project. He'd been distracted at the time by the fact that she was naked and warm next to him, and not a whole lot of what she'd said had actually penetrated his brain cells. This might be an interesting place to shoot a storm, even if the signs forbade it. Nobody was around. There was a lock on the gate, but they'd get a fine shot right here.

"Listen, everyone," he called, and his crew gathered around. "I have an errand to run."

"An errand?" Ernie asked, puzzled. "With the storms brewing?"

"It's a secret mission," he said, hoping it sounded important enough that they wouldn't ask any more questions. "I want you all to stay here for a bit. Film the approaching storms. I'm going to take the van, and I should be back before things get exciting. If I find I can't be back, I'll call and tell you when to launch the drone." He was starting to picture it: dramatic video of him inside the Bubble, flying into a tornado, all captured by the UAV. Why not? He never got anywhere thinking small.

"But you'll be back, won't you?" Evie asked. "My story about you just won't be the same if you aren't with us."

Aurelius considered her open, optimistic face for a moment — the young reporter, the ambitious influencer, another tool in his box, another avenue for promotion and fame. "Why don't you join me, Evie? The rest of you can stay here."

"Evie?" Ernie asked her with the worry and possessiveness that comes of a new romance.

"I'll be fine," she beamed, kissing the young weather geek on the cheek before getting into the passenger seat of the van.

"But not us?" Thing Two asked as her husband rejoined them after his visit to the lava-tree.

"I need you here," Aurelius said. Wynda would freak out if his crew came, too. "I'll call soon. And I'll be back." Right after I return from my flight into history, he thought.

JACK and the Palatable team headed east to the best paved road option, then south, pushing the speed limit, trying to get into position on the developing storms. There were two cells that looked particularly promising on radar, especially the southern one, whose returns showed yellow with a hint of red. That storm was intensifying more rapidly, and the velocity image showed the beginnings of rotation. That was the one Jack targeted.

"Is this it?" Brad asked from the driver's seat of Van One as rain started to spatter the windshield. Saffire was next to him, with Devlin and Andre in the middle seat.

"This is anvil precip from the northern storm," Jack said from the back. To their west, the golden light of late afternoon silhouetted a nebulous cloud base, with multiple rain shafts pouring out of its middle. "You should be seeing the storm we want in a few minutes."

"Is this our storm?" Wynda asked over the radio. She was in the crew vehicle with Michiko and Razor, and Pole drove the Bubblevan. Just like old times.

Jack repeated the information into his radio.

"All right," Wynda replied. "Devlin, be thinking about our road options in case we have a chance to deploy."

"We're a long way from that point," Jack spoke into the radio. "These storms are still pimply teenagers. They have to grow up a little."

"All the same," Wynda said, "I want to be ready."

Devlin sighed and took the mike from Jack. "I'm on it," he said, tapping through images of the road network on the laptop mounted in front of him.

"It's flatter than a butterfly wing out here," Saffire said, looking into Andre's camera with a droll smile. "Are you sure we haven't been here before? I'm getting a strong sense of déjà vu." She turned to their star. "What do you think, Brad?"

"Actually, everything seems different and new for me today," he said. "I have so much clarity. I'm ready for whatever comes next."

Devlin and Jack exchanged glances. Brad's mood had shifted yet again, but their shoots always seemed to go better when he felt like a TV star. Let it be, Jack told himself. Get them to the storm and, he hoped, a tornado.

The rain lightened and almost vanished as they escaped the realm of the northern storm and slid into the southern storm's dominion. As they headed south, Jack immediately saw it had more structure and development. The cell was a little farther west than its sister, and its anvil, the cold cloud that blew off the top of the storm as it bumped against the stratosphere, spread east, aided by the upper-level winds. This ethereal flying disc was festooned with the round lobes of mammatus clouds, and stitches of lightning skipped across its surface.

The storm assumed the shape of a classic supercell, with sweeping striations in the aggressively bubbling convection visible on its southwest side as they drew abreast of it. It was growing up fast.

"It looks like it's forming a wall cloud," Saffire said. They were all picking up the lingo, Jack noted. At least they'd leave this assignment as bona fide storm chasers.

"It sure does," Brad said. "I'd bet that's a good hail core just north of it, too."

The shaggy lowering from the storm's belly wasn't very well formed yet, but it looked promising. And Jack saw from the radar image that Brad was right about the hail, which fell in a glowing, greenish-white wave from the cloud's base. Readings suggested the ice balls weren't huge yet, but there was a lot of it.

"Tantalizing," Jack said, mostly to himself.

"Care to comment for the camera?" Andre said, turning around to aim the lens at him.

Jack was starting to react badly to cameras, but he decided not to unload his ire on Andre. "This is shaping up to be a powerful supercell," he said for the future audience. "It's starting to rotate, and I think we've picked a very promising target."

Andre put the camera down. "Thanks," he said.

"I'm only a jerk part of the time," Jack responded, eliciting a grin from the shooter.

"West or east?" Devlin asked.

Jack looked at the radar on his screen and the map displayed on Devlin's. "West for a bit," he said. "Let's get close and see what it can do."

Brad picked up his radio mike for the benefit of Wynda and the cameras that surrounded him. "We're going to head west at this next road and see how close we can get," he said.

The three vehicles made the turn, and Jack got a better look out the left windows at the growing wall cloud. Tendrils of cloud dangled, spinning slowly counter-clockwise, dancing to some half-forgotten Strauss waltz. He almost heard it, but the siren intruded instead. He shook his head immediately. Maybe he was too close to Pancake and Prairie Rock and all that had gone before, the memory of those who'd died when the siren didn't sound. Whatever he'd done to help, whatever they did now with their probe, whatever scientists did in the future, their answers were unlikely to be absolute. The tornadoes would still come, and they would still destroy lives. He certainly wasn't part of the solution now, but he still wanted to be a part of the storm. The craving was indelible to his soul. *I can't imagine feeling differently tomorrow.* The thought he'd expressed to Saffire applied to storms even more emphatically. He was entangled with them, never to be unbound.

If he could become part of that wall cloud, that supercell, he would. As a scientist, he dismissed the notion, but if the afterlife meant dissolving into a dew, traveling the world as a drop of water from the Antarctic ice to the tropical rain forests and, on a good day, to a storm in Tornado Alley, he'd look forward to death.

For the moment, he was feeling very much alive as he confronted the powerful thunderstorm. From here, a few miles out, he could see the curling wisps of cloud braiding and unbraiding themselves as they dipped lower to the ground.

"Should we deploy?" Devlin asked.

"I think we have the luxury of waiting for a tornado," Jack said. "This storm has a lot of spin to work with, and you don't want to put the Bubble down under the first dust swirl you see. That said, we need to get closer. If it gets serious, we want to be ready."

"Why not deploy in front of that nice wall cloud?" Brad asked. "We don't need a big tornado to get good video."

"We don't have any tornado yet," Jack said, hearing their hero's hesitance. As he said so, strands of the lowering cloud coalesced into a slowly spinning funnel. "But we might in a minute."

"Funnel," Brad said over the radio.

"Now we deploy," Wynda responded.

Devlin switched between the GPS map and the radar on his laptop as Jack leaned forward and pointed out the area of rotation displayed on the screen. The engineer got his meaning quickly.

"The track of this storm puts it north of the road we're on," Devlin said into Jack's radio. "In fact, it's crossing the road now. Which means we can't deploy unless we find an appropriate north road, and the closest farm road looks like it's basically a dirt driveway with a giant irrigation rig parked next to it."

"So, not ideal, is what you're saying," Wynda replied, sounding annoyed.

"We can't drive into a farm field," Brad said over his radio, relief in his voice.

"I think we should stop here to watch," Jack said, and Brad pulled onto the shoulder with the other vehicles. As Saffire and Brad got out, the camera crew did, too, to document the storm and the chasers.

Jack took the mike from Devlin. "Don't fret," he told Wynda as he watched the funnel dip toward the ground northwest of them. A spiral of dust rose under it for all of thirty seconds, a brief tornado, before the funnel lifted again. A new meso was just starting to form to their north. "You're going to have another chance. I'd bet a bourbon on it."

THE NORTHERN STORM was beginning to strengthen, Ernie noted as he looked at the radar in the UAV truck with techies Duncan and Phil, but it didn't have the strong rotation the southern storm did. It was, however, getting closer to their position by the bizarre baseball field, and the anvil, extending several miles to the east, had blocked off the afternoon sun. They were starting to see the storm's base in the distance, and it wasn't half bad-looking.

"I can't believe he just left us sitting here," Phil said.

"Well, for us, it really doesn't matter," said Duncan. "Our drone flies. We can deploy as long as we're within a reasonable distance. But that was kind of bizarre."

Restless, they got out of the truck to get a breath of air. "I'm intrigued by this field," Ernie said. "It looks like a bunch of lightning rods. I've never seen anything like it." He heard thunder and wondered how seriously to take the posted warnings. Things One and Two were pretty much ignoring the "no video" sign and shooting whatever they could get from the outside of the fence. Or they were until a yellow SUV pulled up and parked under a metal carport by the gate.

A blond woman in braids and a curly-haired man hopped out of the vehicle and scanned the Zane Films truck and its miniature plane with curiosity before walking over to the crew.

"Can we help you?" the woman said. "I'm Judy Hale, and this is Robinson Marvell. This is our field."

"What is it?" Ernie asked, overcome by curiosity.

"An art project," Robinson said. "We like visitors to ask for permission before they film it. And besides, this isn't going to be the safest place to be in the next hour."

"Sorry," Duncan said. "We're with Zane Films. Do you mind that we got a few shots? We're actually waiting for our producer here."

"It's OK," Judy said. "But I'd prefer that you not be so close, for your own safety."

"I'd think we're especially safe considering you have a field of lightning rods to attract whatever comes our way," Ernie said, hoping his remark would engender further explanation.

Robinson's smile suggested he was only just controlling his impatience. "It doesn't always work that way. This is our parking lot, and we'd like you to leave now. But the road is public, and you can do what you like. I strongly recommend you move to the main road."

The couple went back to their car, pulled out a few bags of gear, walked to the gate, unlocked it and let themselves in. They made their way to the building that was once a dugout and vanished inside.

"What the hell?" Phil muttered.

"I suppose we should get off the property," Duncan said. "Though I don't know what the big deal is."

"Zane told us to wait here," Ernie said.

"So we move twenty yards away. We don't need to go all the way out to the main road. This road is public, too, like they said."

"Not a problem for us," said Thing One, and he and his wife walked with Ernie to the gravel road outside the parking lot while Duncan and Phil moved the truck and parked on the shoulder.

They all leaned against the truck and watched as Judy and Robinson emerged from their makeshift bunker. The pair focused on a handful of barrels that had more elaborate gear mounted on top than the others. They appeared to be flipping switches and otherwise checking out each apparatus, calling to each other, though Ernie couldn't make out what they said. The sound of thunder rolled again in the distance, and Judy and Robinson looked up and hastened their efforts before returning to their dugout.

"Any word from Zane?" Ernie asked, feeling a twinge of nervousness.

"Not yet," Duncan said. "Where could he be?"

AURELIUS WAS HEADING WEST, trying to find Wynda's crew. Specifically, he was calling Wynda and texting Wynda and wondering where Wynda wandered as he drove closer to the storms. He checked the laptop mounted in the front and saw the southern storm already had a tornado warning on it. That, he assumed, was Wynda's target, though he'd feel better if he actually heard from his redheaded paramour. She'd been silent after a series of flirtatious texts at midday.

"So what's it look like?" Evie asked. She'd put away her computer and was snapping photos with her camera. She seemed to have gotten over the gag order he'd imposed after the drone crash.

"Does that shoot video?" Aurelius asked.

"Beautiful video," she said. "Looks like film. I love it."

"If you like, you could shoot a little video of me," he said. "The van's cameras are on, but their video won't be as nice as yours."

"Great idea!" Evie said. She reached into her backpack, pulled out a small microphone and attached it to the camera, and held it up so she could see the display on the back. "OK, you're on."

"We have high hopes for today," he told the camera, keeping one eye on the road. "These storms in southwestern Kansas have all the earmarks of tornadoes, and we'll be attempting to capture them with our aerial drone. In fact, we may be filming a tornado in an entirely new way today, and

I'm excited to be part of the adventure." He paused. "I'm done. Was that all right?" He was sure it was, but he wanted to hear her say it.

"Fantastic!" she said, putting the camera down. "What kind of new way are you going to film a tornado? You don't mean my camera?"

"I can't say just yet. But if it works, it will be *mind-blowing*," he intoned with a broad smile.

She picked up her phone and started typing with her thumbs.

"Are you posting? It's a secret, you know," Aurelius said.

"Just telling people they should get ready to have their minds blown by today's chase," she said. "I want to build the excitement a little. I'll probably get new followers. I always do whenever I offer a little tease like that."

He could imagine. And he wondered if Wynda had been teasing him as he hit redial and got her voicemail again. He'd become her follower in the most literal way as he got closer to the southern supercell, which was starting to dominate the western sky the way a wedding cake fills a bakery window. Only this wedding cake was as dark as it was dangerous. Or, as Aurelius liked to think of it, delicious.

THE SOUTHERN CELL had teased Jack's crew earlier. Now it was like some pretty little thing in a horror movie that spontaneously transformed itself into an alien monster. Its teeth were showing, and it sucked in brown dust as if it wanted to eat Kansas alive. Its rotation was manifest, and not just in the new wall cloud under the base. It had the unmistakable struc-ture of a spinning storm, with rounded, sweeping layers of blue velvet cloud spiraling up toward a well-defined anvil. There might be photos like this floating around the Internet that people claimed were hurricanes and garden-variety storms, but only one thing could look like this: a supercell.

The crew had moved a little east and north, trying to stay ahead of it, and now the cameras had a spectacular view. Jack felt a familiar rush as he faced the stunning storm. His brain processed the cell's features, from the hail core to their north to the dusty downdraft now visible to their west and the clear slot starting to cut around the area of rotation. It was going to produce a tornado. He was sure of it.

Devlin jogged over to him, atlas in hand. "Where?" was all he asked.

"A little more north and east. We might have to put it on a farm road, but you don't want the Bubble sitting in the middle of a highway anyway."

Devlin ran off to tell Wynda, and Jack had only another minute to take a few photos and feel the warm, rapid inflow flapping his T-shirt, which he used to shield his camera from the blowing dust. He didn't mind grit in his teeth when a storm like this was the cause. The most entertaining activities involved getting a little dirty, after all.

"All aboard!" Wynda shouted, and the chasers began to move to their respective vehicles. Jack stood still for another few seconds so he could reach out to touch Saffire's hair as she ran by.

She turned and jogged backward for a moment, her curls and breasts bouncing. "Not the hair," she said, but she was smiling. Again, just that brief touch shot him through with a jolt of electricity. He couldn't decide if he were pathetic or happy.

"Jack, are you coming?" Wynda shouted.

"Almost," he muttered, running toward his spot in the back of Van One.

"North," Devlin said when they were all aboard. "And when we're looking down its throat, we'll deploy."

"This one feels real," Saffire said, articulating the sense of surety Jack had watching the storm. "It's so beautiful and beastly at the same time."

"It's a nice storm," Brad said, underselling it as he started up the van and pulled into the road. "But we'll wait until we're sure it's going to produce a tornado, right?"

"Nothing is sure when it comes to weather," Jack said from the back, "but I'm as sure as I ever am when it comes to tornadogenesis. I've seen a lot of these things. I'd advise you to get ready." He could see Brad's face in the rearview mirror as it transformed into a stony mask. Something was up. Jack was now sure of that, too.

AURELIUS HEARD WYNDA'S crew on the CB, just as he'd about given up hope. They were talking about where to deploy. So they hadn't deployed yet, and they weren't far away, and both of those were good things.

The bad thing: The network of dirt roads around here was not something he cared to broach without any idea of where Wynda's people were. And he still hadn't heard anything from Wynda. "I need to pull over for a minute," he told Evie as he abruptly crunched to a halt, half on and half off the shoulder. A storm-chasing SUV wrapped in an ostentatious combination of logo and airbrushed tornadoes honked at him as it swerved around the van, traveling at breakneck speed toward the supercell, which loomed to their west. The storm was a barrel-like behemoth with a well-defined wall cloud that kept extending stray hairs of vapor toward the ground. The wisps lifted as soon as they lowered, but he had the feeling a funnel couldn't be far off. He'd already heard the report of the first brief tornado, so he had no doubt the storm was capable of more.

Aurelius pulled out his phone and texted Wynda again. "I'm close, darling. Is it time yet? Just tell me where to go."

He was assuming a lot, but persistence often paid. He waited for one minute, then five. Evie stepped out to take photos of the storm. After twelve minutes had passed, a text popped up on his screen — no words, just a photo. It showed the Bubble and, in the far distance, a distinctive barn. He needed no further encouragement. There were no instructions, no coordinates, but it would be enough. He'd find her in the path of the storm, near that barn.

He punched the number for Duncan.

"Where are you?" the techie answered. The connection was noisy.

"Never mind that. Launch my drone. Go for the southern storm. Get as close to the tornado as you can."

"There's a tornado?"

"There will be. Launch."

"Hey, Zane —"

Aurelius hung up. He didn't have time for conversation. He rolled down his window and shouted to Evie. "Time to go! Let's get you something to write about."

JUDY NEVER REALIZED how much she'd enjoy creating multimedia art. Her education hadn't prepared her for this kind of multimedia, when the sky itself became a part of her canvas. She'd always been a photographer and a painter, not to mention a storm chaser, but catching lightning in a bottle was something new. Now, she and Robinson had a decent shot at it.

"Those fools are still sitting out there by the road," Robinson said, looking at one of the half dozen camera monitors mounted in their baseball dugout-turned-bunker.

"They've been warned," Judy said. "If they get in their truck, they'll be OK."

"What are they waiting for, anyway? If I were them, I'd be hauling after that southern cell. Sweet hook developing on it." He pointed to the radar on one of the laptops that sat on a long, narrow counter that served as a desk.

"I hope I'm not holding you hostage," she joked. "Our storm may not produce a tornado, but it's just what I was looking for."

"Just what *we* were looking for," he said, kissing her on the cheek. "Everything's ready, right?"

"Cameras are running. Field mill is active. Rockets are set." She felt a surge of glee as the storm churned toward them. "I can't believe we finally have one coming to us. And I'm still amazed we're allowed to do this."

"I've learned there are a lot of people out there launching model rockets," Robinson said. "Ours are only slightly weirder than most."

"This is a rare chance," Judy said. "We'd better make the most of it."

Through a narrow window, she could see the blue barrels, the wildly flapping pennants and, well beyond the outfield fence, a dark, seething mass of cloud. A low, expanding rumble of thunder reached her ears, even through the cement walls.

"I'm showing increasing negative charge," Robinson said.

"I would hope so," Judy answered, her eyes focused on the storm beyond the window. "I'm seeing a bolt every minute or two. It's so close." Near her hand was the "Fire" button on a small control console. She'd used it only once, during a test on a blue-sky day.

"Here we go," Robinson said. "Negative three … negative four …" A flash from a nearby bolt lit up the field, but the thunder lagged by about two seconds. "Still a half mile away, and now we have to wait for the charge to build again," he said. "Just need the big five-oh-oh-oh."

Another bolt hit even closer, but not within the realm of their art project. On the camera monitor aimed at the gate and the road, they saw the Zane Films crew hastening to cram itself into the pickup truck holding the peculiar small plane.

"About time," Robinson said.

Judy regarded her pennant-clad lightning rods. "We might get a freebie without the rockets," she mused as another bolt hit a few miles away.

"Maybe, but it'll be a lot more fun to launch. All in all, I'm glad I left CG with your uncle. He's not crazy about thunder."

"Poor baby," she answered absently, focused on the storm.

"We're getting close. OK, negative three … negative four …" Robinson's voice rose with each number. "Negative five! Three, two, one, fire!"

Judy pressed the square red button, and a three-foot plastic rocket flashed toward the sky from the pitcher's mound, trailing its copper wire. A long second elapsed. She let out the breath she'd been holding. "Fail," she said, punching buttons to switch control to the next rocket. They had only five, and she wanted to make them count.

"More where that came from," Robinson said. "This thing is really active." Next to the computer showing radar, another laptop displayed lightning data. A cluster of white dashes was building on the map just to their west, moving their way.

"It's beautiful," Judy said, looking out the window again at the slow-moving storm's heavy rain and hail core, still a few miles away, and the smooth doughnut of cloud surrounding it. She wanted to feel the wind on her face, but that wasn't advisable just at the moment.

"Get ready, sweetie," Robinson said, bringing her wandering mind back to the bunker. "Looking better ... Negative three ... negative four ... negative five ... Three, two, one, fire!"

She pressed the button, and the rocket at second base flew upward with a hiss. In less than a second, a brilliant bolt of lightning struck their barrel, with a rapid succession of strobing return strokes and, a trice later, a blast of earth-shaking thunder.

They were both stunned for just a second, and then Judy let out a whoop and threw her arms around Robinson's neck.

"That was awesome!" he shouted, hugging her hard.

Judy, still seeing the afterimage of the flashes, now felt the power of this most formidable paint brush. She stepped back to throw him a crafty look. "Yes, it was," she said, grinning. "Let's do it again."

❧

"HE WANTS US TO LAUNCH," Duncan said, putting down

his phone just as the rocket brought the first thunderbolt to ground in the infield.

"What the fuck was that?" Phil shouted from the back seat of the UAV truck, where he sat with the monitors and controls. In the front seat, Ernie was crammed up against Duncan as Thing Two sat on Thing One's lap.

"Badass!" Ernie said. "Triggered lightning!"

"You have got to be fucking kidding me," Duncan said, starting up the truck. "We have to get out of this lightning before we launch. He told us to target the southern storm, so we'll head that way."

"Oh, come on," Ernie said, sounding more excited than he'd been the entire trip. "This is awesome."

Another rocket fired from the field, this one from first base, and everyone else in the truck ducked. But this one didn't trigger a bolt.

"What the hell do they think they're doing?" Phil shouted again, a note of panic in his voice. His specialty was computers and toy planes, not dodging lightning bolts. Things One and Two were unsuccessfully trying to disentangle themselves and their cameras to get some kind of shot.

"Calm down. We're leaving. Now," Duncan said, kicking up a cloud of gravel and dust as he accelerated. They all saw the flash and heard the bang as another lightning bolt crashed to the field, presumably hitting another of the barrels. They hadn't even seen a rocket that time.

"Unbelievable," Ernie said.

"Zane told us to wait here," Thing One said.

"He said he'd be back," Thing Two added.

"He said he wants us to launch," Duncan said. "That's my priority, after keeping the plane safe. There's no way we can do it here. I'm concerned about hail, too."

"But it would be so fun," said Ernie, who struggled to avoid Duncan's armpit in the crowded front seat.

"Yeah." Duncan's tone was grim as he made it to the main road and turned right. "This is fun, all right."

Just driving on a paved road made everyone feel better, until lightning hit the power pole in front of them with a fountain of sparks and a deafening boom. Everything in the truck blinked for a second.

"Shit. Are we OK?" Duncan asked. "Did we get hit?"

"I don't think so. Maybe we got a transient charge." Phil looked at his monitors with concern. "I think it's all working."

"Except maybe your phone," Ernie said, looking down at Duncan's smartphone, which was plugged into the inverter. The screen was black, and it didn't respond when Ernie picked it up and tried to awaken it.

"Goddamn it," Duncan said, still driving east. "It must have hit us."

"I think everything would be fried if it hit us," Phil said.

"Could have been a streamer," Ernie said.

"What's that?" Thing Two asked.

"It's the charge that builds up on an object and reaches up to the cloud to connect with the leaders, that is, toward the opposite charge building in the cloud, to make a lightning strike. There was a case in North Carolina where they figure the victim died from a streamer, not from being struck."

"Goody," Duncan said. "We're still moving, and I guess that counts for something. Let's get out of the firing zone and get in a position where we can launch. If you think it's safe, Phil."

"I think it's all working," Phil repeated, hitting a few buttons on his keyboard. "Just a fluke."

WYNDA QUITE ENJOYED TEASING the hell out of Aurelius Zane. Did he really think he would ride in her Bubble? She almost giggled at the thought. Her crew had found an isolated intersection of hard-packed gravel roads east of the paved road. Judging by Devlin's excitement and Jack's rare animation, they were in excellent position. Pole helped Devlin activate the Bubble on the grassy shoulder, Saffire narrated for the cameras, and Brad stood with his arms crossed, looking west at the storm with a determined expression on his face.

"Very well, it appears this is it," Wynda said to the group. "Our big chance."

"Again," Pole noted.

"I'd say our chances are better than ever," Jack said, looking to the west, beyond a pretty barn and the small farmhouse next to it. The others followed his gaze. Their striated storm had a serious, solid wall cloud now that was, as they watched, morphing into a bowl-shaped funnel. Even Wynda had to concede that it looked ominous.

"Are you ready?" Devlin asked, opening the curved, clear door of their device. He sounded nervous.

"No," Brad said.

There was an awkward silence for a few seconds as they all tried to discern if they'd misheard. "Pardon me?" Wynda asked.

"I'm not getting in that thing again."

For once, Wynda hated being right. And since this did not appear to be just one of Brad's little fits, she adjusted her tone accordingly. "My dear boy, you have been an extraordinary asset to this project and, in fact, you are our star. We have been filming you for nearly three weeks with every intention of completing this show with you as the star. And one thing the star must do is get inside the Bubble and fly."

Brad, his arms still crossed, kicked the dirt. Jack's face had a look of *get the fuck on with it* as he kept an eye on the growing funnel, which now pointed toward the ground less than two miles away.

"I've had my lawyers, well, my dad's lawyers looking over my contract," Brad said. "See page eleven. If the Bubble is proven to be unsafe, I have the option to back out."

Wynda stamped her foot, and her tone changed swiftly from delicate to domineering. "Well of course it's bloody unsafe," she said. "It's supposed to fly in a tornado. That is the entire point."

"Anyway," Brad continued, his tone blasé, "I have another opportunity. I'm going to be the host of a show about unexplained phenomena. It's a great gig. I don't have to travel much; I just film my parts in California. I don't have to visit the exploding cows. And I don't have to get inside a tornado. I don't need this show anymore. I have a better offer."

"You are ignoring an important detail," Wynda said, talking faster now, feeling the world crumbling beneath her and her show. "You are under a contract whose terms you are wildly misinterpreting."

"There's something I should say," Devlin interjected. "I've been meaning to; it's just that you never let me run all the tests I wanted to run."

"Somebody decide something," Jack said through his teeth. The funnel had connected with the ground to their west, and a swirl of chocolate dirt was wrapping around the thin, gray point, the dusty inflow assisting in its veiled dance. Thunder resounded over the plain as lightning hit nearby.

"It's just that the airbags fail to deploy automatically in

one out of five simulations since the lightning strike," Devlin confessed. "I was never really sure we'd get to the point of deployment again, and I was hoping we'd get more garage time. But here we are."

"That's it," Brad said. "Definitive proof. I'll be in the truck."

He walked off to the Bubblevan and got in the front. Wynda felt a chill come on, a cold sweat. Saffire appeared disconcerted. Pole raised his eyebrows and looked up at another cloud of dust approaching them from the south. It was the Zane Films van, roaring up to their location on the road they were blocking.

A thousand thoughts raced through Wynda's brain at this confluence of events. Brad quitting? They had a lot of B-roll that showed Brad manning the Bubble. If it wasn't Brad in the Bubble, there was no show. But then there was Aurelius, who wanted desperately to be in the Bubble. Aurelius, who didn't look anything like Brad, but who was more than willing and could save her ass.

"Darling!" the adventurer shouted as he jumped out of the parked van, dashing in his exquisitely tailored jacket. "I knew I'd find you in the path of the beast!" A young woman stepped out of the passenger side, filming them awkwardly with a digital camera.

And who the hell is this? Wynda thought when she saw her, but she held her tongue. She had to figure out something, and fast.

"I'm ready," Aurelius said. "Are you ready for me? I want to help you."

"What a bloodhound you are," Wynda said. "Your timing couldn't be better."

Aurelius grinned. "I couldn't leave you without a hero. Did Brad tell you about his job offer?"

Wynda felt her eyes widen. Her brain went click, click, click. "You knew about his job offer?" she asked, her voice careening from disbelief to fury as she put it all together. "You knew he wouldn't fly?"

"Um," Aurelius said. "Just coincidence, really. I knew a producer who was looking for a host, and we adventurers like to help one another out."

"You manipulative bastard," Wynda hissed. "Take your camera bunny and go."

The young woman with the DSLR lowered her camera and assumed an indignant expression. "I'm a journalist," she said, stomping off to the van.

"Wynda," Aurelius whispered. "My flower. We can work together again. We can be together. The tornado's coming. Your show will be even better than you imagined."

She'd had it. "I wouldn't have you fly in the Bubble if my career depended on it," Wynda said, knowing it did. "This is *my* show. Now piss off."

JACK WAS WATCHING the tornado more than he was listening to Wynda confronting Aurelius Zane. Its funnel was now a narrow column that flowed upward into the swirling meso, a storybook tree of water and air. Vines of brown dust wrapped around its almost white trunk as it spun in the field, moving relentlessly toward them.

"We'd better put that thing away," he said, gesturing to the Bubble as Zane left in a huff.

"Just a moment," Wynda said.

"Not sure we have a moment," Jack said.

"Come into my office," she told him, walking a few feet away from the group. "How would you like to fly in the Bubble?" she asked in a low voice when he stepped next to her.

"You're crazy," Jack said. "Devlin just said it doesn't work."

"It mostly works," Wynda said. "Anyway, it'll probably just roll. Look, if you do this, we can do a little creative editing, and I'll still have a show."

"Give me one reason," Jack said.

"Brad just forfeited half his fee. It's yours, plus your contractual payment and your bonus if it flies."

Jack shook his head. He didn't like the idea of taking such a foolish risk for money. But even as he dismissed the idea, a yearning to see the inside of a tornado sparked to life in him. To have that experience would render all other experiences obsolete. It was insane — insanely tempting.

"I won't use the footage," Wynda said, interrupting his thoughts.

"What?"

"Anything with you and Saffire. I won't use it."

Jack looked up and saw Saffire watching them with concern. She had another offer, too, when this was over, as long as her chances weren't ruined. They would be if this production became a seedy reality show. "What's my guarantee?"

"You'll know what happened here today," Wynda said, her brow furrowed. "Do you think I want anyone else to know what happened here today?"

Jack couldn't say it was a good decision, but he made it,

imagining himself inside the storm, a place where the siren would be silenced. A great adventure.

"I'll do it." He felt a spike of adrenaline. "I'm not sure how you'll explain the body away after I smash to Earth, but what the hell."

"*Yes*," Wynda said, clenching her fist. "Look lively, everyone!" she shouted, hastening back to the group. "Jack will ride in the Bubble. But according to you, it's Brad. Understand? Wide shots only. Let's do this."

The tornado was growing and now less than a mile away. Jack ran to the Bubble and got in, folding himself awkwardly into the chair. Saffire ran up to him.

"Why?" she asked. The wind whipped her hair around her face.

"What's the point of all this if someone doesn't try it?" Jack asked, trying to convince himself as much as anyone. Devlin and Pole worked quickly to strap him in, but Jack focused on Saffire.

"That's your reason?"

He held her gaze. "I made a deal with Wynda."

Saffire looked away, then turned her eyes back to him. "I could go."

"Please. You couldn't pass for our hero, even at a mile away. No matter how pretty he is."

She smiled. "I thought you said the Bubble was just a hair this side of stupid."

"But in a good way," he said, unhappy to have his own, inconvenient words thrown back at him. "Besides, you of all people know I'm capable of being stupid."

Devlin secured the last strap and looked up at Jack. "Are you sure?"

"It'll be fine," Jack said, continuing in a mordant tone. "I'm going to be run over by a tornado. What could possibly happen?"

"We have to go!" Wynda shouted.

"One second," Jack growled back.

"That's all you have," the producer said, backing off.

Saffire touched his cheek. "I told you. You always leave first."

"But I'll be back." He reached out and pulled her close for a brief, molten kiss. As soon as he released her, Devlin and Pole shut and latched the door. Jack donned the helmet and watched them run to the vehicles.

"Locked and loaded," Devlin said. "Radio check," he added. Jack heard the voice in his ear and caught a glimpse of Saffire driving the van south, the other two vehicles close behind.

"I hear you five by five," Jack said, his mouth still tingling, his brain short-circuited by emotion and sensation. He put the noise aside. "Hey, did you know there's a tornado coming this way?"

"I have no idea what you're talking about," Devlin said, dry as always. "We don't expect you to fly high enough to need the parachutes to slow you down, but if the alarm sounds, pull the lever above your head to release them. They won't do you any good at the lower altitude we expect you to hit — that's why you need the airbags. The manual deploy for the airbags is just by your right hand. You have to flip up the cover to hit the button. Don't do it unless you mean it. They should blow automatically, but just in case —"

"Got it. I read the specs for this thing when I signed up for the crew. Chances are, I'll just roll around anyway," Jack said, echoing Wynda's words. He knew he sounded calmer than he felt as he looked at the small camera monitor above him and then peered west between the metal struts, boxes and instrument cases. The sinuous tornado was dark at the ground and almost silver near the cloud, and it was getting wider. As it grew, it almost appeared to be standing still, and that meant only one thing: It was headed right for him.

AURELIUS'S PHONE made a pitiful beep, worn out by his endless texting. And a lot of good it had done him. He took his hands off the wheel and quickly plugged the phone into the charger. The van hit a pothole and started careening off the dirt road until he grabbed the wheel again and straightened it out.

"Careful!" Evie said. "She was kind of bitchy, wasn't she?"

"Perhaps," Aurelius acknowledged, "but sometimes you need to be a bitch to get things done." And he could never think of Wynda that way. He still couldn't believe she had refused his offer, yet he admired her reluctantly for doing so. He also couldn't understand how furious she was. She worked just as many angles as he did. That's why they were so perfect for each other. He sighed, wondering if they'd ever have another chance. And now that his dream to fly in the Bubble was dashed, he had but one recourse: Make sure the drone shot the tornado.

The funnel was receding behind them, and he recalled Ernie's storm-chasing rule: Never leave a rotating storm. Well, rules were made to be broken. And he planned to come back.

He picked up the phone, which was happier with its power feed, and punched Duncan's number. There was no answer, just voicemail. "It's Zane. Call me. I need a status report.

We're coming to meet you." He hung up. "Must not have a signal," he muttered.

"That's odd," said Evie. "You called him before."

"It's Tornado Alley," he said. "Every other mile is a black hole."

He made his way to the main road, heading east so he could start stair-stepping back to their rendezvous point. A quick radar check of the mounted laptop showed the core of the northern storm was about to overtake the baseball field. He figured he'd have just enough time to catch his team and drop back south for tasty footage of the tornado. The weather radio was looping warnings for both storms, the one behind them tornadic, the one ahead of them severe.

"That looks kind of angry," Evie said of the radar. "I wish Ernie were here to tell me what it means."

"It means it's raining," Aurelius said. He wasn't great at reading radar, but he could tell where the storm was, at least. "No harm in a little rain. I just hope they got the UAV flying before it moved in. That thing behind us is producing a real tornado, and I need to have a few shots of me in front of it. It's not real unless I'm in it, at least for the purposes of the show."

"I could shoot you," Evie said.

"You could," he said, not wanting to tell her that he lacked confidence in her camera and her skills. He wanted his pros and multiple camera angles, the big guns to capture his big presence. "We need the others so you can be on camera, too," he fibbed. "You could be the next big star."

"You think?" she asked wistfully. "I'm considering switching to broadcast journalism, only no one really majors in journalism anymore. It's all marketing and multimedia."

"Everything is marketing," Aurelius said as he found his

north road and turned left, soon entering the fringes of the northern storm. He went east, then north, then east, ripping down gravel roads with the bravado that comes from being in the middle of disasters a lot worse than a little rain and lightning. In half the time it would take a lesser man, he spotted the baseball field to his northeast and made the turn onto the narrow gravel road that would take him there. As he drove north, something flew up from the field, and a brilliant, pulsing lightning bolt followed its path back to the ground. He felt the almost instantaneous concussion of thunder in his chest and slammed on the brakes.

"Is that what I think it is?" he asked as rain hammered the windshield. Now a few pebbles of hail were falling, too.

"I don't see the truck," Evie said, sounding nervous.

"They probably moved. Wisely, given the lightning," Aurelius said. "Though they could have told me."

The hail increased in size from pebbles to nickels and quarters, with correspondingly louder impacts on the van's metal roof and the windshield.

"Maybe we should move, too," Evie said, but she gamely held up her camera to film the barrage.

"In a moment." Aurelius tried Duncan's line again but still got voicemail. "Why don't you try Ernie? I'm going to see if we can get in position on that southern storm. They must have gone that way."

"OK." Her voice was uneasy as he did a three-point turn and headed south. The small hail was now interspersed with golf balls, and one hit the windshield with a thwack that created an instant star in the glass, accompanying the small chink they'd earned earlier in their trip.

"Confound it," Aurelius said, driving faster as Evie waited for the call to go through.

"Ernie? Ernie, is that really you?" she asked. "We've been trying to raise you. Where are you? ... OK, what are the coordinates?" She grabbed a pen out of one of the dashboard cubbyholes and wrote the numbers on her hand. "I know it's loud," she said into the phone. "We have hail. ... OK, see you soon."

"Well?"

"I'll punch in the location," she said, entering the coordinates into the laptop's GPS software. "Looks like they are south of that southern storm now."

"Excellent," Aurelius said, distracted by even larger hail. A baseball-size ice rock hit the windshield next, creating an impressive ringed crack.

"When are we going to be out of this?" a worried Evie asked, trying to decipher the radar on the laptop.

"We'll know when we are," he said tersely as the onslaught intensified. He wasn't sure what meant hail and what meant rain on the radar. Though he'd chased storms in the past, he'd always hired experts to do the scientific stuff. His specialty was throwing himself into the path of danger.

He slowed to a crawl as numerous baseball-size hailstones began to smash into the van from the right side — Evie's side. She slid left across the seat, away from the window, placing her young body next to Aurelius's. Any other time, he might have enjoyed it, but not while the van was being destroyed. It sounded as if cannonballs were hitting them. Some of the hail shattered on impact; other missiles bounced high off the hood and the roof and the road ahead of them, rolling into the green fields on either side.

He reached the paved road and turned west in hopes of getting to the southern storm. He also turned directly into the wind-blown hail. The windshield almost instantly filled with prismatic craters, spider-web fractures accompanied by sick crunching sounds, and in moments, it erupted in a cascade of glass. Evie screamed, burying her head in his arm. One hailstone bounced in and hit Aurelius directly in the left shoulder. It hurt like hell. Another nailed the dash cam with an unpleasant cracking sound, knocking its viewscreen right off.

"It's OK! It's OK!" he shouted, but even he didn't believe it as he tried to cover his eyes while wrenching the wheel to the left. He completed a hasty U-turn so at least the back of the van was facing the hail, and then he stopped, not wanting to drive east with the core. It had to pass sometime, he thought, as a hailstone took out the back window. Moisture coated the exposed dashboard. He reached between the seats for a towel and covered the laptop and the broken dash cam. He hadn't realized hail could be so vicious. He felt he had missed yet another opportunity for glory. With the proper helmet and armor, he could have stood outside and let it beat him up. The footage would have been spectacular.

JACK PRIDED himself on being rational. On enjoying women for just as long as it took to forget them, rarely more than a day. On chasing tornadoes with surgical precision. For the past couple of weeks, he had done almost anything but these things, culminating in the exotic madness that had overwhelmed him into saying he would ride in the Bubble. That was the feeling he had as he stared down the tornado and felt the human hamster ball roll slightly toward it, the gyroscope lazily righting him. Now was a hell of a time to become rational, just when this fucking thing might actually fly.

He still had his doubts that it would ever lift into the air, but anyone who'd seen train cars or tractor-trailers flying around a tornado probably had their doubts, too, until it happened. He took a deep breath. "I'd put it at a quarter mile now," he said into the mike in the helmet. "This thing is starting to vibrate."

Indeed, the Bubble shuddered as the gusts surrounding the tornado reached him and dust and tiny pebbles flew against its curved surface. The wind made snapping and whistling sounds as jets of air forced their way through and around the metal struts and vents. These noises were tiny distractions, however, compared with the terrible magnificence of the tornado that approached him. It had evolved from a white cone wrapped by cascading curtains of brown dust into a massive, rusty cylinder of rotating ripples, a barber pole of violence. A collar of cloud rotated so fast above the darkening funnel, it looked as if it had been filmed and then sped up for his viewing pleasure. A horizontal vortex formed and dissipated and re-formed around the main funnel, licking into the air like a giant tongue.

Jack felt as if he were entering a vortex of his own, a queer place where, as the tornado spun faster, time slowed. The Bubble rolled hard to the right, and he started to understand why it made Brad so sick as the gyroscope caught up. "Rolling," he said.

"We can see that," Devlin said. "We're just over a mile south of you and filming. The Bubble looks like a toy in front of it. Wait a minute, what?"

"What?" Jack asked. The Bubble took another roll toward the encroaching tornado. He realized Devlin was talking to someone else before their resident geek came back on the radio. He sounded breathless.

"Is there a key in the manual override?" Devlin asked.

"Key? What key?" Jack looked down. Oh, yeah. He remembered from the technical papers that a key was required to open the clear plastic box that covered the red button, an extra layer of security so no one would inadvertently fire the airbags. And he dimly recalled Brad inserting the key every time he got into the Bubble. It wasn't there.

"I guess I was hoping for a miracle," Devlin said. "Brad just confirmed the key is still in his pocket."

"That's ... unfortunate," Jack said as the Bubble took another hard roll northwest and whipping dust, weirdly loud dust, howled around it.

"The airbags should work automatically. Don't worry about the button," Devlin said, sounding worried. "And let's hope you don't get to parachute height."

Jack was dumbfounded. "The key controls that, too?"

"Uh, yeah. It seemed like a reasonable safety measure," Devlin tried to explain. "I mean, you don't want the 'chutes or airbags exploding in the middle of the lab during routine maintenance, right? We tried —"

"*Devlin.*" Jack cut off the gushing geek. The tornado was almost upon him. "Can we discuss this another time?"

"Yes. Sorry. It'll be fine," Devlin said. "It'll work."

Jack steeled himself as the dark, towering tornado overtook him. "It probably won't fly anyway," he said.

And the Bubble went airborne.

It was as if he'd popped into a pocket of anti-gravity, as if he were floating. At least at first. The sensation was so subtle, so pleasant, it took him a moment to realize what was happening. And then time slowed even further, the ride became rougher, and he realized he was climbing.

He couldn't see a whole hell of a lot that wasn't a blur — chunks of debris, a disembodied door, bits of branches and boards and scary sheets of metal that must have been picked up west of his position. A few objects banged into the sphere with startling force. For brief moments, these things seemed to be suspended alongside him, hurled along with him in the tornado's winds, which he thought had to exceed a hundred and fifty miles per hour, maybe two hundred. It was impossible to tell as he traveled, feeling its dizzying power carrying him. There was dirt and rain and small hail that pinged against his craft and, behind it all, a throaty roar, deep and resonant, almost heard more in his bones than his ears. He caught glimpses of sky and flashes of lightning through the maelstrom as the Bubble rotated and rolled and the gyroscope struggled to keep him anywhere close to upright. He was twirling as the sphere spun around the massive vortex. And for one second, he thought he saw something else sharing the sky with him, albeit much more distant: a tiny plane.

Jack knew the Bubble was too heavy to be lofted for long, though he'd seen train cars fly for several seconds in the Pancake tornado. He tried to think faster in his slow-motion world, but he was mesmerized by the sensation of flying around the funnel, of seeing patches of green below him; even, perhaps, the film crew far to the south. The south? He must have made a full rotation around the tornado. Maybe two or three. He heard a crackling on the radio and tried to respond. "OK," he said. "Still airborne. Monitor shows cameras recording. Looks grungy. At least they should survive the crash."

"Hang in there," he heard Devlin's faint voice. "Your altitude looks good. When it starts falling, the airbags should deploy."

Jack realized there was a one in five chance they wouldn't, but in this instant, he didn't care. The tornado's dusky arms enfolded him. Seductive oblivion. A place where all the dull rules of existence were suspended, obliterated. The vacuum.

The vacuum. He thought of Saffire. And then, with a snap into crystal-clear, full-color focus, time shifted into high-speed reality. He decided he didn't like his odds.

He glanced down at the box covering the button, tried to jiggle it with one hand, realized it was hopeless. Maybe the airbags would deploy without help. But maybe they wouldn't. He reached up and yanked off his helmet, not an easy thing with his body being tossed about in the straps. He sucked in a deep breath and brought the headgear down hard on the clear box covering the manual override button.

There was a satisfying crack, but it didn't break. And he felt the Bubble teetering as it launched forward into brighter air, being thrown clear of the tornado. Gravity was taking over. He slammed the helmet down again on the box, and the crack grew.

And the Bubble began to fall.

And the airbags didn't deploy.

Jack slammed the helmet once more onto the box, knowing it was his last opportunity. It shattered, and he jammed his finger on the button.

The Bubble shuddered violently as tiny, controlled explosions in the generators forced gas into the double-walled airbags and their boxes burst open. They expelled bulky bunches of huge, flexible balls tethered to the struts, surrounding the outside of the sphere with space-age cushions. It had worked, and not a moment too soon. The Bubble, now a colossal cluster of grapes, fell far and away from the funnel and bounced hard and high on the Kansas earth.

Jack gasped at the impact, unable to utter the curse on the tip of his tongue as the Bubble flipped him head over heels, still strapped in. The gyroscope had no chance to catch up as the Bubble again careered to the ground and sprang upward, though it didn't feel quite so high this time. He couldn't see a damn thing except the undulating airbags, and the monitor showed a blur of sky and ground. The ball tumbled down again. He lost count at twelve impacts — twelve jarring, stomach-flipping rebounds — and was more than ready for the carnival ride to be over when the Bubble did a hop, a bump and a roll and came to a slow, merciful stop.

A thrill ran through his sore body. He was alive. And he'd flown in a tornado.

He was also sick to his stomach, and his neck hurt, and he heard a strange buzzing. He realized it was the helmet, now lying on the floor of the Bubble. With some difficulty, he popped himself out of the straps and fell against the curved interior of the contraption. Unsteady, he reached down for the helmet and held it up to his ear. Devlin was screaming.

"Jack? Jack! Are you there? Are you OK?"

Like an astronaut back from orbit, still not fully readjusted to being on Earth, Jack took a second and savored the silence of this womb, this would-be tomb. Then he held the mike up to his mouth. "Still here," he said. "How do I get out of this thing?"

"We're on our way!" Devlin sounded unbelievably excited. "There's a button by the door, under a plastic box. It deflates the airbags."

"Do I need a key?" Jack asked sarcastically.

"Um, no. It just flips up. Press it."

Jack found the clear box, flipped it up and pressed the green button there. With a wheezing sound, the airbags' tethers came undone and the bladders of air deflated, collapsing. The Bubble settled in place. He found the latch and popped open the door, which mercifully was not facing the ground. Stumbling outside, he fought back a wave of nausea. They should call this thing the Barf Bubble, he thought, as he stood with his hands on his knees, catching his breath.

When he lifted his head, Van One was pulling up on the nearest dirt road, thirty yards away. He was in the middle of a plowed field. He struggled forward a few steps and fell to his knees. Jack decided he could stay there indefinitely, facing the sky with his eyes closed, letting the lingering raindrops run over his face, letting his body shed its rush of adrenaline. What a strange thing, to see Oz and live to tell about it. He heard the dwindling wind and the distinctive whistle of a Western Meadowlark. In the distance, another called back. The birds always seemed to sing more joyously after a storm passed. It was mercifully peaceful. And there was no siren.

He opened his eyes and saw Saffire running toward him. She fell on her knees next to him and hugged him. He wrapped his arms around her tightly, burying his face in her shoulder, her hair. Devlin ran up behind her, practically dancing.

Jack held on an extra second before he let Saffire go, and they got to their feet.

"I can't believe it worked!" Devlin said, reaching out to shake Jack's hand.

"That's comforting," Jack said dryly. "And it didn't."

"But —"

"I pressed the button. Then it worked."

Mystified, Devlin walked over to the Bubble and peered inside to see what Jack was talking about.

"Where are they?" Jack asked Saffire. "The cameras?"

"Wide shots only," she said, smiling. "They're way over yonder."

"Then come here." He pulled her to where the Bubble blocked the view of the crew. With his hands in her hair, he kissed her, reveling in her world of pleasure and discovery. "I came back for you," he said as he came up for air.

"Looks to me like you didn't have much choice about coming back, with gravity and all," she said with a teasing smile.

"Just the same," he said.

Her eyes were unreadable as she touched his cheek. "We're on," she finally said. "Wynda's having a cow about now."

Saffire stepped away, back to where the cameras could see her. He followed, suddenly unsure of where he'd landed.

Devlin dashed past them toward the van, his glasses spattered with rain, his grin as wide as Texas. "I'll tell them you're OK," he shouted, still gleeful. "I can't believe it worked!"

THE ZANE FILMS van was trashed. Three big windows were gone — one in the back, one on the rear passenger side and the windshield — making it a perfect mobile wind tunnel. Most of the lights were broken. There was no way Aurelius was chasing anything, and he counted himself lucky he wasn't stuck in front of the large tornado reported with the southern storm. Instead, he hobbled on to Pancake, the nearest town, in hopes of getting a new rental while Evie dialed Ernie.

"Ernie? Are you OK?" she asked when the call went through. Aurelius thought it funny that the budding meteorologist was her first thought and not herself. Ah, love. "Really? Oh, really? That's fantastic!" She turned to Aurelius. "They got footage of the tornado, from the ground and from the air! They said it was incredible!"

And Aurelius Zane had not been in front of it. He was not prone to depression, but he felt his spirits sinking. He anticipated a chunk of green-screen work before his show was done. He couldn't appear to have missed his most important storm of the season. On the bright side, if the drone got the tornado footage, at least the terms of his contract had been met. He would get paid.

"Um, no, we can't meet up with you there," Evie said. "We got in a real bad hailstorm. We have to stop in Pancake. Meet us there? OK? We'll reserve the rooms." She hung up. "Isn't that fantastic?" she asked Aurelius. "You got exactly what you wanted!"

Did he? They got into town, and he used the GPS to find what had to be the world's smallest car-rental agency. The neatly groomed clerk, with short, brown hair, khakis and a red golf shirt, was outside the door with a handful of keys, just about to close, when he saw the beat-up van drive up. The young man sighed visibly and reopened the shop, beckoning Aurelius inside.

Evie got out and shot pictures of the van and its pockmarked magnet-mounted logos with her smartphone. Then she set her thumbs loose on the screen. "Posted it!" she said with enthusiasm.

"Oh, you did, did you?" Aurelius replied wearily, pulling papers out of the glove compartment and realizing that even though his drone had triumphed, he'd have to admit he'd missed the best part of the tornado. It had been a tactical error, trying to reunite with his crew, in his natural assumption that the storm would wait for him, Aurelius Zane. If he'd followed Ernie's advice, he never would have left a tornado behind. If he'd accepted Evie's offer, he'd have footage of him looking brave in front of it. He anticipated more weeks of chasing the unlikely recurrence of the opportunity he'd blown today.

Inside, Evie sat on one of the hard plastic chairs and called a local hotel to reserve their rooms. Aurelius went to the counter and explained the situation, producing the soggy rental documents and requesting another van. He was relieved to be out of the hail and back in action, at least until he saw the look of concern on the clerk's face. "What is it, Ken?" Aurelius asked, noting the nametag.

"You didn't get the hail insurance."

"I got full coverage. I always get full coverage."

"We offer hail insurance now," Ken said. "It seems you didn't sign up for that. I'm sorry, but you'll be liable for the body damage to the van. My guess is, it'll be totaled."

"Impossible," Aurelius said, his voice assuming its deepest, most authoritative tone. "You will give me a new van, and I will not be paying any more for this one. I had full coverage."

Ken seemed unimpressed. "I'm sorry, sir. Acts of God, that is, acts of nature are not covered in the policy you signed. That's why we have an additional option for hail. I mean, we do live in Tornado Alley, sir."

Aurelius looked into Ken's apathetic brown eyes and saw no quarter. He also saw his finances again evaporating. His reward for the drone's success would barely cover his debt to Rodney, and the rest would go into a van he didn't own and would never see again. Here he was, meant to be in the middle of a tornado or tsunami or pyroclastic flow, instead held hostage to the fine print in a shabby little office in the middle of nowhere.

"We can provide a replacement vehicle, sir," Ken said, oblivious to Aurelius's despair. "Would you like the hail coverage on that?"

"ALL RIGHT, put down your burgers and pick up your beers. This is a toast," Wynda called out, garnering the attention of her crew in a dark, loud sports bar in Pratt, Kansas. She was buying the drinks and, on her third gin and tonic, was as happy as Jack had ever seen her. Jack was on his second bourbon and was sipping instead of guzzling, but it was helping ease the pain of the flesh bruised by all the tossing about while he'd been strapped in the Bubble.

"You have done it," Wynda continued. "And even better, this means we can all go home on Friday. First, of course, we have to interview the hell out of you about how impressed we were by *Brad's* feat today. Meanwhile: To the Bubble." She brandished her glass and took a sip.

No one knew whether to laugh or frown, even in Brad's absence, so they followed suit.

"All right, that's enough." Wynda giggled. "You're a sorry lot, but you got it done. Thank you." She turned back to a conversation with Andre and Devlin, and the others dispersed and resumed their eating and chatting. Jack finished his drink and ordered another, looking around for Saffire. She hadn't been avoiding him, exactly, but she wasn't staying close, either. He felt they were safe from prying eyes now. And he really wanted to be near her.

He got his bourbon, walked through the crowded bar and pushed through the door that led to the patio out back. With a half dozen tables and several benches, it was just as crowded as inside. Flower-filled planters lined the space, clear and colored party lights were strung above, and rock music blared from the speakers. A cool breeze underscored the storms' passage and seemed to lighten the patrons' collective mood.

Unlike Jack, normal people were always happy when the latest round of violent weather was over.

Saffire sat on a bench next to one of the tables with Michiko and Pole. She was glowing, in denim shorts and a loose-fitting white blouse. They'd all put aside their beers and had their smartphones out. "Did I spell that right?" Saffire was asking as he approached. "OK, I'm emailing you both my contact information. Just don't share it with my stalkers."

The others laughed, and Saffire looked up. "Hey, Jack," she said with a smile, putting her phone back in her purse. "You'd better not forget me either, mister."

"I'll at least curse your name every time I crave a cigarette."

"Good to know," she said, as Michiko and Pole made a quick exit.

Jack held up his hands. "Something I said?"

"For some reason, they must think we want to be alone," Saffire said coyly. "Why don't you sit down?"

"Thanks." He straddled the bench next to her. "I'm glad we don't have to look over our shoulders now."

"Not much point, anyway, since I'll be heading back to California tomorrow." Her eyes sparkled. "I got the job. I'm going to host the *Mini Monsters* show."

"*Mini Monsters?*" He was trying to take in everything she just said. She was leaving tomorrow? She wasn't waiting until Friday?

"It's all about the creepy critters that live among us, in cities and towns and homes. We'll be interacting with real people and doing close-up stories about the critters, including *lots* of bugs." She sounded so excited. "Macro photography and the secret life of insects, vermin, all the things that creep people out. Travel and a real show. No more stupid celebrity gigs. At least, I sure hope not." She was beaming. "Thank you, Jack."

"I didn't do anything," he said, taking a sip from the glass he just remembered was in his hand. "It's all you." He looked her over, his thoughts turbulent.

"What is it?" she asked. "Look, let's go back to the hotel. This place is too loud. And I want to say goodbye."

"I don't want you to say goodbye," Jack found himself saying. He felt keenly an unfamiliar role reversal.

Saffire looked uncomfortable. "Then *au revoir*."

"You could visit. Wishwell's only a few hours from your mama, a nice place to get away from the bright lights. Or I could come out west for a while."

She seemed startled by his suggestion. "You'd go crazy. It's all concrete and traffic. And there's no weather. This is where you belong."

"I don't belong anywhere."

"Yes, you do. I understand what draws you to this place now. What keeps you here. You showed me that. The endless skies. The power of the storms. I'll always picture you on the prairie." She grinned. "Or in bed."

"It's not forever. It's just a simple visit."

"Simple," she mused. "I don't know." She looked everywhere but at him, then turned her golden-brown eyes to his. "You know I find you irresistible. I mean, that was the idea, right?" She smiled her sexy smile, and he wondered why he didn't shut up and go with her to the hotel. "It's not that I don't want to see you again," she continued. "It's just that I can't afford any complications right now."

Something in her tone made him keep talking. "It doesn't feel right, you going."

"Don't tell me you actually feel *something*." She was joking, but again, there was another note in her musical voice, a minor key.

He drained his bourbon, put the glass down and looked her in the eye. He put a hand on her knee and moved it a couple of inches up her thigh, her smooth skin. Emotion flitted across her face, but she recovered her cool and brushed a hand through her hair.

"Are you about to surprise me?" she asked.

Jack had a feeling that he was about to crash to Earth again, a feeling that he was about to surprise himself. "I —"

But her finger touched his lips, followed by her mouth, pressing on his in a way he took to mean goodbye. He wrapped his arms around her, delving into her kiss, feeling the familiar heat coursing through his body. He had her. And then she pulled back.

All the darkness inside him welled up like a wave. "I can't imagine feeling differently tomorrow," he murmured, just loud enough so she could hear. "Or the next day. Or the next."

Saffire looked down, then lifted her gaze to his. Her eyes shone, misty, reflecting the strings of lights above them. The bright lights.

"Wait a week," she said softly. A bittersweet smile tugged at the corner of her mouth. She got up and walked into the crowd, and into the bar, and was gone.

◣

THE PALM-TREE SHADOWS lengthened on the narrow beach outside the rental villa in Islamorada, and Jack knew it was almost time even before Marcus texted him. "I'll pick you up in fifteen," his friend wrote. "The crew wants to take the boats out at three."

"No problem," Jack texted back from his lounge chair. He set the smartphone on the table next to his beer, picked up the cold bottle and took a swig. He felt the weight of the cigar in his shirt pocket, the one he'd bought at the Miami airport three days ago and hadn't found the right time to smoke yet. The Atlantic stretched out before him, calm and blue-green, its nominal waves glittering. Puffs of summer clouds promised lightning later.

Late afternoon was prime time for Florida Keys waterspouts, and chasing them on a boat was nothing but fun. When he got the call for this two-week TV gig, he'd found it hard to resist. Who knew a recommendation from Wynda would result in such a pleasant summer job? He could afford to take time off thanks to the payout from the Bubble show, but it was always cool to be paid to chase storms, especially if he could be in the background, off-camera, where he could reap the joy without the hassle.

Wynda had emailed him a link so he could preview the documentary series' finale. He had to admire the editing, which made it look as if Brad were flying in the Bubble. Quick cuts and extreme close-ups from the Twister Tracker's two weeks in action, combined with rough-and-tumble footage shot by the Bubble itself, told a captivating story, even if it was more fiction than reality. The wide, soft-focus shot of Saffire running up to "Brad" and hugging him after the Bubble bounced to a stop was especially moving, or would be to anyone else. Jack never wanted to see it again.

Marcus showed up in the rented red Mustang, top down. Florida's summers were way too hot for it, but when a couple of guys used to being landlocked in Oklahoma get two weeks to traverse graceful bridges over turquoise waters, they rent a convertible.

"I took them to the hurricane monument," Marcus explained. "They'll probably use it in the show."

It didn't take long to get to the marina. The Australian crew had rented two boats. Jack's job was to drive one of them; Marcus, the other. Jack had to steer them to the most promising towers and storms and herd them close enough to get their shots. His expertise guided him, but memories of youthful trips to Florida fueled his instincts.

A line of cumulus clouds was already building in the Gulf as they headed out and navigated the channel that would get them on that side of the islands. The heat was so deep and moist, it swathed Jack's skin like a blanket. He didn't mind the slow burn. He felt it melting away his resistance as he soaked up the sun.

The clouds were soaking it up, too, translating the heat into updrafts as the hard towers reached toward the sky. They weren't violent like Tornado Alley supercells, but they were entrancing, newborn storms. One tower reached toward the sun faster than the others, swelling with energy until rain began to fall from its base. Next to the rain shaft, a nub of cloud soon became a pointed funnel, and the emerging spray ring on the waves below betrayed the waterspout's consummation. The funnel filled in, becoming a stout, silvery column of rotating vapor. Jack waved at the other craft to come along. The crew brandished cameras as the boats pushed forward.

"Looks like a nice one!" Marcus shouted from the other boat.

Jack could barely hear his voice from across the waves, but he smiled, feeling the wind on his face, as he accelerated toward the spinning synthesis of water and sky.

NOTES AND THANKS

While the essence of *Tornado Pinball,* like *Funnel Vision* before it, is inspired by my experiences as a storm chaser, its characters and situations are fictional. Though I have sought to be authentic in all aspects of the story, I have manipulated geography and technology when it suited me. While many of the towns are real, a few are fictional, as are most of the hotels, bars and restaurants. A notable exception is The Big Texan, one of my favorite stops. The Bubble is certainly an invention, perhaps an outlandish one. Still, given the extremes to which chasers seem willing to go, I don't think a probe like it would be out of the question.

I am deeply grateful to several people for the inspiration and expertise that helped me in writing this book. I alone hold the responsibility for any inaccuracies, but their guidance was invaluable.

TV news helicopter pilot Johnny Rowlands, who not only chases storms by air out of Kansas City but is offering helicopter storm chase tours (helichasers.com), endured a barrage of questions and offered me precious insights into what his job is like and what a helicopter pilot might experience in a perilous situation as described in this novel. His kind feedback was hugely helpful and a great supplement to the terrifying videos of helicopter crashes I found online.

William McMillan gave me an air traffic controller's perspective on the airborne follies I describe. Chaser and engineer Dave Lewison patiently answered my questions on what materials might work in a device like the Bubble. If anyone could build it, I'm pretty sure he could. The NASA airbag technology was used on multiple Mars probes; granted, no person was inside them, but isn't it fun to think one could be?

I'd like to thank chaser Scott McPartland for telling me what it's like to quit smoking, and Nicole Desmond for a conversation we once had about the charms of bugs. Also, Christina Jordan's nagging was a great motivator, and if it helps you sleep at night, Christina, Jack's personal car is currently a 1977 Plymouth Volare wagon.

I'm grateful also to Becky Lee, a fine video producer who answered my questions and let me mention her as the charming cousin of the character who might be her evil twin.

Thanks to my old friends at *Florida Today* for their continuing support, including Suzy Fleming Leonard and Christina LaFortune, and to other publications in my part of Florida that continue to write about authors and books, *The Beachside Resident* and *SpaceCoast Living*.

I want to honor the brave women I've interviewed for articles about domestic violence; their courage found their way into Saffire's story. I also must give a nod to the appealing attitude of the group Saffire: The Uppity Blues Women and their song "It Takes a Mighty Good Man," to which my character Saffire alludes.

Thank you to my storm-chasing friends and companions for sometimes great, sometimes disastrous, but always memorable moments on the road. I'd also like to acknowledge the storm chasers and other folks who have been kind enough to read *Funnel Vision* and this book.

Eternal thanks go to George Jenkins for his encouragement and support of my writing and storm chasing obsessions; for caring for our furry children while I travel; for making exquisite cocktails when they are most needed; and so much more.

For positive, powerful conversations, thank you to wonderful writers Susan Hubbard and Dianne Marcum.

Finally, I must toast the talented scribes of the Harbaugh Literary Salon for their feedback and friendship as I wrote this book: Pam and John Harbaugh, Annette Clifford, Rachel Wilkerson, Billy Cox and especially Cathy Mathias for her vital early reading of the manuscript and excellent notes.

As Shakespeare put it, "I can no other answer make but thanks, and thanks."

Don't miss the third Storm Seekers adventure!

*The mission is electrifying,
but danger can be twisted …*

For tornado chaser Jack Andreas, an invitation to a lightning study means double the danger. As he sees it, what's not to love? He's intrigued by the job and fascinated by pilot Maribeth Lisbon, who must fly a research plane into the zap zone. Maribeth suspects he's trouble, especially when his charms set off all her alarms. In their way are scheming TV chaser Brad Treat and down-on-his-luck adventurer Aurelius

Zane, intent on filming a wedding in front of a twister. The eccentric billionaire who funds the study has a secret agenda. And a mystic with a food truck tests them all. As fearsome storms put them in mortal peril, Jack and Maribeth find their toughest challenge may lie within.

The sequel to FUNNEL VISION and TORNADO PINBALL, ZAP BANG continues Chris Kridler's Storm Seekers Series with action, drama, humor and romance.

Learn more at ChrisKridler.com/books

BOOKS BY CHRIS KRIDLER

The STORM SEEKERS Series

Writing as Chris Kridler

FUNNEL VISION

TORNADO PINBALL

ZAP BANG

Storm Seekers Series Boxed Set: Books 1-3

BOHEMIA BARTENDERS MYSTERIES

Writing as Lucy Lakestone

These funny mysteries star Pepper Revelle and a team of mixologists who travel to colorful events where life is a cocktail of fun — until it's shaken into madcap mayhem … and murder.

RISKY WHISKEY

BAFFLED BY BITTERS ~ *story free to subscribers*

WRECKED BY RUM

VEXED BY VODKA

JIGGERED BY GIN

BEGUILED BY BOURBON

SHOCKED BY CHAMPAGNE

WHY OH RYE?

BOHEMIA BARTENDERS COCKTAIL COLORING BOOK

The BOHEMIA BEACH Series

Writing as Lucy Lakestone

Award-winning hot contemporary romance

In a beautiful small city on Florida's east coast, artists meet, create, laugh and love. Where restless hearts are fueled by secrets and imagination, romance is impossible to resist. Welcome to the seductive tropical escape that's home to drama, humor and lots of heat – Bohemia Beach.

BOHEMIA BEACH

BOHEMIA LIGHT

BOHEMIA BLUES

BOHEMIA HEAT

BOHEMIA NIGHTS

BACK TO BOHEMIA ~ *story free to subscribers*

BOHEMIA BELLS

BOHEMIA CHILLS

Bohemia Beach Series Boxed Sets:

Books 1-3 | Books 4-7

ABOUT THE AUTHOR

Chris Kridler is an award-winning writer, photographer and storm chaser who lives in Florida. She travels every year to Tornado Alley in search of the perfect storm. She also writes mysteries and romances as Lucy Lakestone. Learn more about her work and travels at ChrisKridler.com.

.